THE EAGLE AND THE SUN

This novel is an imaginative reconstruction of an astonishing and little-known epic. In 25 B.C., Augustus Caesar ordered the conquest of Arabia, and launched the Tenth Roman Legion into a waterless land to seek the riches of Arabia—a mirage which drew it to a point from which there was no retreat; and on south for two thousand miles to the climax at the walls of Mariba. Lord Belhaven, with his long personal experience of the desert, tells the story with all the direct excitement of an eyewitness's account as he details the difficult personal relationship of men committed to a hazardous enterprise; the devotion of Antonius Valens to his commander, the treachery of Syllaeus, the cross currents of intrigue between the rulers of Arabian Kingdoms in their selfish and half-hearted defence against the Romans and, most vividly, the character of the Commander, Gallus, upon whose decisions, against conflicting advice, the survival of the legion depended, in a land where life hung upon a tenuous and unknown string of wells.

THE EAGLE
AND THE SUN

AN HISTORICAL NOVEL BY
LORD BELHAVEN

LONDON
JOHN MURRAY, ALBEMARLE STREET, W.

FIRST EDITION . . . 1951

Printed in Great Britain by
Wyman & Sons, Ltd., London, Fakenham and Reading.

DEDICATED

by his permission

to

the late

FIELD MARSHAL THE EARL WAVELL

OF CYRENAICA

P.C., G.C.B., G.C.S.I., G.C.I.E., C.M.G., M.C.

CONTENTS

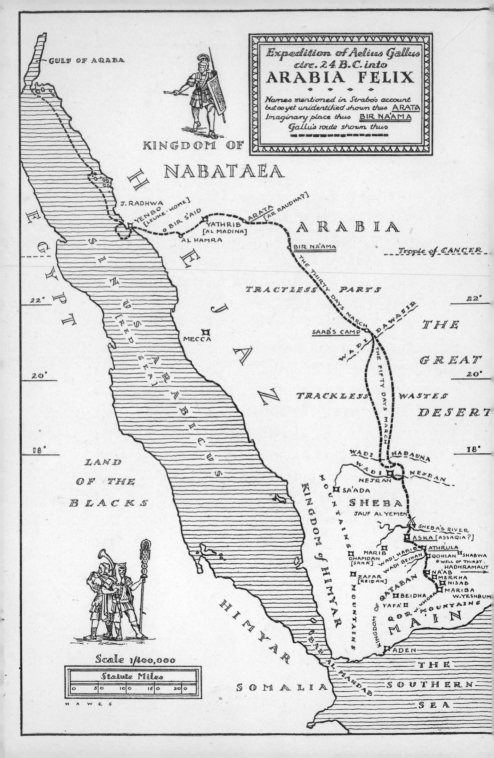

GULF OF AQABA.

KINGDOM OF

NABATAEA

Expedition of Aelius Gallus
circ. 24 B.C. into
ARABIA FELIX
Names mentioned in Strabo's account
but as yet unidentified shown thus ARATA
Imaginary place thus BIR NA'AMA
Gallus's route shown thus

ARABIA

J. RADHWA
YENBO
[LEUKE-KOME]
BIR S'AID
YATHRIB
[AL MADINA]
AL HAMRA
ARATA
[AR RAUDHA?]

BIR NA'AMA

Tropic of CANCER

22°   22°

TRACTLESS   PARTS

EGYPT

S I N U S

A R A B I C U S

[RED SEA]

THE THIRTY DAYS MARCH

SAAB'S CAMP

WADI DAWASIR

THE
GREAT

20°   20°

TRACTLESS   WASTES

DESERT

THE FIFTY DAYS MARCH

MECCA

H E J A Z

LAND

OF THE

BLACKS

18°   18°

WADI HABAUNA

WADI
NEJRAN   NEJRAN

SA'ADA

SHEBA

MOUNTAINS

JAUF AL YEMEN

KINGDOM OF HIMYAR

SHEBA'S RIVER
ASKA [ASSAQIA?]
ATHRULA

MARIB
GHAMDAN
[SANA]

WADI HARIB
WADI BEIHAN

QOHLAN   SHABWA
WELL OF THIRST
HADHRAMAUT
NA'AB   MERKHA
NISAB
MARIBA
W. YESHBUM

ZAFAR
[REIDAN]

QATABAN
BEIDHA
YAFA'I

QOR W.WHORE

MAIN

MOUNTAINS

JEBEL AL MANDAB

HIMYAR

ADEN

THE

SOMALIA

SOUTHERN

SEA

Scale 1/400,000

Statute Miles
0   50   100   150   200

HAWES

The Legend

As the whirlwinds in the south pass through; so it cometh from the desert, from a terrible land.

(ISAIAH, 21.)

LONG ago Augustus Caesar sent a Roman Legion to conquer a mirage, in the land of Arabia the Happy. The Legion he chose was the famous Tenth *Fretensis*, who, led by the valorous bearer of their Eagle standard, had been the first to plunge into the Kentish surf, some two decades before, under Julius Caesar; and who were destined, close on a century later, to breach the high walls of Jerusalem. This Legion Augustus took from Judaea, as a man might choose a spear from his armoury, and he cast it far to the south, into the uttermost deserts of the earth.

You may go, if the Kings of Arabia permit you, if you are strong and inured to hardship and have studied the wild Arabian, down the long road the Romans trod. You will take with you a few guides, wise in desert lore, and a hardy camel-man or two. You will carry water in sewn goat skins, for you must chance your way from settlement to desert well, from hill spring to water-hole over two thousand miles and more of desolation. You must take a small, skilled party for this expedition; there is not enough water in the land for numbers of men. And, when you come at the end of that long road to the lost city of Mariba and look down upon her tumbled altars and her broken walls, ghosts will touch your sleeve, like the fingers of the wind, and voices, faint after two thousand years, will whisper, "Hurry! Hurry! For the horns are calling and we must scale the walls of Mariba, at the rising of the morning star!"

Often I had wondered where Mariba could be. "And he came," says the story, "to the city of Mariba, in the country of the Rahmanitae." Mariba became in my mind a city of fantasy, high walled, impregnable, standing in some tall mountain, its battlements alight with spears.

One night I sat by a camp-fire, near the ancient town of Nisab, in south-west Arabia, waiting for the moon to rise. It pleased my Arab companion at such times to point out here a mountain peak, there a star which showed where, in the vast land, this tribe lived or that village lay. A light wind stirred the fire. The rising moon was as yet no more than a glow behind the sharp mountain peaks. To our north stretched the empty lands, far into the desert heart of Arabia. Presently my companion leaned across the fire and pointed with a crooked arm, so that the firelight flashed from his bracelet of silver and cornelian and caught my eye and my wandering attention.

"See you," he exclaimed, "yonder tall mountain peak? Beneath it and a little beyond, lies the village of the Well of Lead. Once, long ago in the ancient time, there came a great army into the land from the north, an army of the *ahl fareng*, of the Frankish people. They had fought and destroyed all the length of the land until they came to the Well of Lead and there they halted, dismayed. That mountain was once a place of many springs. They blocked the springs, they broke down the cisterns and the water

2

channels and thence they departed into the setting sun, no man knows whither. Thus is the land dry these many years and no water flows in all that mountain."

"Is there," I asked, "a ruined city on that mountain?"

"Assuredly," he answered, "there, by day, one may see the fallen houses of the city, with ancient writings on the walls, and fragments of marble and alabaster, such as you have seen elsewhere. It was a great city. Now it is fallen, deserted, a dwelling of djinns and evil spirits. None venture there by night, no *billah*! For they say lights shine there and cries are heard in the dark of the moon. They call that city Mariba."

The night was less still than before, there was a stirring of the sand about our fire. There was more than air in the wind. I have since imagined that, had I closed my eyes and listened, I would have heard the shuffling of many feet, marching through the night by our fire, on the way to Mariba, a lost host who would find that the long road ended in the dawn at the city of disillusion. And contemplating, in after years, the strange sensations which then assailed me, underlying all I felt some deep personal appeal to remember that sudden stirring of the sand and of the spirit. So vivid was that appeal that I looked into the shadows beyond the fire, thinking to see ghosts marching through the night, faint with the long centuries, on their way to Mariba in the mountain of springs.

And for a moment, from the wind-blown fire, I heard the sound of distant trumpets.

3

CHAPTER I

The Trumpets Sound

" The Roman expedition to Arabia under Aelius Gallus which took place recently . . . the friendly alliance with the Nabataeans urged him (Augustus Caesar) to great expectations . . . relying upon them Gallus set out with his army but Syllaeus deceived him . . . not guiding them in an easy crossing but in the midst of hidden reefs and by shoals where the tide in its ebb and flow was most opposed to them.

STRABO[1]

THE trumpets blew, two thousand miles from Mariba. The strident *Lituus* of the cavalry and the melodious *Cornu* of the Legion cast up their voices to the bare rocks of the gully and the mountains caught them and threw them, echoing ever fainter, back and forth, until they melted into the silence of the still sea and the evening sky.

In the shadows far up the gully the sand rose, a pale mist against the dark rock walls. It moved billowing to a sharp edge of sunlight and there became suddenly a golden, shimmering curtain hanging across the gully, torn for a moment by a gust of mountain air, rejoining its folds, rising higher, spreading out, while from its edges and before it sprang whirling dust devils, wild dancers of a desert

[1] The eminent Geographer, a Cretan, who was a friend of Gallus the Commander of a Roman Legion sent *circa* 24 B.C. to conquer Arabia. This, and subsequent chapter headings, are from Strabo's description of that enterprise.

5

prelude, which fell to the ground as the first of the actors rode out upon the stage.

A Centurion came riding from the gully with one hundred and twenty armoured horsemen, their heavy spears slung across their backs, the mounted wing of the Tenth Legion of Rome. Their little slim-legged ponies fretted and danced, sensing the end of a journey, excited by the tang of sea air. They rode out of the curtain of golden sand into the broadening valley, looking expectantly to where, beyond the walls of a newly fashioned camp, a fleet of ships lay at anchor on the blue waters of the Gulf of Aqaba.

Behind them the curtain thinned and parted. There was a sparkle within it of arms and accoutrements and into the clear sunlight rode a smaller party of horsemen, spreading out as the valley widened. These carried their heavy spears across their knees and in their midst Aelius Gallus, *Praefectus* of the Legion, gentled his dancing Arab mare. He sat his mare easily, a broad-shouldered, powerful figure, his pale blue eyes alight under sand-dusted lashes, his full lips closed. The thin, shifting evening breeze stirred his close-cropped, golden curls. A smile would come seldom to those lips, a frown as seldom to his broad brow. He had seen much of fighting in his years of service and was a warrior of mark and distinction, having held the rank of *Primus Pilus*, 'First Javelin', twice in the last five years. He was a knight of Rome. He had reached the height of his career in the Legions, outside the Emperor's Principate of Egypt; for elsewhere the Armies of Rome were commanded by Legates, well-born Romans, of rich and ambitious families. Within Egypt, only, was high command possible for the promoted Centurion. No high-born

6

Roman could enter Egypt, for Augustus Caesar feared that the temptation of a throne might overset the doubtful balance of their loyalty. The Emperor governed Egypt through such tried and trusted soldiers as Gallus and it was towards Egypt that their eyes turned, where there were Legions to be commanded and the prize of prizes to be won —the Governorship of Egypt itself. Gallus might well expect in time to fill that post.

The treasures of Egypt were vast indeed. Yet they seemed as nothing to the treasures of that fabulous land, deep in the south, Arabia the Happy. From there came wealth untold, gold and precious stones, silk and spices, ivory and strange beasts—and incense, .the very breath of magic and religion. Augustus would have Arabia the Happy for his own and so the Legate and the Tribunes of the Legion had been recalled from Judaea and the Legion, under its professional commanders, had awaited the arrival of its new General, the *Praefectus Legionis* Aelius Gallus.

He had come to them in their camp in the Judaean hills on an evening of storm and mountain thunder, with his group of servants and his staff of writers. Some few days later a curious, outlandish company had camped beside them, northern Arabs from Nabataea, hook-nosed black men from the distant land of Punt, and dark Arabs from the south, under the command of a silent Centurion from Egypt, Antonius Valens. A dark-complexioned, blue-eyed Gaul was Valens, who spoke strange tongues and with whom always went a great chest of papers over which he worked long into the night. Valens was a man of secrets, a confidant of the *Praefectus*; but he had not stayed long in the camp in Judaea; for a column of some seven hundred mounted men rode by the camp one late afternoon, wearing heavy brazen helmets with chain cheek-pieces, great scimitars aswing on their hips, led by a giant of a man, who smiled through his black, curled beard. These, the Legion knew, were the warriors of the tribe of Judah, King Herod's men. The Legionaries had watched the long column riding by, with a dull clank of armour and equipment and had noted their heavy-lidded eyes, their incurious expressions and their air of ferocity and purpose. As they passed the camp, the Centurion Valens had joined them, with his wild crew, and had left with them on the road to Petra, the capital of Nabataea.

Many months had passed since then. Rumour had had its long and inevitable day. Now as their long column emerged from the airless hills, the Legionaries looked expectantly towards the sea, where lay the ships which were to take them far into the unknown south. Behind the mounted wing and their General came long lines of mules and camels, burdened with the great balks and throwing arms of catapults, the frames of heavy dart-throwing balistae and panniers holding brazen-headed darts half a span long, the heads as broad as a hand. This was the mobile field artillery of the Legion and beside the beasts of burden marched the skilled crews of the machines and the masons, whose task it was to shape the great thirty-pound balls of stone which the catapults could sling three hundred paces and more. Then followed the *Primi Ordines*, the senior Centurions, with their orderlies and runners. Hardened veterans these, grim of face and lithe of body. Behind them came a forest of brazen standards. First the thirty standards of the Maniples, their shafts hung with commemorative medallions of shining silver and glowing brass. Then, surrounded by its devoted guards, the most doughty

8

warriors of all, famed each one for some desperate feat of arms, came the Eagle of the Legion, the holy symbol of the Legion's unity, a golden eagle borne on a white shaft, cruel beak open and wings spread. Behind the Eagle strode the trumpeters of the Centuriae, the companies of a hundred men, and the declining sun shone redly on the long, curved horns, slung across the shoulders of the bearers.

Behind the trumpeters the dust settled. The sun lay, a polished brazen disc, above black, sharp-pointed hills, which rose beyond the near arm of the bay. Then, their heads bowed to the light, came the warriors of the Legion in their ten Cohorts, each of six hundred men, trudging through the sand. They marched out of the gully into the wide bed of the open wadi, the last red gleam of the sun striking dusty fire from their round iron helmets, their articulated shoulder armour and their swinging aprons, of brass-studded leather straps. Behind them the sky darkened to deep purple above the black mountains. Before them a sharp peak of rock for a moment divided the sun's disc and then from a vanished sun a flood of scarlet light rose into the sky and hung there, failing as it spread, and the night came down and there were only shadows and the sound of marching feet.

*   *   *

The long cadences of a horn had marked the third watch of the night. In the camp above the bay where the fleet lay, lights burned in the General's private tent in the camp centre, an orange glow through the walls. It would soon be dawn, but Gallus had not slept. All night he had read and studied the three reports he had received from the Centurion, Antonius Valens, who was already far down the road to the south and had by now reached the port of Leuke Kome, for which the Legion was due to embark that morning.

Valens' first report had been received when the Legion had arrived, a month before, at Aqaba. He first commented upon the week he had spent in Petra, the capital of the Arab Kingdom of Nabataea, where Gallus himself had spent some days, as the guest of King Abodas. He confirmed Gallus' own impression of Abodas—or 'Abud, as the Arabs called him—whose treaty of friendship, so easily negotiated, had spurred Augustus Caesar's determination to conquer all Arabia. Valens wrote that Abodas was, "fat and lazy, a Bacchus at his orgies rather than a Satyr." A gross old man, this Arabian King, detested by the more virile of his subjects. On his first evening at the Nabataean court Valens had met Syllaeus, the chief guide appointed by the King, "energetic, fearless, dangerous to his own King, an enemy of Caesar." Syllaeus had forced his way to this appointment with the help of the rich merchants, and it was through him that the fast trading ships, now lying below the Legion's camp, had been prepared. "Let the sailors keep far from the Arabian shore," wrote Valens; "the faction of Syllaeus are opposed to our venture. Have a care of them, should they insist on sailing at the new moon, for it is under that that their most desperate ventures are undertaken." Gallus had watched the new moon rise that night, a thin chip of silver above the black hills.

Valens had found none whom he could trust, but a black man among his own company, one Buralo. The warriors of Judah, who marched with Valens, and on whom the Romans depended as the most reliable of their Allied

Force, were not liked by the Nabataeans. "Be sure," the first report concluded, "this is no easy venture. Beware of treachery at all times. I leave from here with King Herod's men at daybreak. Syllaeus and some five hundred of his Arabs accompany us and I leave this with those who prepare your camp by the ships; greetings."

Between this first report and the second was much time and distance. The second was a report on the road to the south, a confusing roll giving name after name of places and the distances between them, yet each name of something inconsiderable—a single well, a hut village, a grove of palms. Here and there through the precise details of distances and outlandish names, Gallus could form a picture in his mind. One picture in particular, towards the close of the report, caught Gallus' attention and after he had read it, he remained for a time pensive, his eyes half closed, trying to visualize the things his subordinate had seen. "The road," wrote Valens, "is but a channel of untidy tracks, covered sometimes by sand, sometimes cut deep in the rock of hills or in the dead lava of vast plains. We halt and fill goat skins with water, wherever there are wells or wherever the people have built water cisterns to catch the rain, which they say falls seldom and only after much sacrifice. It is a long, narrow road, leading us across deserts the like of which I have never seen. Only on the road can water be found. To left and right there is no water, nothing but a wilderness of sand and rock in which, should a man stray, he would swiftly die. These deserts, they say, are the home of evil spirits. Yet it is a road of riches, up which comes all the treasure of the world; therefore, at the end of the road, there must be some land such as men have named Arabia the Happy. No man would travel this road, were it not that, at its distant end, he should find a great treasure for his pains."

Did Valens doubt the existence of that land at the end of the road? Gallus shivered a little, in the cold of early morning. He unrolled again the last report, written some months before at the port of Leuke Kome, and delivered to him a few days ago by ship. Its opening words had shocked him: "Those of Judah have turned back from me," he wrote: "their horses sickened in the lowland heat under this sun, which is the enemy of all. Their leader died suddenly by night and after this they left me, some in groups and some singly as they wished and I doubt but that they are lost and that King Herod will see his men no more. I am left with Syllaeus. Some of my own men are loyal to me. Have no doubt of it, all here and to the south oppose Caesar's venture. All know that, should we take even a part of this long road into our hands, the source of their riches will be taken from them. Now, with the defection of those of Judah, we can look for no Allies save those chosen by the guide Syllaeus. I send this by the hand of the black, Buralo, in whom you may trust. He is of a distant, nomad nation, the Somal, who have no part with the Arabians. He is a seaman and I counsel you to keep him with you, when you take ship."

The Roman Legions depended much on the use of auxiliaries in their mode of war and the loss of the Jewish Allies was most serious. Gallus could delay his departure and seek to make up his strength—but from where? If indeed Syllaeus was disloyal to his King, Gallus would be ill-advised to increase the number of Arabian Allies. Perhaps, in such conditions of travel as Valens had described, a smaller force than the fifteen thousand men he had been

12

granted might prove to be advantageous. He had resolved to leave these matters until he could assemble his whole force at Leuke Kome, but in his heart lay the first seed of misgiving. For a moment doubt grew in him. He pulled aside the curtain of the tent door and stood for a space, looking at the sleeping camp and then, as if to answer his fears, the strident voice of a trumpet called the camp from sleep.

*   *   *

Gallus sat in the after cabin, his back wedged in the corner of a bulkhead against the rolling of the ship. The north-west wind, which had filled the great lateen sail throughout the night, had failed with the dawn and his fleet lay scattered, rolling in the short swell, the running rigging swinging and jarring. There had been one hundred and twenty great ships when they left the little port of Ala, in the Gulf of Aqaba, fifteen days ago. Now there were eight less and they had not strayed. They had been lost on a dark night close at hand to his ship, when the thunder of the suddenly encountered reef and the tumult of the sea had not drowned the cries of four hundred drowning men. If what the Master of his ship said was true— that water spirits raised rocks in the deep sea to trap wayfarers—no ships would sail on these waters.

He dreaded the night, the fire in the iron basin on the poop throwing its flickering, red light on the straining sail, the leap and shudder of the ship in a sea of white fire, the spray thrown from darkness over the plunging prow, the feeling that he controlled nothing, not even this labouring ship which bore them into the unknown. Not least he hated this morning calm, from dawn until the sun was quarter risen, the foul air, the rolling of the ship and the pale, grim faces of his men, staring out over the glassy ocean, with who knew what dreams behind their eyes.

He turned as a tall, angular figure darkened the narrow cabin door.

"Ah, Clemens," he said, "enter."

Julius Clemens, First Javelin of the Legion, the Commanding Centurion, lurched through the doorway and sat down upon a bale of straw, which did duty as a couch. Clemens was an older man than Gallus, past his fiftieth year. His hands and arms were knotted with muscle, his body thin and sword-straight, his movements like the jerks of a marionette. In his pallid, hawk-nosed face, with its thin, bloodless lips and its fringe of grey hair upon the chin, his eyes—large, dark and alive with humour—were an arresting contrast. He spread his long legs, to steady himself.

"You sent for me, *Praefectus*," he said.

"Yes, Clemens, I am troubled. The Master of this ship has told me that, when the wind rises, we must close the shore, since we are near the port of Leuke Kome and he must make a landfall to guide him before night. Buralo, the black, is no navigator; but he swears that Leuke Kome lies yet some days ahead. Such men, I believe, have the power of knowing their place in the sea, from long experience of it. And we are not far from the shore, for all yesterday and this morning I have felt sand between my teeth. What think you, Clemens?"

"We could order the fleet to be anchored at nightfall," replied Clemens. "The Master has himself said that these waters are dangerous by night."

"The water spirits?"

Clemens smiled. "Let us call Buralo and an interpreter," he suggested. "We are children in the hands of these

14

seamen, on the sea. If we demand that the ships should anchor, the Master will reply that we must find an anchorage out of deep water."

Buralo entered, salaaming in the doorway, and stood straddle-legged, his broad back jammed on the low cabin roof, like a black Atlas supporting the world. He listened as the interpreter, a young servant of the court of King Abodas, put to him Gallus' questions. Then he spoke, a deep voice and a rolling, tripping tongue:

"He says that Your Excellency should in some fashion warn the fleet. On each ship, only the Master and three or four Arabians are of the faction of Syllaeus. The crews are seamen, mostly of no race. On this ship there are five who serve the Master and fourteen who distrust him and who follow Buralo. Should Your Excellency desire, he is ready to slay the Master and his men and to take over the ship, but he says that he has no true skill in navigation."

Clemens and Gallus consulted together. Then Clemens spoke again to the interpreter:

"Tell our friend Buralo," he said, "that we will find some way by which we can make the soldiers in the other ships alert to-night. Should there be real danger he must not hesitate, he must take over the ship and lead the fleet to open sea as best he can. After that we will have only the dangers of the sea to face together, and the dagger of treachery will be no more."

In the mid-morning, the wind rose, a few breaths which darkened the water and then a steady, rising wind from the north-east. The sails filled and the ships heeled over, driving smoothly through the swell with the freshening wind on their port beam. Gallus stood for a while by the silent steersman on the poop, who leant his bare breast against the great tiller. Below, in the waist, an Arab seaman crooned to himself, absorbed in some task with a fishing line. Gulls circled the ship as the sun sank, and night came down over the fleet, when the eye could no longer see, and the ear was filled with sound. Gallus wrapped his cloak closer about him and returned to his cabin. He slept a little.

The sound of running feet awoke him. He stood in the doorway and looked out into the tumultuous night. The great yard had been half lowered, seamen were weird shadows against a deeper blackness in the bows. From a ship far to the south a drum began to beat, a dead, empty sound over the sea. Men stood up and gathered their cloaks about them, staring into the darkness.

Bin Ja'ad al Bahri, the Master of the ship, stood by the steersman, two others beside him. He waited for a call which he knew must come from the look-out in the bows.

"Reefs ahead!"

Bin Ja'ad turned swiftly and called into the darkness: "Helm a-lee! Lower away! Secure yard fore and aft, let go anchors thirty fathoms!"

But there was confusion forward, a cry cut short, the sound of running feet. The ship lowered her prow into a steep sea and bore on her course. Bin Ja'ad's hand fell to the hilt of his broad dagger and his teeth showed through thin, parted lips.

Gallus had heard the shouted orders from the poop above him. He stepped from the cabin door and glanced upwards, when a dark figure suddenly confronted him and he saw the glitter of an iron blade. It happened in an instant of time, the thrust parried by his bare arm and the feel of a man's throat strained beneath his fingers, while

16

his own dagger grated on a rib bone, sank effortlessly deep, twisted and flicked clear of the body he threw from him. In a stride he was at the foot of the poop ladder, knife in hand; but he was thrust aside by a great, black arm swinging out of the night, as Buralo bounded past him and, before he had found his balance, pandemonium broke out above on the poop-deck, there was a gasping cry and a splash, and a deep voice, urgent, commanding, calling into the night.

Black shadows sprang into the yard halliards, heaving, groaning deep in their chests, while the great yard, the sail freed and billowing, crept up the forward-slanting mast. The fire in the iron bucket on the poop blazed up in a flare of tinder and oil, showing the rising sail like a chip of fire-lit ivory. From the forepart of the ship he heard Clemens' staccato voice—"Sound the alarm and the rallying call!"

The curved horn's voice ruled the confusion of the night. From ship after ship the call echoed, first the loud insistence of danger and then the invitation of the rally. The sail of his ship, rising fire-lit in the night and the call of the war horn had spread their warning far, for north and south and behind them showed dim fire-light on other sails as ship after ship turned and followed them to open sea. There were others to whom the call came too late, for the reef was long and the tide-set was towards it. Gallus gazed into the concealing night, imagining the rending timbers and the clutching hands. He did not see three hundred of his men drowned and four of his ships lost with their precious cargoes of metal and sinew rope but, when the first light tinged the sail a faint rose, he still stood looking to the east, where a distant line of white water marked their graves.

17

A sudden triumphant shout from Buralo at the tiller woke him from his misery of doubt. He found the young interpreter beside him, his face alight, his words tumbling from his lips.

"It is the port! It is Leuke Kome!" he cried.

Buralo was beside him, pointing to a distant headland, no more than a smudge on the face of the sea. "Tell him," said Buralo to the interpreter, "that I know that *ras*, that headland; it stands in the sea a little to the north of Yenbo' al Bahr, which they call Leuke Kome—by the gods of Ma'in and of all travellers, Bin Ja'ad was right and I was wrong! By as little as a man might walk in a winter's morning, by so much did he err. May Allah of the djinns and spirits of the sea have pity on him—for I myself slit his throat and threw him from the ship!"

CHAPTER 2

Flood Tide

*After many sufferings and in great distress he reached
Leuke Kome in the country of the Nabataeans . . . the Army
was sorely tried by scurvy of the gums and legs, diseases of
the country. He was compelled to stay there during the heat
and colder weather whilst attention was given to the sick.*

THEY had given Valens a small, mud-brick house for his
use on the landward side of the town of Leuke Kome,
isolated from the main group of coral and limestone
buildings by a grove of palms. It stood in a high, walled
courtyard, containing a well and a stunted tamarisk tree.
The window of his chamber opened to the north-east
and, on a clear morning, he could see in the distance the
flat-topped summit of Jabel Radhwah and, to the east,
the rocky plain which led to the great caravan centre of
Yathrib.[1] From this house he could not hear the sea,
but the sea haunted his every dream and his every waking
thought. Somewhere in its rolling wastes it held Gallus
and a Legion of Rome and day by day he scanned it, a
shining expanse, on which no ship sailed.

This night Valens could not sleep. The wind blew
strongly off the land, warm with the first fire of summer.
He put his sword sling over his shoulder and buckled his
belt, with its hanging apron of brass-studded leather straps

[1] Now the city of Al Medina.

19

and its dagger sheath, over his long tunic and, opening the courtyard door, stepped past the sleeping watchman into the windy night.

The rubbish heaps, with their packs of mangy yellow curs, were on the south side of the town. Valens walked briskly to the north and, when the houses of the town could no more be seen, he turned westward towards the sea, over low heaps of sand and past the stunted trees, which marked the watercourses of the delta of the Wadi Yenbò'. Soon the coarse grasses of the dunes were behind him and he came down upon a rocky, coral beach. He seated himself on a rock and let the cool sea water surge up and back over his bare feet.

Out here in the night there was peace from nagging anxiety, peace from Syllaeus' wordy compliments, so belied by the mounting triumph in his dark eyes. Here the sea had, it is true, little comfort to give, but its rhythms of wave, of ebb and flow, had a timeless quality and the tired mind emptied itself of thought and drifted with the movement of the waters.

Valens sat unmoving, his chin in his hands, his dark hair ruffled by the gusty wind, his eyes on the changing patterns of the flowing surf. It had been his task now for two years to study this land of Arabia and never had there been a more elusive quest. He had hoped that here, at Leuke Kome, he might find himself at last within this strange land. This was the first port of the Nabataean Kingdom, its prosperity linked with the trading centre of Yathrib and with the holy city of Mecca, which held in its small, cubic temple, the Ka'aba, the images of all the gods of Arabia. Here, surely, one should find some pattern of the country, its government, its trade and its people. He

had found no pattern of these things. The road from
Yathrib to the north passed through here. To the south
was the road, to the north was the road and, to the west,
the road of the sea. Was there, indeed, a happy Arabia?
His search had not revealed it. Yet somewhere, deep in
the south and far more distant than the Roman world
supposed, must lie that land of the desire.

A plank, borne in on the flooding tide, touched his
foot. He bent down to it and picked it out of the water.
Under his strong fingers it felt smooth, slippery with sea
water, not long immersed. Close by him another tapped
in its passing on a coral rock. The dawn behind him
shed a faint, white light. He looked again at the flooding
waters of the little bay. It was full of broken timbers
floating in on the tide and then, while he watched, he saw
a round object, turned by a movement of the surf, which
a wave rolled almost to his feet. He sat there staring at
it, fear holding the door against comprehension. It was a
pannier of wood and basket work and, as it rolled again,
he saw the familiar "X" branded on its base. With this
sign the Tenth Legion marked all their gear.

He sat for a while unmoving, as the flotsam of disaster
drifted in from the sea. In the mouth of the bay something less buoyant than timber rolled between two rocks
and the gulls circled and screamed above it and dropped
down upon it, their wings beating. Then a sound from the
shore came to him and he turned swiftly, his hand on
his sword.

The dawn was a handsbreadth above the horizon, a
line of yellow light below the paling blue of the sky. The
morning star still glowed unwinking, a jewel in the dark
heaven. He saw, silhouetted against the band of yellow

21

light, the horseman he had heard, his mount stretched to full gallop towards the town, the beat of its hooves thudding in the loose sand.

Valens looked once more towards the sea and then rose and walked southwards down the beach. If he could know the extent of the disaster, his course would be clear. If the whole Legion had been lost, then he must return, if he could, or make sure that, in the quickest possible time, news of the calamity reached Caesar. He could, perhaps, overawe Syllaeus and remain here in safety until new forces arrived or he heard that the venture had been abandoned. But there was one thing which must first be done—he must confront Syllaeus and the Governor of the town. Search parties must be sent up the coast at once. There might be injured men to be succoured; there might be sailors who could tell how the tragedy had occurred. It might even be that as many as a Cohort of men could be reformed and, given arms, six hundred of the Legion could hold this port in the Emperor's name. He quickened his pace towards the town, his tall, spare body erect, his eyes troubled with thought.

*   *   *

Syllaeus had been awake before the dawn. It was his custom in the dark nights of late spring, to pay the dues of worship and genuflexion to Allat, the goddess Moon, after the setting of a certain star in the early morning. Allat was the mother-goddess, all fertility was hers. She was the goddess of merchandise, of all profit, of all that accrued to a man, an animal or a coin. He had purified himself in the smoke of incense before his worship and he stood now, his mind composed, the heavy smoke undisturbed by his still body. A man of middle height, slim waisted, strong with the wiry strength of the horseman, his face, ascetically pale, yet glowed with virile health. His pointed beard was dark and oiled. His large dark eyes, remote in their expression, were narrowed between long-lashed eyelids. All the beauty, all the force of the Arabian were his. Those calm eyes, those long-fingered hands could bless and fondle any young thing and, in fanatical anger, the eyes could look without doubt on death and the hands could take any life, unhesitantly.

The messenger came to him as he stood, void of thought, in his private room. He had heard the challenge of the watchman, the waking of his servants and the footsteps of the messenger to his door. Now, without turning, he called, asking who came and at once the messenger entered, a half-naked Arab, his breast heaving, his head cloth awry.

"It is done, Excellency!" the man cried: "The whole shore is littered with their gear and their corpses! We watched five nights. Last night, at sunset, we saw the Roman fleet, like a thin mist of blossoms fallen on the sea, bearing in towards the coast, in the last light of day. At midnight the first of their torn planks reached the shore and then came the corpses of their soldiers. For a day's march up and down from the headland the sea brings in all that is left of Rome!"

Syllaeus, his contemplative air unchanging, regarded the messenger. "Tell me," he asked, "how much of the shore did you see, before you came to me?"

"The wreckage drifted in where we watched, south of the headland and some to its north; from the headland until you come to the fishermen's huts, all is littered with floating timber.

"Go then and call the Governor. Tell him your news and that I shall come to him directly and that I must speak also with the Commander of the soldiers."

As Syllaeus raised his feet in turn to allow the slave to bind on his sandals at the outer door, his mind remained placid. He had long since visualized this chain of events and the things which he must do. There was no need for haste and caution must yet rule him. If the Legion were indeed no more, then little remained to be done but the murder of Valens and a messenger to the fat old King Abodas—let the King have the unenviable task of commiserating with Caesar. In the town and camped among the dunes to its west, he had some two thousand men at arms, all mounted. If only a few Romans survived, having struggled through the rocks to the shore, the fishermen could be trusted to deal with them. If a shipful or more survived it might be necessary to let the soldiers land in peace, to march with them a few miles into the hills away from curious eyes and there to fall upon them with the sword.

He found the Governor in the reception-room of his house, overlooking the little port and, beyond, the open sea. A large room, its beams of imported teak—since no timber of any size grew inland—it opened on to a wide veranda through a tall, oriental arch. The room was white, carpeted with many rough mats, blue, red and white striped, an industry of the country. A few pillows lay against the wall, but the Governor and the hastily summoned gathering of soldiers and merchants stood in the archway, their backs to the sea. As Syllaeus entered, all turned towards him, their speech held in mid-sentence, their eyes wide with question.

24

"You have heard the news?" he asked, when he had given his hurried greetings.

"Praise the gods!" cried the Governor. "We have heard it indeed! And now, honoured one, it remains only to send men along the sands, to slay such of these devils as have come up out of the sea alive!"

The Commander of the soldiers stepped forward: "It shall be done with despatch! And this Roman who lodges with us, what of him, the spy? This *Walein*—if such be his accursed name—but give the order and my sword shall sever his dull head from his foul body!"

"*Nesr*, the god of victory, must have his sacrifice!" exclaimed an old merchant. "Let us bind this *Walein* and let his blood flow at the god's feet!"

"Peace!" said Syllaeus. "Peace! There is time for all these things, once we know how many of the Romans now live—the sword of action will not be less sharp if we hide it for a while in the cloak of patience!"

"Patience!" cried one. "If this is not the time to strike and to have done with Rome, then I am a slave! The gods of the sea have cast away their fleet, now let us take this spy we have borne with too long and let him die like a sheep upon our altars!"

Syllaeus had raised his hand for silence, but the flood of their words burst upon him. Anger, lust for slaughter, hatred of the stranger they held at their mercy brought dire words to their lips and their hands to sword and dagger hilt. Their rage hung above Syllaeus, a great curling wave which must sweep him away, as they pressed their bearded faces close to his and shook the sleeves of his cloak in their vehemence—and the wave remained suspended and their words caught back, as the door of the room opened and Valens entered, his face stern and his eyes unflinching. He stopped a few paces from Syllaeus and a grim smile twitched the corner of his lips.

"Peace upon you," he said. "Does the tempest of words fan the fire of audacity? I heard you from the street!" And he laughed.

"By God!" gasped one. "Why do we wait?" and he stepped forward, his sword half drawn. But there was an answer to his question. It was in the calm of the blue eyes and the threat of the smiling lips. Valens knew that he stood on the doorstep of death; but he had a deeper knowledge, a conviction that there was some part of his fate which remained unfulfilled and that the last door was yet closed to him. This knowledge came to him swiftly, profoundly. For a moment the men he confronted, their anger and their menace, became of no importance. He looked away from them and through the broad, oriental arch towards the sea. His eyes widened and the smile left his lips.

Syllaeus, who stood closest to Valens, turned slowly and gazed also at the bright blue water and one after another they all turned and silence fell upon them. Far away, on the very rim of the sea, the sails showed, lit by the full, flooding light of morning, tiny, motionless and white. For a long time no one spoke. Then Syllaeus murmured: "A thin mist of blossoms fallen on the sea; it was well said!"

"What was that?" asked Valens, turning towards him and curious to hear the phrase again.

Syllaeus' eyes met his, a friendly glance: "So a man once described to me a fleet of ships, seen thus afar off; he said, 'A thin mist of blossoms fallen on the sea.'"

"He was a poet?" asked Valens.

"No," said Syllaeus, "no, he was not a poet; he was a fisherman."

* * *

Gallus pitched his camp on a rocky knoll to the east of the town. It was like a dead town, half deserted, its merchants fled. Only the fishing community remained undiminished, in their village of grass huts on the beach to the north, and throughout daylight the triangular sails of their canoes moved back and forth beyond the reef. The Governor and all who had stood with him looking through the archway at the distant sails, except Syllaeus, had gone. Syllaeus remained, grave, thoughtful, dignified, ever ready when advice or help was needed. It was natural, he had explained to Gallus, that the people of the country resented the intrusion of a Roman Army and its professed desire to march in their desert trade routes, which could ill support, in food and water, the caravans which already moved in them. He could not deny that Valens had heard threats against the Romans, from the merchants and commanders of the town. He, Syllaeus, heard such things daily. But he protested his own innocence with vigour. Valens had been in some danger that morning but so had he and from him the danger had not lifted. Had not Valens heard him argue for caution and patience? And while the others had fled, he had stayed, a loyal servant of his King, who was a friend of Rome.

Gallus treated Syllaeus with cautious urbanity. If he were in truth the real enemy, as Valens insisted, it was better to have him close at hand, where he could be watched, than far away. Moreover, from the moment of

27

his arrival at the port, the Legion had encountered difficulties and dangers of which they had not been forewarned. Here was no grain such as formed the bulk of a Roman soldier's rations, there was no olive oil and the wine was raw and scarce and soon consumed, nor could more be brought in the summer's heat. The Legion had embarked on a treacherous sea and they had landed in a strange world. The grain they ate here was a coarse, red millet, hard to grind and bitter to the taste. Their palates had to become educated to new and foul-tasting foods—the sour, lumpy milk of goats, taken from ancient skins, the nauseating *samn*, the clarified butter of camel's milk, the flacid flesh of undernourished sheep and the raw country oil. There was no green food. Valens consulted Syllaeus over the health of the men, who sickened and died under the fierce sun, itself a bitter enemy, as they were to know full well.

"The scurvy?" said Syllaeus. "It is a common ailment here among the folk and comes from the sea. Let the men eat no flesh and drink no milk and let them march a day or two into the hills where the air is not sea-tainted."

Valens thanked him. He went to the headman of the fishing village, a small brown man, with a straggling grey beard, his body bare except for a loin cloth knotted round his broad legs. He found him dragging his canoe towards the sea.

"Let the men eat fish!" cried the headman. "See," he exclaimed, taking a fresh-caught Bonito of about fifteen pounds' weight in his hands and digging his sea-wrinkled thumbs into its firm flesh. "See, this fish has all that the belly desires; here is flesh, so sweet that a man may eat it raw, and in the flesh is oil, such as comes from no plant in hill or valley!"

28

Valens could not deny that this fish seemed strangely unlike any other fish he had seen except, perhaps, the sardine or the herring. He returned to the camp and found old Serenus, the Quartermaster, sitting outside his tent near the camp centre, regarding a growing ulcer on his right calf, his bearded face a study of gloom.

"Syllaeus!" exclaimed Serenus. "He would have us eat sand. A Roman soldier must have wheat and oil and wine."

Clemens the First Javelin and Gallus stood outside the hospital tent, where Valens joined them. He told them of Syllaeus' advice and of the words of the fisherman.

"I believe the fisherman," said Gallus, "and he must bring us all the fish he can catch. That will be little enough."

A bearded Bedouin, concerned in some business of the supply of milk or flesh, walked towards them down the stone-bordered path, a soldier escorting him. Valens stopped him.

"What is your name?" he asked.

"Salih! *Ana* Salih!"

"The son of whom?"

"Bin Ma'tuk!"

"Come with me."

He led him into the hospital tent. He showed him the men there, their bleeding gums and ulcerous limbs and then led him apart, outside the tent.

"Now, *ya* Salih bin Ma'tuk," he said, "have you seen this illness before?"

"It is the sickness of those who cannot eat! It is a townsman's sickness and the bane of the sailor. *Wullahi wa al Illahat!* I know it full well, when the sailors land here and languish, crying out for flesh and camel's milk.

29

They lie in the shade of trees, drinking and gorging until their stomachs are like Jebel Radhwah! Then, when they are stout again, the humour leaves them and they seek work again in the ships." He warmed to his subject: "*Bin 'Ami*, my uncle's son," he cried, "found once such a man. When he came to us he was like a dead shark, black and coarse skinned and his ribs like a half-built boat. *Wullah wa Tillah* and my name Salih! Never was there so sick a man! But he drank the fresh milk and ate flesh with us four moons and one night, being swollen with food, he craved a wife from us—he a great black man—and he raged like a stallion camel and struck my uncle's son a blow which threw him upon his back without speech and thus, mark you, was the custom broken and in defence of our women I drew my sword and slew him in the tent door——"

Valens pushed him gently to the waiting soldier and he left, still telling the tale to the startled camp.

"It seems," said Valens, when he had rejoined his superiors, "that we must overset Syllaeus' advice. The men must have fresh milk, flesh and fish and rest in the shade, until their bellies are like the mountain yonder!"

"We will try it," said Clemens, "you will make the arrangements, Valens, and Serenus will see to a just distribution. We are all like to perish here, unless this evil is overcome."

The sickness continued a danger to them and the cooling winds of autumn brought little relief. Dysentery and other stomach ailments took their toll of the Legion and malaria carried a few, even of these men so hardened to it, to their graves. In tribulation of mind and in pain of body the

Legion fought its invisible foes with its armament of discipline and its weapon of resolve. Slowly, as the winter passed, the sickness lessened, until one bright morning, five thousand four hundred men paraded in their full equipment and ninety stallions of the mounted wing, off saddled, rolled and kicked happily in the warm sand and Clemens knew that the men he had made from ghosts were ready now for adventure and for war.

* * *

It was a night of the new moon and they brought a messenger from King Abodas to Syllaeus. The King wrote that he had heard of many men of the Legion lost at sea. He counselled Syllaeus to have a care of his friends. But the messenger had another letter, written to the Governor of the town and for his eyes only.

"I am the Governor of the town," said Syllaeus, "you will give the letter to me."

The messenger demurred. These were words written by the King with his own hand and to the Governor by name. Syllaeus would doubtless hear from that functionary the purport of the orders it contained.

"Search him!" said Syllaeus.

He opened the letter, which had been heavily sealed. The messenger, the rough search over, lay panting against the wall. Syllaeus glanced towards him—the grey face, the weakly moving hands. He read the letter slowly, his heart unstirred, his mind placid.

"To His Excellency, the Sheikh Mubarak bin 'abd al Qasim the Governor of the port of Yenbo' may he be long preserved, you shall at once have my emissary, Syllaeus, taken and slain, showing this letter as your authority, and sending me his ring as a proof of your obedience, in the name of Allat, mother of the Nabataeans and of your Master, 'Abud, the King."

"Let all the doors and windows be closed," said Syllaeus.

They waited in the room in silence, the guards motionless by the door, the messenger gazing wide-eyed at the floor, his mind flooded, overfull with fear.

"Now," said Syllaeus, "let a sack and a strong cord be brought."

The messenger fell forward on his knees, his hands outstretched. "Excellency!" he cried, "I only bore the letter, it was not from me!"

Syllaeus' large, dark eyes opened wide and he turned an astonished, a humorous glance towards the speaker: "You knew its purport," he said and turning to his men he nodded.

There was no noise. For a bare minute the hooded body of the messenger jerked horribly, while Syllaeus held the King's order to the flame of the lamp and burnt it and pressed the ashes to powder between his fingers. Then the man who held the cord relaxed.

"He is dead," he said.

"The rubbish heap," said Syllaeus evenly, "the one yet too hot for the dogs. Bury the body deep, where the flame still burns."

"It shall be done," they answered.

When they had left him, he sat alone, the still flame of the oil lamps illuminating the table before him. He wrote on the hard papyrus with firm, clear strokes of his wooden stylus and the words he wrote to his friend at the King's court were comely and innocent, a simple cipher for the orders he conveyed. But his thoughts as he wrote were neither comely nor innocent. As he ciphered and wrote, evil things in the dark corners of his mind spread outwards from the illuminated table and stirred in the dark corners of the room. A cup of wine for the King, a cup of the best wine, cooled with snow, and the thin yellow drops stirred therein and death, foul and agonizing, for Abodas of Nabataea.

In the Roman camp beyond the town a horn blew to herald the coming day. A breath of parched air stirred the leafless thorn trees. Sentries changed at the guard tent and at the gates. There was the sound of the awakening of disciplined men.

CHAPTER 3

The Narrow Road

*Gallus again led forth his army from Leuke Kome by
parts such that water had to be carried on camels. . . .*

In the starlit hour before the dawn the camp was astir.
Voices, hushed in the darkness, sounded clear and thin.
Beyond the main camp gate, over a high dune, the camels
passed, an endless line, their long necks stretched forward
as each struggled to the crest and, plunging from it down
the slope of sand, was followed by another. All night
they had grumbled and snarled while they were saddled
with their carefully apportioned loads. Long before they
had risen from their kneeling places, the strident *Lituus*
had sounded for the departure of the mounted wing. Now
the thirty maniples of foot soldiers, each of two *Centuriae*,
filed out of the gate to halt in the open and to await the
dawn. Behind them rose bright flames from the empty
wooden storehouses and the unwanted gear, while some
remained to break down the camp walls into the surrounding dyke; for it was the custom of the Legions to destroy
the camps they abandoned.

The men carried their rolled burdens and their helmets
slung on strong, forked poles, resting the shafts on their
shoulders. They were heavily laden, in their armour and
with their weapons. They trudged through the sand in

silence, glad to leave this camp where so many had died, to be at last on their way to the land of promise.

As the morning star rose above a dove-grey dawn, the long column moved forward. Their first stage was to the town of Al Hamra, and between it and the camp was a single well in the hills, Bir Sa'id, the Happy Well, a name of good omen. Syllaeus had provided five hundred mounted Allies but, since they were doubtful of the capacity of the Happy Well, these had left for Al Hamra on the previous morning, where other Allies, archers and slingers, had been promised. The Legion moved forward with a vanguard of mounted men, behind which, also mounted, came the survey and the pioneer parties. Some five hundred paces behind them rode Gallus with his escort of horse and foot, followed by the mounted wing of the Legion. Then came a long column of camels, bearing the engines of siege and war, followed by the senior Cohort commanders and the massed standards, the Legion's golden Eagle in their centre, and their guards. Behind these marched the burdened foot soldiers, the strength of the Legion, the long column of baggage camels, and, far in the rear, a single Cohort of lightly burdened men.

It was a strange caravan to set forth into Arabia. Gallus and his staff had barely yet comprehended the nature of the land they were invading. It was a vast, inhospitable land which was to reveal itself to lonely travellers slowly and painfully through the centuries; it was to retain the mysteries of its emptiness for two thousand years after Gallus and his gallant army were dust. He had planned as a man might plan to invade the moon, unknowing the inimical conditions, believing the barren to be pregnant with treasure. The world the Legion knew possessed water. Here, in few and widely separated places, water lay deep in ancient wells and, except after violent thunder floods, when for a few hours the earth drank thirstily from torrents in the hills, the land was dry. In their world wheels carried the reserve food and the heavy equipment. Here wheels sank in the sand or broke in the jagged lava of the plains and only the slow-paced camels moved freely through the wilderness. In the world they knew, the sun brought light and strength to men. Here and in the south, where indigo-stained Kahtani Arabs worshipped her as a goddess and the moon as a god, the sun drank the moisture from their bodies and struck them down suddenly in the noonday. And there was the road—the narrow track of Valens' report—the hard road which one must keep, for left or right of the road were tall dry mountains or wastes of sand. One must not stray from the road. It alone could lead one to the next well, to the next habitation, a thin path, dusty yellow by day, shining in the starlight, ancient, impersonal, leading on and on, south to the kingdoms of the sun, east into emptiness.

They travelled to the east. In a short hour the coastal sand dunes gave way to gravel plain. No longer, now, could they look back on the sea. Tall dunes hid the sea from them and they had entered a new country, a bare plain, rising imperceptibly towards the hills before them and to their left. Here and there grew a stunted thorn tree or a foot-high tuft of grey-green weed. The long column moved forward slowly, men halted to adjust a burden or quickened their pace to preserve their distances. Midday passed. There was no fresh thing, no interest to attract the eye. The land had nothing, only small lizards and little birds the same drab colour as their earth. The hills lay across their route, a low, scarred screen below the sky.

In the late afternoon they made camp. The surveyors had mapped and marked it out, as was their duty, and the pioneers had done what they could with the stony ground. Firewood was scarce. When the light faded from the sky, the Legion slept behind their low perimeter wall and the camp was dark and still, except for the voices of the sentries and the calls of the horn, which marked the watches of the night.

Dawn saw them again on the move, their direction south-east, across a plain intersected by dry stream courses, full of tumbled boulders. There was a little more contour to the ground, a low hill here and there and the mountains before them took shape, dry and steep and uninviting. That night their sleep was short and their awakening hastened by lack of water. Gallus summoned the senior officers to his tent after midnight, while the baggage was loaded and asked Valens to describe the next day's march.

"The Happy Well," said Valens, "must be reached before nightfall. We should be in mountain country by midday and there is but one track; but the march to the well is safe, I am assured of that."

"Is this road," asked one, "truly the great caravan road?"

"It is," replied Valens.

They all laughed. Receptus, of the First Cohort, spoke jeeringly: "Where are the rest houses, the hostelrics and the pedlars' encampments?"

"There is no water," said Valens. "We have to carry water for our horses. The Arabians travel this road on camels, which water seldom. It is a long road. Should

37

people settle where there is a well and not a copious supply of water, the merchants of the land would drive them away into the deserts, for all the water is needed for the caravans. You will see no people until you reach Al Hamra, which is a day's march from the Happy Well."

They looked at each other wonderingly. A fear, a distrust of this empty country, which yet opposed their march and menaced them with hunger and thirst, entered among them from the night. It was to remain with them, that fear, many of them to their last hour, a fear of emptiness, opposing them, yet drawing them on, whispering an invitation in their hearts. And their hearts answered the whisper with challenge.

They moved out of camp, men and camels unrolling into the dawn on to the narrow road, like a long thread pulled from a tangle of cotton. Their baggage train alone, the camels head to tail, bearing tents, palisade stakes, catapults, ballistæ and their ammunition, reserve food and the hundreds of water skins for men and horses, lengthened their column by about eleven miles of our reckoning—almost a day's march in theirs, so heavily laden was the Roman soldier. By midday they were marching between high mountain walls, the pageantry of standard bearers, in their lion and bear mask head-dresses, the horn-blowers with their great shining horns, compressed to single file. Night found more than a third of them still moving, stumbling up the dark ravines. At the Happy Well reigned dire confusion. The men drank thirstily, leather buckets rose and fell. The mounted men—the surveyors, pioneers, Gallus and his staff and guards and the mounted wing—had watered their horses and filled their water skins and had moved away into a gully, to clear the well-head. They felt naked here, in the dark, unknown country, without a camp.

Clemens found Valens among Gallus' staff. He called him apart.

"There are eight hundred men and over a thousand camels yet unwatered and many still marching," he said. "The water is low in the well and muddy—is there no other water near here?"

"There is none closer than Al Hamra."

The old First Javelin glared at Valens. Then he turned and strutted away to the well, where Gallus watched the half-filled buckets lurching out of the well shaft. They conferred together. The skins must be filled here, they would need to rest the well and there would be endless delay. They agreed swiftly and sent for Antonius Valens and Publius Sabinus, the swarthy Centurion of the mounted wing.

"You will take the survey and pioneer group and the mounted wing. We must make sure of Al Hamra. Leave all your kit but one day's rations, ride fast to Al Hamra and surround it. I will send after you, as fast as they can march, two unburdened Cohorts. The rest of us must stay here until all are watered and fed. March at once."

In a short time they were on the road, some three hundred mounted men, their horses' hooves raising the echoes of the steep gorges. The path turned and twisted. Mountains towered on either side, bright stars shone down from above, striking cold light from helmet, shoulder armour and heavy spear. Sabinus, who led them, pressed on, there was no wind and they choked in the rising dust and the heavy smell of sweating horses. In the rear the men rode hard to keep the pace, urging their mounts with heel and voice. The long hours passed as they rode. Twice they dismounted and walked, stumbling, to relieve their horses. Then the pace slackened, there was a murmur of voices and an order passed down the line.

"Silence! Silence! We are close to Al Hamra!"

*   *   *

Rushlights burned and smoked in the long reception-room of the Headman's house at Al Hamra. Some thirty men sat with their backs to the wall, some cross-legged, some lounging on brightly coloured cushions. At the head of the room, in the place of honour on the Headman's right, Syllaeus, his slim body erect and commanding, ruled the *mijlis*. These men met here were no common travellers. They were the rich merchants of the land to north and south. There was Abu Bakr of the Qareish from Mecca, Master of Caravans, hirer of vast camel herds. There was the fabulously rich 'Abd al Ya'uk of the city of Najran, designer and maker of fine jewellery and a merchant of precious stones. Old and white-bearded, his red-rimmed eyes flashed at the Headman with hardly restrained anger. There was Bin as Seil from the distant port of Dhufar, a dealer in the magic incense and in precious gums and woods, and many others, rich and powerful men. All were angry, impatient, their minds on the waiting caravans of thousands of camels, delayed by the Roman invasion in town and village, all down the long road to the sea. This Legion was an intolerable thing.

"Picture them to yourselves," said Syllaeus, "as I have seen them. At sunset yesterday they were lost and scattered in the narrow defiles. They will not find water enough at Bir Sa'id until they have sucked it dry three times. When their first camel kneels here in the camping place, their last will be more than a half day's march away!" He turned to the Headman: "My five hundred men will hold them in front, and your young men will have them, the General first and all his leaders, throat by throat!"

The old Headman gestured weakly. "But the King 'Abud?" he asked, querulously. "What order have I from the King?"

He did not like this work. The curse of all the gods upon the Romans, the merchants and Syllaeus! He was in a cleft stick. Should his ambush fail, he knew full well that Syllaeus would turn on him and swift death was the most he could hope for, for him and his family.

"I am the King's messenger!" snapped Syllaeus.

"Let them go on," pleaded the Headman. "Between here and Najran are endless deserts. Here we are too near Rome."

'Abd al Ya'uk of Najran leant forward and tapped the floor with his cane: "My caravans lie still," he croaked, "and I have suffered enough from this delay. Not a beast moves from here to Marib and from Shabwa to Azzan the roads are empty. Why should the Romans march in our paths and drink dry our wells? Here, at Al Hamra, is the opportunity to slaughter their whole force, piece-meal among the hills."

"Here is our opportunity," affirmed Syllaeus, "and for your service in the matter, their arms, their stores of brass and other metals, which I have described to you, even the camels which carry them are yours, for yourself and for the people of Al Hamra."

The old Headman glared round the room in despair. What could he do, what could he say which had not already been said? They were all against him. Tired and browbeaten, he leaned back against the wall.

"It is well," he said, "it is well; let the young men prepare themselves. We shall strike. But, Syllaeus, bear with me a little—who shall strike first? There is no——"

"I have borne with you from dusk until near dawn!" exclaimed Syllaeus. "Now get you up, I pray you. Let the men arise——"

The door burst open and a young man entered, armed with bow and spear.

"The hills are full of men!" he cried.

"Men——?"

"As I lay on the spur below, I heard a falling stone. There, on the hill-top above I saw three men. They are all round us in the hills, their lances are like blades of grass against the sky!"

Syllaeus rolled on to his elbow and opened the nearest wooden shutter. He closed his eyes for a space and then looked into the night. A dark spur of granite across the wadi bed showed dimly in the first, faint light of early dawn. For a long time he watched and then he saw a little movement of shadow upon shadow and the faint sparkle of polished metal. He turned away, a slight smile on his lips.

"We have talked too long," he said. "I am tired and must sleep."

*　　　*　　　*

The first camels of the Legion filed into the kneeling place below Al Hamra in the early afternoon. From the forts and hills above them their own comrades saluted them and their Nabatean Allies vied with each other to welcome the brave soldiers of Rome, to draw water and to stack the heavy burdens.   Here at Al Hamra were many little springs and if one struck the rock where it was damp, water flowed from it.   Until far into the night the long column came in, the slow plodding camels and the tired men, their beards yellow with dust and their eyes red and sunken.

There was an abundance of fodder at Al Hamra.   The people were friendly and the old Headman hummed to himself in the morning, as he saw to the watering of his garden.   Syllaeus was the affable ally, never intruding, always there.   On their third evening at Al Hamra, he sat with Gallus and his Staff on the broad, flat roof of the Headman's house.

"Now," said Syllaeus, "when you are rested here, we will go to the city of Yathrib.   We shall not enter the city, for it is full of caravans, but we will camp near it, in easy reach of the water.   You will find space there to make your customary camp.   Yathrib is on the main route, a city stored with provisions of every kind and you will find there all that you require.   From there it is easy marching to Raudha, 'the restful place', a name of good omen, where lives a cousin of our King, one Aretas, who desires to entertain you.   We will add to the number of your auxiliaries there and we will find there guides to the south.   From there we set out on the long march to Najran.   To reach the incense lands, you must pass through Najran, which is the most fertile land in all Arabia.   There you will prepare yourselves for your journey into the southern kingdoms, which hold all of the south and the land of the blacks across the sea."

"A long road," murmured Valens.   He was standing, his elbows on the wall of the roof, looking down on the plain. Below him, some two hundred of the Legion's horses were being walked in a circle in the centre of which stood Publius Sabinus, the Centurion of the mounted wing, and two other Centurions, watching the horses critically. He saw Sabinus lift his *vitis* stick and beckon to one of the riders and, in the still evening, he heard his voice, sharply commanding: "Dismount and bring your horse here!"

The man dismounted and began to lead his horse to the centre of the ring. But the animal moved slowly and then stood, lifting and replacing a hind leg. Then it took a lumbering pace forward and fell over on its side. For a moment it lashed out with its hind legs and then lay still.

"Poison!" whispered Valens.

In the morning, when they had hoped to march, one hundred and seventy horses lay dead. Valens sent for the Headman and for Syllaeus.

"The General requires two hundred horses," said Valens, shortly.

"Two hundred!" exclaimed the Headman. "From whence, two hundred?"

"From the men of Al Hamra, and he wants horses which do not die."

"But these horses are owned privately," protested Syllaeus. "Surely the General will not take horses from men who are not soldiers but are private citizens? Let him take horses from my auxiliaries who can march on foot, until more can be found."

"No. We require the horses of Al Hamra."

"He will compensate the owners?"

"Their owners will march with us," replied Valens. "Should a horse die its owner will die also. This is the General's order."

44

The Legion left Al Hamra in grim silence. Women and children, crowded upon the house-tops, watched them go. The surly Nabataeans had ridden from the town by night, with no word of farewell. The villagers, those who did not accompany the Legion as hostages for their horses, walked among their low crops and spat. Even the village dogs were silent, cowed among the dung heaps.

Many blamed the old Headman to his face, but he was happy. His houses still stood and his crops were unharmed. Let who would fight Rome. And that Syllaeus, too, a pox on him, the cunning man! The Legion marched to the incense lands—he laughed. That was a long road, a bitter road. Here, at Al Hamra, they would not be seen again.

The road rose gradually and, at sunset, the Legion pitched camp below the steep pass of Al Jadeida. The village here was deserted, but there was water in plenty and here they rested for two days, under the shade of palms. The third night found them moving again over rough, rocky ground and, after a night and a day of toil in the fierce heat of the hills, they halted in two separate camps on the track. At dawn they reformed into one column and marched through unchanging country until nightfall brought them to a place of springs, and there they camped. During all this time they saw no one and marched along a twisted road in a land which was dead.

From the springs, they plunged again into the furnace of the hills. All day they laboured in the dusty, windless heat. They staggered onwards in silence, their lips caked by thirst, their breath heavily drawn in the burning air. At evening the long toil began of watering at a single well, and when at last it was done, a horn blew and the leading

45

men marched into the dawn. Night saw the column still on the move and at midnight they reached another lonely well, which ran dry before a third of the Legion had tasted its water. They pressed on and at dawn the mounted men led their exhausted horses up a path of rough steps, hewn in a high wall of lava, black and broken against the sky.

"This is the very path to the gates of death!" gasped one.

None answered him. They staggered up the steps, their minds dazed with fatigue, and halted and gazed in wonder on the scene before them.

There, made a thing of mirage by the rising sun behind it, a city stood, on a wide plain, a light breeze stirring the palm trees in its green gardens.

CHAPTER 4

The Valley of the Green Doves

After many days he came to the country of Arata where there was a kinsman of Abodas . . . but the treachery of Syllaeus . . .

THE Legion made camp to the east of the city, beyond the Bakia cemetery, on level ground. The people of Yathrib avoided the Roman camp; they had no greetings for these strangers and passed them by with averted gaze, or looked sidelong at them with hatred in their eyes. The Romans kept their hostages from Al Hamra under close guard. There was still a pretence of friendship between the Legion of Rome and the Kingdom of Nabataea, but the pretence became hard to sustain here, where the northern and the southern Arabians met and where Abodas, the northern king, no longer ruled.

It was clear, now, to Gallus, that he had no more than completed the first step of his long march. The old First Javelin, Clemens, busied himself in the complex tasks of the Legion's armament and equipment. Serenus, the Quartermaster, fat and vulgarly humorous, scratched his greying beard and studied his subordinate's suggestions for reducing the length of the baggage train. In a vivid flash of memory he pictured the long strings of camels and, a whiff of camel-stench being wafted into his tent,

47

grim and curious oaths from Gaul and Egypt and Syria flowed from his nimble tongue. Publius Sabinus of the mounted wing supervised the grooming and feeding of the horses and the hostages from Al Hamra watched them with anxious eyes, praying that the high scale of horse rations would not result in colic. Repetinus, a Centurion, expert on siege engines, examined the thick sinew ropes of the catapults and the ballistae and whistled between his teeth. They had stood the dry air well and had been kept covered from the sun.

To Antonius Valens, the camp at Yathrib brought a deep depression of the spirit. Syllaeus had always resisted and blocked his efforts to obtain a full knowledge of the country. Yet he knew much and he was sure that their next march should be made to Mecca and on from there, by easy stages, down the route of the great caravans. Gallus insisted on accepting an invitation from the King's cousin, Aretas, to visit Raudha, hoping there to plan their subsequent march in detail. Gallus distrusted all but the court and the faction of the King. He pointed out that Abodas, the King, had proved himself a friend of Caesar and that only through Roman help could the King either stabilize or extend his kingdom. Valens knew that this was true; but was Prince Aretas truly of the King's faction? The whole pattern of Roman war demanded auxiliaries under Roman command. In their place Gallus had depended upon allies and he blamed Valens for the defection of the only trustworthy ones, the men of Judah. He had not seen these men, as Valens had, overburdened with their heavy armour, in desert country which, to them, was terrifyingly unfamiliar. They had been promised five thousand mounted Arabs at Raudha, a dangerous

48

number, should they prove to be Syllaeus' men. And again—thought Valens, his tired mind turning on itself—should they prove loyal, how long would the vulnerable column be, with the addition of five thousand horses? The largest trading caravan on the main route numbered no more than three thousand camels.

On the afternoon of their last day at Yathrib, Valens sought audience with Gallus and was admitted to his tent. He looked down at the powerful, broad-shouldered figure and into the stern, pale blue eyes. He had come to argue, but he saw that his argument would only tire a man who had already made up his mind. Gallus' eyes were critical. He knew and trusted this tall fellow. He had watched him in council and on the march, a man with a career before him, should he survive this venture. Not perhaps a career commanding men, nor in a great administration, but a career on the fringes of the Empire, where a lonely man of integrity and courage, loyal to Caesar, might be of more worth than many Legions.

"I have made up my mind, Valens," said Gallus. "We go to this Prince Aretas at Raudha, or whatever the name is. You should rest now and have no thoughts until we reach the place. It is not good to think overmuch, even when thinking is your trade. The body should tire first, then the mind and last of all the spirit. The mind should not, by tiring, overbear the body which carries it."

Valens sought his tent. Lights in the camp were being lit. There was no need for guards to escort strangers from the camp here—none came to the Romans. The Legion here was far from the world it knew, isolated in an unfriendly land. The golden Eagle shone all day above the camp on its tall white staff. The sun flashed down upon it, a god of Arabia in the north, a goddess in the south, but god or goddess, it ruled the sky and burned down upon the Eagle with venom and hatred. Valens left his lamps unlit and stretched himself on the hard floor in the dark tent, his head rested on the bundle of his kit. Whatever Gallus said, to whatever plan he had made his mind, of one thing Valens was sure: if to-morrow they stepped off to the right, to Mecca and beyond, it would be a pace with the right foot, a matter of good omen. But if they set out to the east, it would be like a pace with the left foot, a dangerous step to a precipice of disaster, where no good fortune awaited them.

Prince Aretas lived in a castle on a hill—this Valens knew. He pictured the castle in his mind, as it stood to-night awaiting them, a great black tower with a light shining on its summit, a light where the Prince sat in his high belvedere, his dark counsellors about him, considering this matter of a Legion of Rome. And beyond him, under the moon, lay the vast red lands of a dead world.

Valens slept. He stood now, in his dream, below the tower, which looked down at him with two lit windows, red jewels in the night, like eyes. The tower ruled the world. He went towards it cautiously, lest it should stoop upon him suddenly and strike, like a snake. He kept to the shadows of the hill, in the dark, for fear of the tower. He turned past the shoulder of a rock and there lay at his feet a pool of still, clear water. He knelt down and looked into its depths. He knew in his heart that deep in that clear water was a thing which had been promised to him a long time ago, a thing he had searched the world to find. He stretched his right arm into the water and felt something with his fingers. He drew it up and regarded it in wonder —a beautiful, shining thing, full of pale light, it lay in his hands. It was the silver crescent of the moon.

He looked up at the tower, but its lights had gone. It stood blind and impotent in the night. As he watched, one of its walls toppled and fell soundlessly down the hillside. It was a tower no more, only an empty ruin on a hill.

The watch horns sounded, the sentries changed. Here a man spoke, there one laughed gently in his sleep. A horse neighed and another stamped its hooves and rattled its head chain. Time slipped away from them. The bright star rose in the east, the wind dropped and the morning horn called them to their tasks. Swift dawn sprang into the sky. A strident trumpet woke the echoes of the distant hills and they rode out of camp and turned east into the face of the rising sun. If we rode to the south, thought Valens, the sun would shine on our shields, but now we face it full. We are committed to error. We have stepped out with the left foot.

Four days march to their east, in high mountains, Prince Aretas of Nabataea lived in the Valley of the Green Doves. Mountains towered above the valley, sharp pointed as the blades of spears, their steep corries boulder strewn. Monstrous pillars and horns of stone jutted from their sides. In the dim past the earth's breast had here been rent in torment, nor had the winds of ages blunted those great spires forced from the billowing earth. It was thus that a rift was made between the mountains, wide and deep. From its southern end poured a rivulet of warm water, which flowed all the length of the valley and at its extremity

51

dropped down, by deep and unknown chasms, back into the earth.

All the length of the valley wild fig trees grew and, in their deep shade, all day the green doves, which cannot put foot to earth, fluttered their wings or, launched in swift, curving flight, flashed their orange breasts in the sun. Prince Aretas had come here many years ago, a young and ardent man and had chanced into this hidden valley, deep in the strange mountains. He had ridden in silence beneath the trees, and, from the source of the rivulet, he had looked back down the valley and had asked what name it bore. His guide replied that it had no name, that there was nothing here but the leopard and the red lynx and the wild ibex, with his great curved horns.

"I shall name it then," the Prince had said, smiling on his companions, "I shall name it the 'Valley of the Green Doves'. It shall be my valley."

Here, on a spur overlooking the spring, he had built his tall castle, a square tower of red granite hewn from the spur itself; a castle of great rooms and winding stairs and, on its high battlements he built a belvedere, a graceful house of marble and alabaster, where he could look down upon his valley and watch for the rising of the new moon. Beneath the castle his people lived, in a village of stone, and he called it Ar Raudha, 'The Restful Place'.

Aretas in his life had loved three times. First he had loved his valley, tending it, making it a place of beauty, seeing that it was fruitful and its people happy. Then he had brought here his beautiful wife, his cousin. Seventeen years ago he had taken her in his arms for the last time and laid her in the cold, carved marble of her tomb, near the pool she had loved, below the spring. Lilleth was her name, 'the devoted to the Moon'. Her head was pillowed on the finest silk, her white dress shone and whiter than the marble were her pale cheeks and her hair a cloud of darkness, lit by soft stars of jewels. A single heart-shaped ruby glowed between her breasts.

She had given him, in dying, his last love, his daughter, naming her Lilleth as she died. He had watched her grow, fascinated as the years brought back to him in her speech, her movements, even the small gestures of her hands, the mother he had adored. He was old now, for lost love had gored his spirit with an unkinder spur than he ever used to a horse. He had ridden far in the service of his King, his lips stern, his eye unrelenting, his body tireless. For many months at a time the little community of the valley watched expectantly for his return, while their master rode forward on far missions in distant lands, pressing his tired companions, working long into the night, so that his sleep should be deep and short and without dreams. Then, returning, he would hold his daughter's shoulders and look upon her, the dark cloud of hair, the deep brown eyes, the pale, soft cheeks, the smooth ivory of her neck, and the past returned and held him, lost in memories and wonder.

He sat now in his belvedere alone. Before him on a marble table there lay a letter, written on thin parchment, sealed with the heavy seal of the King. His hand fondled his grey, pointed beard and his eyes were sombre and his lips hard pressed together. Here was mystery. Syllaeus should arrive here with the Romans in four days' time. Yet here, in this letter from the King, the King himself wrote that he had ordered the Governor of the port of Yenbo' to execute Syllaeus. There was more. The King had been suspicious of Syllaeus and, on his departure to Yenbo', he had arrested Syllaeus' agent and had put him to the torture. The agent had revealed the whole conspiracy and had given them secret papers which gave name after name of the men and women involved, many of them among the King's closest companions. The King had roused himself and there were no more revels, no more royal banquets in the rose-red city of Petra. He had shed much blood. And he sent here a list of Nabataean merchants and commanders who must be seized and executed, trusting his cousin to see that his orders were carried out without loss of time.

Valens had imagined the Prince seated among his counsellors. Prince Aretas had no counsellors but his heart and head. He had a writer or two for his private affairs. He had skilful and loyal agents, spread through the land, a net of listeners. He had trusted friends among his own people of the valley, who carried his letters and brought to him his affairs of state. He had no soldiers here, the community of the valley were his tenant farmers, peaceful subjects of the King.

He looked through the wide door of the belvedere down the valley. In the still morning air smoke rose from fire on fire, in every glen and corry of the mountainsides, where five thousand warriors lay encamped. These were Syllaeus' men, Syllaeus who should now be dead, deep in his grave in the sand.

Far down the valley rode a party of horsemen. More of Syllaeus' men, no doubt. But were they? His interest quickened. They rode fast, disappearing into a grove of trees on the winding path. He waited, his eyes on the place where they must reappear, and as they rode from the

grove, he recognized their leader. It was his agent in
Yathrib, an old man now, one Sa'id. He took a silver
handbell from the table and rang it, ordering the servant
who came in answer to prepare for Sa'id's reception and
to show him at once to the belvedere.

Sa'id entered and greeted him, somewhat out of breath
from the long climb up the stairs. He seated himself,
puffing out his cheeks and straightening his headcloth, a
stout old fellow with a full white beard, slow of speech
but as yet alert of mind. He asked now if a servant could
be stationed on the stair, as he had ridden fast with news
which was for the Prince's ear alone.

"Aretas," he said, leaning forward, his eyes earnest
under their thick grey brows, as yet dusty with the sand
of his journey, "there is danger. We are all in great
danger. Now listen to me, I am old but I still hear well
and I see better; the Romans are coming here; you invited
them, and that is your affair. But on their journey certain
things happened to them. First, they were but a wave of
the sea from destruction on the reef to the north of Yenbo'.
This was not an accident. The Governor of the port fled
—you knew this?—but he has since died in Mecca, of a
knife thrust. Perhaps he knew too much. Then for a
long time the Romans waited by the sea and, while they
waited, messengers came and went through all the length
of the land. There has been much talk, open and secret,
and the land has joined"—he pressed the palms of his hands
together—"joined in treaty and promise against the
Romans. There was a plot to destroy them at Al Hamra
—it failed. Their horses were killed. They were not
delayed and they took hostages from the people of Al
Hamra——"

"Hostages!"

"They took the men of Al Hamra as hostages and marched on. This was a grave error. Now all the land say that they are enemies, that the King is their friend and the enemy of his people. That the King and the Romans will take our land and our wealth and we shall be enslaved. War is declared between the people and the King and it is here, here in your valley, that they will strike. It is arranged. They have five thousand men here, but they are not enough for the thing they have to do. More and more are coming, the paths to this valley are black with warriors, moving in for the kill."

Aretas was silent. He did not doubt that he had been told the truth.

"I must send this news to the King," he said. "I must warn the King——"

"The King!" Sa'id leant back, his heavy brows drawn together. "Who will find his way to the King? You may enter this valley as I have done. You may not leave it. Those are the orders. Armed men are there, in every glen, on every mountain between here and Yathrib. By day they watch from the hills. By night they are on the paths. None may pass unseen, by day or night. Those entering the valley pass unharmed. Those who try to leave it will be slain. This is the trap, here beneath your castle. This, Ar Raudha, is the place of blood and sacrifice."

"You came to me," asked Aretas, "knowing that you could never go?"

The old man smiled: "I have lived many years in your service," he said; "something may yet chance to save you and you may yet live to bury your old servant Sa'id in peace at Yathrib; but if death now comes to you in your green valley, I will go with you, no road too hard or too long."

"Tell me," asked Aretas, "do they strike at once, when the Romans come?"

"That night. They have watched them at Yathrib. The Romans send before them mounted men, who plan and build their camp and into this camp the rest move as a body, each one to his own place. They could attack them on the road, but this plan, to slay all in one place, and to slay you and your people also, has been accepted by the Chiefs."

"And my daughter?" Aretas' mouth felt suddenly dry.

"Alas! They have no pity."

Aretas rose from his chair and, leaving the belvedere, looked down from the battlements towards the spring. There, far below, he saw the dancing water of the pool and a white arm waved to him. He turned away.

* * *

The Legion had entered again the oven of the hills. They toiled in the gorges and the pale faces of thirst and hunger menaced them. They marched between walls of burning granite in the lifeless, dusty air, steadily climbing, counting the days from sip to sip of their evaporating water skins. At last on the evening of the third day they came upon a patch of river bed where the sand was damp under foot and where, when they scraped it away with their hands, they discovered slowly running water, while the mountains seemed to shake with heat above their heads. There they camped.

In the morning they entered the Valley of the Green Doves, rejoicing in the shade of the trees and in the sight and sound of running water; and, as the last Cohort behind the long baggage train passed through the gorge into the valley, others rejoiced also. Long caravans, carrying incense and spices and all manner of precious merchandise, broke camp and moved northwards from Yathrib and Mecca; for the news had reached them that the Roman Army was dead.

Valens had come to Raudha on the previous day, with the mounted advance parties and all day they had laboured, preparing the camp, in the wide valley below the castle. This morning he rose before dawn and left the camp when the horn roused the men to labour. He wandered up the valley under the tall trees, stopping by the stream to bathe his face in the crystal-clear runnels of water. He walked on, watching the grasshoppers spring away before his feet, taking deep breaths of the scented mountain air. Suddenly he laughed. "I am taking Gallus' advice!" he said aloud. He looked up at the tower. It was dark and very high, but it did not rule the world, like the tower of his dream. It was a friendly, unobtrusive tower, the same colour as the hill on which it stood. Perhaps at night it might dominate and overawe. More probably it would invite one to look through its windows to the light and comfort of its rooms. He had not yet seen the Prince.

He walked on, paddling his feet in the water. The small barbel minnows sped away from him and a bright blue bird flashed in a bush, regarding him with a hard, red eye. He turned a corner in the path and hesitated. There was something familiar about that jutting rock and the smooth precipice above it. It caught his attention, puzzling him. He walked to it and looked back for a moment instinctively at the tower. Then he walked round the rock into the place of his dream.

The pool lay there in the bright sunlight, sapphire blue with the reflection of the sky, and standing in it a dark-haired nymph, the water to her shoulders, looked at him surprised out of eyes as deep and mysterious as the pool was clear and revealing. He gazed back at her, startled, his left hand on the smooth rock. She stood as still as he, a growing wonder in her eyes. He had come! She had, in her day-dreams in this pool, imagined that he would be fine and proud, seated on a horse, with a long, curved, golden scabbarded sword, pointed beard and jewelled finger rings. Now she knew she had been wrong. He was a tall man, dark haired and his eyes were blue. The sword slung from his left shoulder was straight, its leather scabbard worn and his face was pale and tired, his lips parted but unsmiling.

They looked into each other's eyes, until the colours of the world, the red mountains, the trees and the blue water were no more and they were alone in a dream. As in a dream they spoke and the spell which bound them was not broken.

"You have come——" she said, in wonder.

"Yes."

"Far?"

"From the sea; and you?"

"I have always been here."

"I know."

They were silent. This was a new world and an old world—a man and a woman and a pool in a garden.

"There is a magic in this place," said Valens, nervously.

"You brought it with you."

59

"Is it mine? I have no magic. What is your name?"

"Lilleth."

Yes, he thought, that is what her name should be—Lilleth, the devoted to the moon. He had held her symbol in his hands, the lovely, silver crescent.

"My name is Valens," he said, "Antonius Valens, a Centurion."

"Antonius—then you are one of the Romans. Yet you speak our tongue?"

"It has been my task to learn it."

"How did you come here, to this pool?"

"Some fate led me here," he answered her. "I dreamed that I came here a few nights ago. I cannot be mistaken. It was dark, but the water glowed with the light of the crescent moon I drew from it. When I turned, the tower was empty, its wall fallen, a poor ruin on a hill. I am afraid."

It seemed to her that the sunlight suddenly darkened. He was afraid. Her father, too, was afraid. He had turned from her in the midst of speech. The castle had been silent, these three days. Laughter had died in it, and she had felt fear too. But now she knew it, a strong hand at her heart.

"Of what are you afraid?" she whispered.

"I do not know."

They had stepped out with the left foot. A shadow marched with the Legion, the shadow of disaster. Now the shadow spread over the Valley of the Green Doves. It spread over the valley and over the pool, where fate had led him, where he had held the silver crescent, glowing in the night. Roads met here, they parted here. The way here had been hard, a weary road. The way from

60

here would be no easy way for them, for Valens and the dark-haired girl.

Far up the valley a horn blew. He turned at the sound. Then he looked at her again and spoke, a deep urgency in his voice:

"To-morrow," he said, "at this hour—will you be here?"

"Yes. I will wait for you, Antonius. I have waited all my life."

"I leave my heart with you," he said and he was gone.

* * *

All that day the Legion marched into the camp. Gallus sought audience with the Prince, accompanied by Valens, and the door of the long reception-room was guarded by armed men. Many entered the room and left. The Prince was silent, after he had listened to Valens' long questions, and to Sa'id's replies. He leaned back on a cushion and heard the steady flow of orders, in a language he did not understand. Gallus' voice was clear and resonant, his face untroubled. Clemens spoke in sharp, staccato sentences, with quick, jerky gestures of his powerful hands. Before sunset Gallus rose and turned to the Prince.

"Tell the Prince," he said, "to have no fear. His services shall be remembered and Caesar himself shall thank him for his timely words. To-night he and his daughter and his people are my especial care. No harm shall befall them."

* * *

Night came to the Valley of the Green Doves. There were no fires, no lights in the camp. There was no sound among the soldiers, not even the steady pacing of sentries in the gravel by the wall. Like statues of long dead men

61

the sentries stood, the pale starlight reflected from helmet, shield and drawn sword. The dark and twisted mountains rose about them, full of stealthy life, their jutting heads dim-lit, their shoulders sunk in darkness. In the high tower two windows glowed, like eyes in the night.

Lilleth looked out on the night from the window of her chamber. Below her, the spur on which the castle stood was steep and smooth, sloping away from her to the mountainside. In the shadow of the wall there was a deeper shadow and it moved, little by little, up the spur. She caught her breath and, turning from the window, she ran to the door and threw it open. There she stayed, her hand to her throat. The light in her chamber streamed out upon the head of the stair, and there, turned half away from her towards the stairway, stood an armoured man, his iron helmet glowing dully, the light striking a red flame from the blade of his drawn sword! And, outside the castle, the night split into tinkling, empty sounds, which the mountains caught and threw one to another, a sudden meaningless confusion that was held and overridden by the fierce sound of a trumpet call.

They hurled themselves at the palisade on the strong wall and the javelins struck down at them. They pressed forward against the camp, a torrent of men, filling the deep dyke before the wall, trampling their fallen comrades, their sword blades swinging and at the palisade they met the swift thrust they could not parry. They recoiled, shouting, their blood staining them, their beards foam-flecked. From the gates of the camp into their packed thousands the heavy darts flashed, with a smack and a hiss, driving through them, bearing them down. They rallied, their leaders urging them, and once more they breasted the wall. Once more, in slaughter, they were hurled back. They surged round the camp raging, indisciplined, exhorting each other to the assault, which should have been so overwhelming. The camp remained, its wall unbreached, dark and menacing and from the dyke, from the twisted confusion of limbs there, rose cries of helplessness and agony. They rallied again and once more they stormed at the wall and the iron men behind it and were struck down upon the dead and dying below. Then the remnant fell back, calling to each other, the sound of their shouting growing faint as they withdrew into the hills. And the cries from the dyke grew less as the hours passed.

*　　*　　*

In the morning Gallus looked down upon the bodies of his foes. "I did not know," he said to Clemens, "that there were such numbers of them."

Clemens shook his head.

"They will bring more to-night," he said.

"Let them come," said Gallus, "for we shall not be here. We cannot remain here, however long we hold the camp. Our stocks of food will hold for a few days, no more. No, we must march and the Prince must prepare himself for a long journey, for they desire his blood as well as ours. To the east of here, they say, are empty lands and we must pass through them to Najran. If we go back to Yathrib and to Mecca, we shall find too much for our swords."

"That is so," replied Clemens, "of what nature are these empty lands?"

Gallus put his hand on Clemens' bony shoulder.

"We have gone too far," he said, "and we cannot return. If we cannot go back, we must go forward, whatever the land is like." He laughed: "Caesar desires the incense lands for his own and I go to take them, my old fighter!"

*   *   *

That day they broke their wall and tumbled it down upon the bodies in the dyke.   They set fire to the tower. As he rode out into the unknown mountains, Valens looked back to the pool of his dreams.   It lay there, still and blue and, while he looked, a wall of the tower tottered outwards and fell, crumbling, down the mountainside.

CHAPTER 5

Into the Desert

And so he wandered on for thirty days through trackless parts. . . .

THERE was no road through the mountains, no camel track such as had before guided their feet. They toiled up steep gullies behind their pioneers, who cut through rocks and heaved and levered at boulders, making a way for the animals. That first night the hills were alight with Arab watch-fires and the Legion slept in the open, on the hard ground, while lightly burdened Cohorts held the heights above them. The wild, jumbled mountains had no pattern in their spurs and ridges and through them they cut their narrow path, now this way, now that but tending always to the south-east. The third day, as the Prince had prophesied, their scouts sighted a mountain with a double peak to the east and, by evening, passing it to the north, they dropped down into a deep canyon, the dry watercourse which drained this lofty wilderness.

They marched on between high walls of mountain, in the dark of the canyon, all that night. The sky lightened above them in the dawn, the sun rose, but they were still in shadow, marching to the south in silence. The sun climbed into the sky and its hot light sparkled on the slim javelins and flashed from the heavy cavalry spears. All that day and half that night and all the long day following they marched in the narrow, winding canyon and, at evening, the mounted men led their horses down a steep incline on to the level gravel of a limitless plain. Here, where the foothills met the desert, was a small well.

"This well is Bir Na'ama," said the Prince. "Once, when I was a youth, I came here to hunt ostriches. It was arranged for me. A small family lived here then, grazing their goats in the fringes of the plain and in the foothills. They have gone long ago. See, the sand lies untrodden and no mark of their sojourn remains, not even the dry dung of their flocks by the well, where for many years they watered. I met here, on that journey, guides and camels from one named Sa'ab, a chief of the nomads who roam this desert country. He was in his prime then, a famous warrior, but I did not meet him. We rode for seven days to the south and found water, in a hollow of the ground. Then for four days we travelled north-east, to another place of water and thence for three days back to this well. But from here, you will understand, I am ignorant of this country. You might find men and water a half-day's march from here. You might pass through all the country and see no one. Only the nomads know where there is water and they graze their flocks, following the scanty rains."

Gallus and his senior Cohort commanders listened to his words as they were translated. Then they turned and looked out across the plain. It stretched away from them, a red expanse, here a low, flat-topped berg, there drift dunes tumbled in a hollow, there wide stretches of gravel. Beyond, in the far distance, hung a faint red mist, a mirage of slowly dying heat, stretching farther than the mind dared contemplate or the heart could bear. Only one desert

66

in the world was greater than this one and none more terrible. They could not know of its size nor of the lifeless country it held in its depths. They stared across it in the fading light, searching it with their eyes, stout-hearted, uncomprehending.

The short dusk of upland Arabia passed and night came. Far away in the mountains behind them a fire glowed, where their foes watched them. At the well the work went on, endless, exhausting, the creaking wheels, the splashing leather buckets, the water gurgling into the trough, the lowing and the roaring camels. When they could, they lay down in the cooling sand and fell into the utter sleep, when mind and body feel no more. They had cleared the well of the sand which the years had swept into it. Its flow was strong, undiminishing, but the shaft was narrow and very deep. All night the buckets rose and fell. For three days they must remain here, so their Centurions had told them, watering their beasts, discarding everything which might later be replaced, before they set out to the south-east to find the land of the nomads, and of Sabus, King of the Sands.

The Prince had pitched the camp of his followers some distance from the Legion, in the mouth of the canyon, where overhanging rocks made caves of shade at midday. The people of the valley had lived long in peace and they had many children. Three had died among the mountains and, this first night at the well, a child was born, taking its mother with it to the grave. The men, hardened by lifelong labour in the fields, were yet bewildered and like to be unmanned by this sudden oversetting of their fortunes. The women were wide-eyed and silent. They heard that the Romans prepared themselves for a march into the wilderness. Must they go, then, with the Prince and lay their bones out there, in the devil-haunted wastes? Had they escaped slavery, or the swift death of the sword, only to find a fate more terrible—the swollen tongue, the protruding eye, the madness of thirst? And their children —how could children endure in that treeless, waterless country, under the fierce sun and unsheltered from the burning wind?

They came to Lilleth, an unhappy concourse, the men hanging back behind them, silent and unhelpful. Miriam spoke for them, an ageing matron, gentle-hearted and soft of voice, from whose breasts Lilleth had drawn life, seventeen years ago.

"We can go no farther," she said. "What shall we do?"

Lilleth looked at them helplessly. It was true. They came to her because they were her people. At this marriage among them she had rejoiced, at that death she had mourned and now, when calamity had come upon them, she was empty-handed in an empty land. And if they could go no farther, she must leave them, for her fate lay with her father, in unknown and untraversed lands, where these people could never live.

They could not go on, but they could not go back. Lilleth had known nothing of the bitter evil of men's minds, the violence of their hands. Now she knew both and feared them. She had heard the wolfish howl for blood in the night. The sprawled corpses on the spur below the castle testified to the violence and horror of her death, had the Romans not held the stair.

The men who had been watching, now came forward and one spoke to her, pointing to the well, gesturing to the country of the foothills.

68

"See," he said, "honoured one—here is water, pure and good. Here we may camp and build ourselves shelters, such as we have made, when as shepherds we watched over our flocks in the hills. Here grows the strong *samra* thorn and we may make bows from its branches and the young boys have skill with the sling. In these hills there is much meat of diverse kinds, the bird of the rocks, the gazelle, the fat-tailed lizard. Here we may live, however poorly, for a time."

"But there is no milk, no bread——" said Lilleth.

Miriam took the sleeve of Lilleth's dress in her hands.

"There are she-camels, a few, among those which bear the burdens of the foreign soldiers, loved one," she said. "If the Prince should speak to the great General, he would leave us, perhaps, a she-camel or two. With milk and the meat in the hills and this water, we can live here awhile, a year or two maybe, until those who drove us out have forgotten us."

"But if they come here?" asked Lilleth; and they were silent, discomposed. Then Lilleth learned for the first time, from their averted faces, that she had lost the people of the valley. A door was closing between them and her and this was farewell. A sorrow, a sharp bitterness came upon her. These, her people, waited only for her to go. Miriam's hands dropped to her sides and she turned away, towards the hills.

"We are poor people," she murmured, "no one will harm us. We shall live here for a little while and then we shall go back to the valley. We have harmed none."

So Lilleth parted from the valley and the people of the valley and they, busy in urgent and unfamiliar tasks, sighed hopefully, grateful, yet not to her, that the parting had been so simple an affair.

The Romans had turned their backs upon the hills. In few and measured words, orders passed among them. They would move in three widely separated columns, their horsemen spread before them; men on unladen camels would ride far out, as far as the eye could observe them, ranging the flanks. Standards and their guards would march with the Maniples of two hundred, and the horn blowers each with his *Centuria*. Gallus, Clemens and their personal staffs would march at the head of the centre column, accompanied by the Prince and his agent, old Sa'id.

Valens had not sought the company of the Prince. It was his duty to interpret between the Prince and Gallus and to give his commander information of the country before him. There was no information of this country into which Gallus now must march. They must steer by chance, a wandering course through unknown terrain. He had been near to Lilleth, when they had listened to her father, looking out across the plain. When he had found Lilleth's dark eyes on him, he had looked away. When she turned from him, his eyes sought her. There had been no tryst that second morning by the pool. He had known a dream and its fulfilment, a meaningless thing, and that was all. Their ways led on together for a while, she chained to her father's fate, he to his duty.

On the fourth morning, as the light spread, the three columns moved off, diverging from each other, and the flanking scouts spread out far to left and right. Behind Gallus and his small party of horsemen, the Eagle flashed in the first rays of the sun. Ahead of them all, Publius

70

Sabinus, the commander of the mounted wing, rode his horse on a loose rein. His handsome, swarthy face was full of mastery, his lips were firm and full. His horse slithered down a low dune and broke into a trot towards the distant haze.

All day they marched and the next and the next, until the mountains were like low clouds on the horizon behind them, and still they marched, until each man moved alone, each in his own hell, across a mighty saucer of hot gravel. Dawn on the fifth day saw them moving still, heard a trumpet blown by thirst-cracked lips and, like three lines of ants, the columns converged upon the dark circle of a water-hole. Here they laboured with buckets and water skins, praising a sand-filled water more sweet to them than any wine—and a sickness came on them, as they worked, gasping in the sun, which seared their bowels and filled their thin bodies with pain; and the horns sounded untunefully, calling them into the desert, like the voices of thirst and hunger leading them on; and the wind veered and the sand began to rise.

Once, by day, they espied ostriches, which appeared like mounted enemies far away, shrank to the size of hen chicks as they neared them and then were great wild-eyed birds which sped through fire and were part of demons' dreams. Sometimes by night the sand burst open before them and herds of oryx sped away across the desert and they saw their tall horns and were filled with terror. "Unicorns!" they cried. "This is the land of Unicorns!" and they huddled together as they stumbled through the sand. Sometimes the trumpets would croak shakily and they lay down, but there was no rest from the fires within them and the hot air would scarcely pass their swollen tongues. Then the trumpets would sound and they would rise up and fall forward again, and their fingers would unlace the belts and daggers of dead men. And the dead men walked beside them in the driving sand and cried out to them, "You cannot leave me there—lie down beside me and sleep!" The dead men plucked the sleeves of their tunics and pressed their faces forward and jeered at them, crying, "You are dead! You are dead! The Legion is no more!" And tears ran down their cheeks, because the Legion was lost—until a lean horse trotted by them in the sand and they saw their golden Eagle flashing above it and they gasped and staggered forward on tottering legs and cried, "The Legion lives! The Legion lives!" But none could hear them.

They passed their dead companions, who gazed open-eyed at the sun, and their dead horses, unbridled and lying where they fell. They passed black rocks which rose out of the sand, like the ruins of burnt cities, and out of the ruins came dread forms of fancy, the ghouls and vampires of desolation and snarled and spat tongues of flame into their breasts; and they stumbled away from the rocks into the desert, where the sand rose up in monstrous columns which reached the sky and the columns danced a ponderous dance to one another.

They came to green water in a hollow of the ground and fell beside it, laughing and drinking and crying, until their stomachs swelled and split; and others pulled them away and plunged their beards into the slime of the water-hole. They wandered on and the quartz sand drove into their faces, so that for many there was no difference between night and day, because they could not see. More dead men marched beside them now and they could hear them calling in the whirling sand and they gripped their sword hilts and marched on.

Then the devils and the spirits of the sand held a council. And they lifted the sand of the great desert on a wind high in the air and they hurled it on the Legion. And the Legion swayed and tottered and fell, with their heads beneath their shields, while the sky shrieked above them and dark, tumultuous night covered them and they lay still.

The *Ghoba*, the great sand storm, raged across the wilderness. It lifted the sand to the sky in whirling towers in its onrush, it rolled forward behind its cliffs and battlements, a red and purple terror. It tore at the dunes and the gravel seas, gathering its fury and hurled its hurricane strength against the tall mountains beyond. In its dark heart the Legion lay, there was neither earth nor sky, the sun was blotted out and time ceased in chaos. As it had risen, swiftly, so it passed, its ferocity spent. After it a thin oven-breath stirred the desert, a rustling sigh of poison-wind, and was still.

It was finished. There had been a Legion. Now there were little mounds of sand where the camels lay unstirring, their long necks outstretched. Above them the serene evening sky; below it the changeless desert, red and empty as it had always been.

They had marched with all their pageantry to the ships. They had striven with the sea, they had pressed on through the furnace of the hills. They had endured the arrow by night and the noonday sickness. They had entered the desert of death. Now they lay still. Soon there would be nothing, only the wide plain and a wind, perhaps, to uncover their white bones.

F
73

The Eagle had fallen. Here was journey's end.

Then a miracle happened. A little sand lifted and broke, and, leaning on a shield, a scarecrow clambered to its knees. Slowly he rose to his feet. He fumbled with a rag dipped in oil and with it parted and soothed bleeding lips. He raised his horn aloft.

It was late evening, there was no breath of wind. High and clear across that desolate plain sounded the call which rallied the Legions. Once it sounded to the still mounds, and twice. Thrice it sounded and the heart of the blinded trumpeter died within him and he fell upon his shield, his horn still to his lips. But the spell of the desert was broken.

The sand was stirring, a ghost army was rising from it, searching in it for spear and shield. Blindly, drunkenly, crying noiselessly to one another, they rose up, hollow-eyed, cracked and bloody of lip—and the ghosts of their dead comrades flitted among them in the dusk, no longer jeering at them but pleading with them, thin, half-remembered voices in their ears. "Did you hear?" they whispered, urgently. "Did you hear? All the trumpets of Rome are calling! Onward! Onward the Legion!" And the Legion wandered onward as the sun sank behind the world.

Then the spirits of the dead made supplication to the gods and asked: "Are we not enough? We are lying back there on the desolate road. We have paid the sea and the land in full."

So the gods strove with the spirits and devils of the great desert and thunder rolled heavily in the distant dwellings of the djinns, where the gods hurled down their thunderbolts and lightning flickered and stabbed the eastern sky.

74

A strange deep sound came to the Legion's ears. amid
the rolling of the thunder and the stars they could not
see were shut out one by one and fierce, cold pains spat at
the Legion out of the night. They stretched out their
hands and lifted their faces to the sky.

"Rain!" they whispered. "Rain?"

And the rain drummed and thundered on the sand about
their feet.

*　　*　　*

The rain fell heavily on the nomad encampment and
Sa'ab, the old chief, slept uneasily in his black goat-hair
tent. Wind whistled through the strained tent ropes.
At midnight the rain cleared. He rose and, wrapping his
cloak about his shoulders, he walked out into the night,
where his wakeful dogs snarled and snapped.

The dogs were uneasy. Far to his east and west, where
families of his tribe lay encamped, he could hear other
dogs barking. This was not the sharp, frightened yap and
whine which betokened the approach of leopard and here,
deep in the desert, leopard never came. This barking was
the growl and cry which heralded the approach of men.
A raid coming from the north? Somewhere, out in the
sands, men were moving.

He turned back to the encampment and kicked a slave
into wakefulness.

"Beat the drum!" he ordered.

The drum sounded a steady, tripping rhythm in the
night. Men sleeping under the stars or in their tents
stirred awake and grasped their spears. A raid? They
stood in the night listening. The dogs were speaking and
the wind was in the north. Somewhere out there men
were coming, closer and closer. They spread out in the

sand before their tents, swords and spears in their hands. Old Sa'ab grew no older—here had been watchfulness indeed! A bright star shone in the east—*Zohra*, the flower —and they felt the breath of the dawn wind.

Dawn found the Legion moving slowly to the south-east on rising ground. Ahead of them all strode dark Sabinus, his helmet and his armour slung from shouldered spear. He paused on the crest of the long rise and looked back upon the Legion as the sun rose. Then his gaze wandered over the plain and he suddenly stiffened and shaded his eyes with his hand.

Spread out widely, coming towards him at a swinging pace, was a line of camels and above them flashed the spears of their riders. He turned to his trumpeter.

"Sound the alarm!" he ordered.

The trumpeter sounded a high, rippling call. The horns of the Legion gave him answer. The Legion halted, the men in the rear of the three columns running and stumbling forward. The Eagle rose, glinting, among its guards.

Sabinus' men closed in on him. He turned towards the advancing camelmen and counted them—perhaps two hundred. They must by now have seen the Legion, but they held on towards him, singing a wild chant until, fifty paces from him, they heaved at their camels' head ropes and halted. Surprised, Sabinus watched them conferring together and then some twenty of them dismounted and came towards him, leading their camels, their spears on their shoulders. Their leader, white bearded and wrinkled with age, spoke to him. He did not understand his words, but he smiled back and pointed to the Legion, still forming its battle lines. Then, inspiration coming to him, he asked, slowly and inquiringly: "Sabus? Sabus?"

76

The old man took his hand and together they walked down towards the gathering men.

At three deep wells women chanted as they drew water. Beyond the widespread black tabernacles of the nomads, the blood of goats darkened the sand. Blue smoke from fires of ancient timber rose in the sky. For Sheikh Sa'ab —King Sabus, the Romans called him—would entertain a Legion of Rome in his kingdom of the sands.

CHAPTER 6

King Sabus

That is the land of the nomads whose King is Sabus. . . .

THE Legion camped like bedouin among the widespread tabernacles of Sa'ab's goat-hair capital. They had few tents, for they had cast them aside during their nightmare march, to spread the burden of their machines the easier on the exhausted camels. They made what shelters they could to shield them from the midday sun.

They had marched to the sea at 'Aqaba at nearly their full strength of six thousand men. Now a scattered roll call found them less than four thousand strong, without vigour, a tired army. In their weariness, they had little rest. Grazing near the nomad settlement was nearly all eaten down. The old chief allotted land to them, a day and more to the south, for their camels. They rode out by companies in turn, to watch their beasts wander in the thorny vales, sitting painfully in makeshift camel saddles, their shoulders drooping, a great lassitude upon them in the fainting land. Illness had delayed their setting forth from the coast for a summer and a winter season. Now high summer reigned. The fiery sun struck out with blistering heat in its uprising. It hung for endless hours in the pale blue, burning heaven. At nightfall, from dens in the cracked earth, came a multitude of spiders, gross, yellow-

bodied and black-haired, which rustled over the land, poison-
ous creatures left in this desolation from some foul and
distant age. Well might they suppose these sands to be
devil-haunted; and haunted they were, for each man strove
in his heart with the devils of doubt and despair.

Clemens, the First Javelin, strutted in the sand, a smile
on his lips, his orders sharp and incisive. The weight of
his years lay on him, a heavy burden, but it could not
stoop the thin, muscled shoulders. In their distress, the
men might well have fallen by the wells, listless and de-
spairing. Clemens' staccato sentences, his well-known,
jerky movements, held them up and set them to their tasks.

Serenus, the Quartermaster, patted his empty stomach,
miraculously preserved in its ample proportions. He set
about his staff, strange and vitriolic oaths bubbling from
his lips, their spate unabated. The Maniples mustered to
their duties, Centurions forced themselves to their tasks—
the tent sites, the water and camp fatigues, the siting of
lavatories, the sentry rosters, the kit inspections, all the
hundred-and-one matters which keep thought from the
soldier and make the strength of an army.

Gallus did not rest. It seemed that their thirst was
hardly quenched before he left camp for the grazing areas
and in four days he was back, working in the sun with
Repetinus at the Ballistae, in conference with the Prince
and Sa'ab, to the hospital tent, where his pale eyes softened
and his rare smile cheered them, to each *Centuria*, sharply
critical, noting the maladjustment of a strap, the roughened
edge of a sword.

To assemble invincible forces, to launch them with
economy on the foe and with brain and sinew to achieve
victory—that is generalship. But, except in adversity,

79

the stature of a man remains obscure. Gallus had thrust with his army into the untrodden sands. Moses might wander for forty years in his pocket desert—it was more than a Moses who led a Legion of Rome into this, the most terrible wilderness in the world! A man with twenty or so skilled and seasoned companions, with expert guides and selected mounts, might hope to pass through that country from water-hole to water-hole and might live to tell the world of his great achievement. But to lead thousands of armed men with their stores and their cumbrous engines of war through these uncharted wastes—what other man ever undertook such a task?

The Legionaries shook off their fatigue and fattened on milk and flesh. What lay before them was not theirs to foresee. What lay behind them they shut from their minds. The camels must be conditioned, every leather strap must be serviceable, every weapon sharp, every water skin sound. They worked and ate and strength flowed back into their bodies and confidence into their minds.

Gallus' eyes turned now to the south. They must take and hold Nejran. He could gain little but vague information from his few interpreters. Prince Aretas had never visited Nejran, but he agreed wholeheartedly that a strong citadel must be held in the south, from which a campaign could be launched against the southern kingdoms, should diplomacy fail. He was not sure of their reception in Nejran—it might be friendly. It was a rich and somewhat isolated community, on brittle terms of friendship with the north and south. There also they would find news from traders and travellers of the fortunes of the Nabataean Kingdom in the Hejaz. To hold Nejran was essential, both for military and for diplomatic reasons. But the journey to Nejran—he held up his hands—how could it be done? It was harder terrain than that which, by good fortune only, they had just crossed. He had spoken to Sa'ab and to many of the nomad men. No army could survive in that country. His daughter Lilleth, too, was a burden on him. He thought of sending her, with Sa'ab's assistance, back to the people of the valley, to await the success of their venture. She had no place here, in this war camp, nor in the desperate businesses of intrigue and war which lay before them, if they were to re-establish the rule of Nabataea over Syllacus and the merchants. No, Lilleth could not march to the south.

Gallus nodded politely. He did not doubt that the merchants would have to be dealt with by Roman arms. Fat old King Abodas, for all the blood he had shed in Petra, could never undertake that task.

Gallus summoned Valens to his tent. He must have a plan of the route south to Nejran at once. He intended to march from here in a month's time. Valens must prepare maps. He must put forward some workable scheme, in conjunction with Clemens, Serenus and their staffs, for moving from here to Nejran and for reaching the oasis ready for war.

"We must arrive there capable of storming a city," he said; "I do not wish to arrive with the men falling about as if they were drunk. Your plan must be ready in sixteen days. Now go."

Valens sought audience with the old chief, who glared at him, well knowing his business before he broached it. He had had enough of this problem of finding water for four thousand men where one-tenth of that number could not be satisfied. The matter was one of plain sense. It could not be done.

"No army can cross those sands!" Thus Sa'ab spoke, when Valens asked for guidance. "The land you traversed is a garden. South from here, a man must twist and turn, from water-hole to water-hole, and at this season the land has little moisture and the water-holes are low. That country is *khala*, it is empty."

They sat in Sa'ab's black tent, made of a coarse worsted of goat-hair, through which the sunlight glinted. A hot wind stirred the sand in the doorway. Valens was patient. Sa'ab was slow, cautious, opposed to any march, but a return, with skilled guides, to the hills. There they would find the true road to the south—there was no other road for such a host of men from here.

"Yet tell me, Chief," said Valens, "what like is the desert between here and Nejran?"

"It is *khala*, have I not said?" Sa'ab rumpled his straggle of grey beard: "See you," he said, "we will speak to Jareiba, my cousin. He knows that country as you know the palm of your hand. *Heyya, ya* Jareiba! Ho! Let Jareiba be sent here!"

Jareiba's skin had the dark lustre of polished teak. He smoothed a stretch of sand before the tent with the palms of his long-fingered hands. Hook-nosed, his eyes narrowed, his strong black beard stirred by the wind, he knelt before this flattened sand map he had made. He spoke in the harsh, slow speech of the desert men.

Valens, sitting cross-legged, listened to him, checking him with a question now and again, absorbed in this unfolding picture of a wilderness.

There was no way, said Jareiba, in the sands for such a host of men. Here—marking the place with a pebble—there was water. Two hundred camels would drink it

82

dry. After that it would fill slowly, in four or five days. To south and east was nought but *khala*. To west from there for half a moon of droving, on higher ground, a place of springs. To the south thence, seven days, there were hills, where water lay after rain. True, he had seen distant lightning ten days ago, a flickering, low in the sky, but that rain might be too far to the west, among the hills. From that water a *gom*, a raiding party, of say, one hundred, could reach a well in four days at walking pace, through dune country. Thence and thence and thence— now south-east, now west, now south went Jareiba's mind, from a place of thorn trees to one where rain had left grazing ten years ago; from a gravel sea, through dunes to the goal to which he contrived his way—water. Sa'ab had leant back on a camel saddle when his cousin began. But the tale was too enthralling and he could not preserve his air of indifference. He now leaned forward, engrossed in Jareiba's words. He knew this country to the south also, although he had not traversed it for many years. He began to interrupt, savagely, striking Jareiba's hand off the sand map, so that the pebbles scattered and had to be replaced, amid further rasping contradictions and argument.

"Here, then," said Jareiba, "you may find a little water——"

"It is not so!" croaked Sa'ab. "Not there, no, by god! There is a hill, flat like this and steep and beyond, a day's march over great stones, there are yellow drift dunes and it is there, on the dunes' edge, that water lies!"

"Yet, rain or no rain, here is water, by Allah!"

Valens, too, became excited.

"Wait!" he cried. "Wait! If from here to here is a

moon of herding and to here but ten days, then it were swifter to turn east?"

"*Sah!* He speaks truth!"

"Swifter to where?" Jareiba spat. "For that water sears the bowels and dries the tongue! Let him turn east—the birds will have him!"

Slowly the pebbles multiplied and crept south on the sand map. Almost, now, they travelled the road together. The country became easier, grazing more plentiful. Sa'ab praised this place for its *ithil* bushes, that for its sweet water. Then here, here are the sands of Wadi Habauna! And beyond—Nejran! They sat back, smiling at each other, three successful travellers—they were there!

"But," said Sa'ab, "suddenly glaring at Valens under thick, contracted brows, "not with your army—no! No! No! It cannot be done."

Valens' smile vanished and he sighed deeply. No, they were not there after all.

Jareiba looked on him with compassion. This stranger, who spoke their tongue, wished to go to Nejran.

"I will take you there!"" he exclaimed. "Let your friends return whence they came. You and as many as two hundred I will take but no more."

Valens suddenly leant forward, his hand over the pebbles on the sand map, his eyes alight with interest.

"You shall take me!" he cried, "I and two hundred. See, we will go thus and thus. . . ."

"Eigh! It is so and to here and rest some days and then on. . . ."

"And from here, a short march, and we shall be in the sands of Wadi Habauna! But listen—there shall be a friend of yours and, when we depart by this route, he will

84

take others of the army and they will march thus and thus. And, a few days after our setting forth, will come another two hundred in our tracks and after them another. And here, in Wadi Habauna, we shall meet.

"Not Habauna," snapped Sa'ab, "it is dry!"

"There is the Green Mountain!" exclaimed Jareiba. "It is here. There is, of a truth, no mountain, but there are springs and there is grazing."

"You can find men, guides for these parties?" asked Valens.

The two Arabs looked at each other. Then the argument began once more, a name suggested—ruled out with an oath and a violent, sweeping gesture of the hand; another accepted with praise, a third left in some airy waiting list. At last Sa'ab turned to Valens.

"They shall be found! They shall be found!" he cried. "Men shall be found who know the land. In a day, the first shall be ready for you."

Valens' staff now numbered only six, two clerks, soldiers of the Legion and four Arabs from the Yemen coast, who wrote their language but knew little of the interior of their country. Through Jareiba, he brought bedouin to his assistance, sharp-featured and skinny-ribbed, who knew the sands to the south. Bit by bit he constructed a rough chart of two separate routes, the distance between water and water marked in numbers of days' marching. A Maniple of two *Centuriae* would leave by each route every fifth day, the baggage split and apportioned equally throughout the Legion.

His calculations showed that the western of the two routes was the shorter by seven to nine days. It was necessary to ensure that a strong force should arrive at the

Green Mountain some days in advance of the first Maniple, to prepare a fortified camp, in which the Legion could be reformed. This could be done if he, Valens, led two hundred pioneers, surveyors and soldiers by the eastern route and Sabinus another party, including his own mounted wing, by the shorter western route, seven days later. Valens' party could march at once. This would enable a force almost equivalent to a Cohort to reach the Green Mountain simultaneously, enough to hold selected ground and to prepare a camp.

He took his completed plans to Serenus, who studied them for some time in silence, before looking up at Valens, his face solemn.

"It is good," said Serenus, "but surely it is very wide of the original intention—dying one by one, instead of all together? But I like it. Now let me see—four days here; *ten* here! But that is the longest—yes, while I cannot say I look forward to all this marching, you shall have my support."

Clemens clutched the papers, his sallow, hawklike face grim.

"Yes," he snapped. "Yes—from here directly east, nine days' waterless march. Hard going for some. But why does this short stretch here take nine days? Your scale must be faulty!" and he glared at Valens.

"High dunes," he replied.

"Hmm. You are sure that you cannot be more accurate in your estimates of days? Seven to nine—that is two days' possible error. You may arrive two days before Sabinus, with only a Maniple of men. However, it is at least a plan. Let us see if the Praefectus can discuss it now."

Gallus studied the plan, his face impassive. He listened

while Clemens and Serenus gave him, briefly, their views as to its feasibility. Both agreed that to march in a body would be dangerous in the extreme. The nomads were friendly and would assist them, if they adopted nomadic ways. Gallus turned to Valens.

"Sabinus returns to camp to-night," he said; "all the men you and he will lead are here now. When can you start?"

"In three days, Praefectus."

"That will do. You will march, I see, by night, with the moon just past its full. The fourth night then. That is all to-day, Clemens. You can have your orders ready in a week's time and yours, Serenus? Good, I thank you. I will send these plans to the writers for copying, when I have shown them to the Prince."

The Prince sat often with Sa'ab, listening while the old chief recalled his long life here, in the great plain. Sa'ab spoke of raid and counter raid and of a desire for peace, which had spread under his guidance, despite the nomads' dusty brains and the bitterness of their hearts, the saga of the making of a nomad nation, a kingdom of the sands.

This afternoon he went to Sa'ab to tell him of Gallus' decision to march, despatching his first party in a few days' time. Sa'ab made place for Aretas beside him in his tent and served him with the roast flesh of a goat, cooked on hot stones. He had long observed his guest, finding him a man of wisdom, honourable and kindly. Aretas had told Sa'ab of the disaster which had led him here and of his determination to restore the fortunes of his master, the King. But Sa'ab felt that this wise man doubted the wisdom of the whole venture. And this Legion—had not

87

Aretas complained that in deserts it was too large and in populous districts too small? And how could four thousand succeed against the might of the Yemen Kingdom of Himyar, the bloodthirsty warriors of the Beni Hilal and the remnants of Sheba and Ma'in? All settled Arabia would turn against the Romans and with hatred against the ambitious Kingdom of Nabataea. Aretas would find no friends in Nejran, of that Sa'ab felt sure. He would go in Nejran perhaps to his death, leaving his daughter alone and among enemies.

"*Ya* Harith," he said, calling Aretas by the Arabic version of his name. "*Ya* Harith, why would you go from here? Now, friend, consider, will you not stay here with me? You shall have a tent and I will find you a young wife, who will tend you, and I will bestow camels upon you, a small herd. You shall be a son to me and a chief among us. You shall help me to judge these folk, who are turbulent when the rains of autumn fatten the land. And your daughter, the dear one, the women find her gentle and motherly with the little children. My youngest son is yet a lad and my oldest—for I have sons thirty and more—is grey of head. But we shall find a strong young man, not yet married, who desires a wife and we shall join them here. Thus shall your seed grow in the shelter of our tents and you shall yet see your grandchildren, strong with the rich camel's milk, young warriors of the tribe."

"May god increase your wealth," murmured Aretas. He looked at the rough mat on the floor at his feet. How good was this old man! For a moment he pictured to himself how he would end his days if he stayed here. The restless, nomad life, the long journeys, the summer's

88

scorching heat. But there were temptations and they crowded upon him. To stay here, to renounce his rank and all claim to his possessions—it would be freedom. He had journeyed much, he was inured to wandering. No longer to be Prince Aretas; to accept the tent, the patriarchic responsibilities of the nomad life; to be a wise and accepted judge among these honest folk of the open range. He could care for his daughter and rejoice in her children, and she would tell them of the distant valley of her childhood as a fireside tale, its reality forgotten in motherhood. The tempting picture! But there were loyalties to be observed and duty to be done. His course was clear to him: he must go with this Roman army to their conquest of the southern kingdoms and thence he must return to the service of his King and to the subjection of the merchant princes.

He answered Sa'ab gently. One birth, one life, one duty—these encompassed a man. He had built; he must build again, of the same substance, in the same pattern. Had he been more alert, had he served his King to better purpose, this disaster and the change in his fortunes might not have been. He could not bow his head to adverse fate. He must endure. He must return, strong enough to rebuild the things which he had allowed to fall.

"By god!" said Sa'ab. "That is the speech of a man! So you will go to Nejran, a far journey." He fondled his beard. "And your daughter," he asked, "must she travel this hard road? She will be a danger and a burden to you. Let her stay here. There is a tent for her here, marriage and a comely life."

Aretas was silent. Lilleth could not return to Nabataea until the way was secure. She could return to the people of the valley, they would not harm her. Lilleth had no place in these desperate affairs of state. Should he ask Sa'ab to care for her? They were kindly folk, they would force no man on her as husband, against her will. And the march to Nejran—it daunted hardened men.

"Send for her," said Sa'ab; "she is a woman, no more a child. Her breasts are grown and among us she would now be a mother of two and more. I will speak to her; let her choose between your wanderings and mine."

Lilleth entered and sat between them. The nomad women had bound her hair. They had put on her a shapeless smock, of blue-stained linen, tied with a cord at the waist and had given her rough sandals for her feet. It pained Aretas to see her thus—the dark clear eyes, the pale oval of her face—beauty in a sackcloth gown. Sa'ab chuckled. "See, Harith," he cried, "already your daughter is one of us. So enters a woman of the desert when you summon her!"

He turned to Lilleth.

"Now, child," he said, "we lay a choice before you, your father and I. To go with your father into the south, a maid alone among strange warriors, who thirst for war. There is a world of marching between here and Nejran! Thence, who knows the road? Nay, dear one, let your father go, unburdened by your softness. We will await word of him here and on the desert's edge. When he has served his King, to here he will return to seek you. You shall be my child, you shall marry whom you will, at a time of your own choosing. And when your father comes again, you shall lay his grandchild in his arms and there shall be a treaty between all the tribes of the sands and the Kingdom of Nabataea!"

Her eyes wide, she stared from one to the other. Her father looked away from her, across the open plain beyond the tent door.

"I must stay with my father," she said, her voice low.

"He has man's work to do," replied Sa'ab. "He seeks revenge on those who have shamed him and his family. Do women shake the spear and draw the sword? Their place is in the tents."

"But my father——" She turned to him, panic mounting within her. "I will come with you—I am your child! You would have me by you?"

Aretas said nothing. He raised his hand and dropped it, a helpless gesture.

"Oh!" she cried: a humble, lonely sound in the still tent. Her people had turned from her, when she had lost the valley. Now her father would leave her, he must do man's work, unburdened by her softness. Only old Sa'ab wanted her, to bear children for his slaves of the sun—the woman's place was in the tents. She was to marry a man here, of her own choosing, among this dark-skinned, alien folk, a simple conclusion for them all. Simple it would be for her also, since she could never love but where her heart lay. She rose. Her legs felt weak, trembling beneath her. She could not speak. As she left the tent, her father leaned forward to restrain her, but she was gone.

She walked unsteadily, a long way from the tents. Then she began to run, stumbling in the drifted sand until, at last, she fell exhausted and lay, sobbing in the dust.

It was sunset before she rose and stared about her and in a moment it was dark.. She climbed a rise of ground and saw, far spread in the distance, the twinkling campfires. She must return there, where she was wanted—

not by her father. He would leave her there, hungry of heart, among these wild folk. If he left her there, she would give proof that she had none of the softness which he feared might burden him. She would not be a burden any more. She felt her body below her breasts, pressing with her hands. There she would thrust the knife blade, it would need no strength to pierce the aching heart beneath.

She took a pace in the darkness, towards the distant fires. The moon was rising, a white glow far down on the rim of the world. She paused. How strange was this naked earth! She watched the moon, a white, glowing disc, rising from the sands—and between it and her a dark figure moved, closer and closer, bent down and peering at the ground. It moved silently, a graceful thing, but here a thing of terror. Then it stood upright, a bare twenty paces from her, watching her in the moonlight.

"Lilleth!"

"Antonius——" Her legs would not support her; she fell forward on her knees in the sand.

He knelt beside her and took her hands in his.

"What do you do here alone?" he asked. "It is not safe to stray from the tents."

"Yes," she said and laughter mounted in her. "Yes, I know. A woman's place is in the tents——"

"I saw you go and I waited for your return. Your father sits with the chief——"

He has man's work to do, thought Lilleth, hysterically; they all have man's work to do and I must sit in the tents, giving birth to their grandsons——

"I followed your footsteps in the sand," he said, "now you are safe. You were lost, perhaps. Rest a little and I will lead you back to the tents."

92

"Back to the tents?" she asked. "Is that where you will lead me? Where I can drink the warm camel's milk and have strong bedouin children, little brown things?"

"I do not understand——" said Valens.

"When you have led me to the tents, will you leave me there? Will you not take me somewhere else, Antonius?"

He looked at her in the moonlight. The coarse blue smock did not disguise the beauty of her slim body. The rough hem of the neck fell low and the curve of her breast glowed soft and white in the moonlight. No Grecian sculptor could chisel the image of those delicate nostrils, those wide brows, those sorrowful lips.

She felt his hands tighten on hers. She heard him catch his breath. She leant towards him a little.

"Will you not take me, Antonius?" she said.

"I would take you to the end of the world!" he cried.

"That is not very far. The world ends here."

"You speak in riddles, Lilleth. I do not understand."

"Look at me," she whispered. "Tell me, truthfully and from your heart, do you desire me? I have said farewell to the people of the valley. My father—my father would leave me here, among a strange folk. But you—do you desire me?"

There was nothing now, the moon unseen, the ground unfelt. The dream—the crumbling tower, the crescent drawn from the water—all was fulfilled. There was nothing, only the breathing of the wind over the empty sand, the night's cool charity to the tired earth and the world turning through the long night hours. And a star rising and two lovers, stirred from their sleep by the music of a distant horn.

CHAPTER 7

The Trackless Wastes

*. . . on for fifty days through trackless wastes as far as
. . . the city of Negrana. . . .*

OVER the high mountains of the northern Yemen, the sky
was thick with gathering clouds. They moved, seemingly
of their own volition, unaffected by the changing wind,
straggle-edged, grey and oppressive. A great, anvil-
shaped thunderhead formed above them, drawing in their
ragged streamers, glowing white above, dark and threaten-
ing below. From its lowering northern face, a cold wind
blew down upon the city of Sa'ada.

The low edge of ragged cloud moved towards the city.
They watched it from their house-tops and their fields.
"It will fall here!" they said. "The earliest rain, may
the gods be praised!"

The billowing, anvil-shaped head glowed with inner
lightnings. The wind whipped up the street dust and
bent the orchard trees before the city. In every house the
shutters closed. A sudden flash stabbed the earth. Peal
on peal of crackling thunder rocked the mountain peaks.
Released, the hail lashed down, a violent blizzard of ice,
isolating house from house, while lightning flashed and
shone. Then, as the cloud encompassed the city, the rain fell.

The five tributaries of Wadi Merwan filled with flood

water. The Merwan bore the spate north and east down its rocky course, a wall of water leaping the boulders, tearing at the dry, stony banks, rousing deep echoes in the mountains, as the rain cleared over Sa'ada and darkness came.

Sixty miles away, from the gorge at Madhiq, where the Merwan becomes the Wadi Nejran, they had seen the thunderhead forming in the early afternoon. In the first, pale glow of dawn, they heard the dull echo of the approaching waters, a low reverberation in the air. They waited until the water-bore, foam-capped, leapt into their sight beyond the gorge.

"*Seil! Seil!*" they shouted. "Spate! Spate!"

"*Seil! Seil!*" They caught up the high-pitched cry, from house to field and house again, all down the wide valley of Nejran. The sluice gates opened, the irrigation channels swelled and flooded. They trapped, seized and claimed this bounty of the gods, dividing and taming the violence of the flood, as it moved down the valley to the east until, by now but a brown swelling of the perennial waterflow, the narrow, eastern gorge for a moment constrained the hurrying waters, before they spread out into the thirsty, barren lands beyond.

The old King of Nejran watched the flood from his palace roof, his eyes dull, his long face impassive. Here, high above his city of Nejran, which divided the waters, it was no more than a discoloration and a swelling of the stream. He watched the approach of the brown torrent, noting a glint of flooded fields far away. He followed its approach until the houses and the city wall to the east blocked his view. Then he shuffled across the roof and waited to see its reappearance to the west of the city, leaning his elbows on the marble parapet, nodding his head and humming to himself in senile approval. At last it reappeared, brown and tumbling where the divided flood met, after encompassing the city. Observing it, he started slightly. He had forgotten, for a moment, why he had climbed to the roof—the *seil*, of course! He had not missed one in fifty years.

But in the interval of time since he had leant here, looking to the east, his mind had turned to other things. Tahir, the confectioner, had brought a new sweet to him that morning, red in colour and of a sugary texture, compounded, so he had said, of the juice of fruits, the essence of certain petals, honey and flour. He dribbled a little, as he thought of it. Such things meant much to an old man, without teeth. He fumbled among his cloaks and clothes and produced a small box and from it he took another chunk of this new, delicious *halua*; he mumbled it, his dull eyes half closed in delight.

His servants stood behind him, respectful, in attendance. At last he turned to them, his mouth still moving. As he tried to speak through Tahir's sugary glue, a great, red bubble grew out of his lips and hung there, scintillating before his bulging eyes. It burst, splashing across his white beard. He staggered a little. Astounding stuff, this new *halua*! His servants hurried to obey the order, which they had anticipated but which he had failed to pronounce.

The King's programme this morning was, indeed, known to all. The first flood of the Great Rains must be greeted by blood sacrifices at Taslal. His Wazir led him down the long stairs to the courtyard, where the mules were waiting, and soon he headed an ever-swelling procession through the city's winding, odorous streets.

The multitude gathered below the great basaltic crag, the Cube of Taslal. This crag was an awesome thing. Half of Arabia turned towards it, when they worshipped or sacrificed. A natural, unornamented block of stone, it was the most venerated of all the shrines in Arabia. Millions of the dead turned their gaping eye-sockets towards it, in their graves. Temples, through all the land, were carefully and scientifically orientated towards the Cube. For here dwelt all the gods of Arabia—Shams and Melik of Sheba, Wadd of Ma'in, Ya'uk the feared, Nesr of Himyar and a hundred more, known and unknown. It was the abode of gods and spirits, pregnant with ancient mystery, fearsome, a thing to be placated.

Where once, long ago, kings had been sacrificed, the King came forward with his sacrifices—two score of camels, seven bulls, and sundry bleating goats. Knives flashed redly and the rank smell of blood rose in the hot air. Others followed the King. In return for the first flood of the Great Rains, let the gods have blood, and the lowing and bleating round the Cube rose in a great lamentation from the animal kingdom, while the people danced and feasted, until the evening.

That night, the King sat in his reception-room, exhausted by his ceremonies, letting his thin back sink into the pillows propped behind him. He had hoped, after the fatigue of Taslal, to be allowed to sleep; or to rest, with vacant mind, while music was played. Now, so Selim, the Wazir, had insisted, there was talk of war.

Opposite him sat Slave-of-the-Sun, Commander of the Army, large, grizzled and loud of voice. By him sat the merchant of precious stones, old 'Abd al Ya'uk, but lately returned from Yathrib and the north. It was on him that

the King's gaze was fixed, in loathing. The King hated
'Abd al Ya'uk's red-rimmed eyes. They are like a rat's
eyes, he thought, his irritation rising. An old rat, long in
cellars and foul places, peering out of somewhere unmentionable. He was rich, too, the old bag of bones, far
richer than the King.

Slave-of-the-Sun began to speak, his voice booming
and sonorous. Like a bull, thought the King, regarding
him. A pity we did not sacrifice him with the other bulls
at Taslal. He talked too loud and all names, names, names
—if one tried to understand one's head reeled. It was better
to lean back on the pillows and consider him as a bellowing
sacrifice at Taslal. They would drag him off by the
hind legs to cut him up; but nobody would eat him, the
useless old fool! What was he saying now?

"And so, Your Majesty," boomed Slave-of-the-Sun,
"we face the danger of an attack from the north by this
Roman Army."

"Eh?" said the King, sharply.

"If the Roman Army can pass through the *khala*, it is
here that they will first attack."

In the name of all the gods and of the Cube, what was
all this? He shook his head, despairingly.

"Listen," said 'Abd al Ya'uk, "listen—the Romans came
to Al Hamra; do you know Al Hamra?"

"There are many places called Al Hamra," said the
King. "It is a foolish name—'The Red Place'—half the
world I have seen is red and the name conveys no distinction.
Names of places should either convey distinction or be
ancient and meaningless. I once, as a youth, rode from
here to a place called 'The Green Mountain'. It was
neither a mountain nor was it green. At the best it might

98

be said to be a little brown, an unpleasant place, full of camel ticks and with a foolish name."

He clapped his hands for a servant. If he had to sit here and listen to old 'Abd al Ya'uk's nonsense, he would do so as near unconsciousness as made no matter.

"Bring wine!" he ordered.

"Your Majesty must understand," persisted Slave-of-the-Sun, "that there may be real danger of attack from the north. These men of Room, the Roman Army, passed from the mountain, eastwards from the Valley of the Green Doves, into the great plain. Thirty days after our men last saw them, marching to the south-east, a sandstorm blew. Since then they have not been seen——"

"But since they went into the desert," said the King, "who but the vultures would see them? You cannot blame your men. And they were no concern of yours," he continued, his temper rising, "no concern at all! Why did they not come by the proper road, the road of the caravans?"

"But they may come here!" insisted 'Abd al Ya'uk.

The King frowned at him, over the rim of his silver cup. Then his eyes softened and he fumbled in his robes.

"Here, old friend," he said, in a wheedling tone, producing the wooden box which held Tahir's new sweets. "Here, take one of these; they are a new confection, delicious, made by Tahir. Take one!"

'Abd al Ya'uk took one, with an irritated snatch, and put it in his mouth. He chewed with appreciation. There was certainly something new in the flavour, more a scent than a taste—a flower perhaps?

"We must be prepared to fight!" thundered Slave-of-the-Sun. "Why should these dogs of Romans invade our land and disrupt our trade? I implore Your Majesty to take the matter seriously. The forts guarding the eastern gorge have long been in disuse. Their walls are crumbling. Money must be found! I have sent men to the Green Mountain to watch all that area. . . ." His voice boomed on, but the King paid him no attention. His eyes were fixed upon 'Abd al Ya'uk, trying to imagine the consistency of the sweet between his jaws. Now, he thought, should be the time. He cut Slave-of-the-Sun's words short with an imperious gesture:

"Let His Honour, 'Abd al Ya'uk, now speak!" he commanded.

'Abd al Ya'uk opened his lips—and a great, red bubble grew from them and hung before his face. It was bigger than the one the King had blown that morning!

"Tee hee!" giggled the King.

The bubble burst. An astonished silence fell upon the room.

"Enough!" roared Slave-of-the-Sun, while 'Abd al Ya'uk mopped his beard and his smock: "Enough! We did not come to Your Majesty for an entertainment! We must have money for these things!"

"*He* has lots of money," said the King, pointing at 'Abd al Ya'uk with a long finger, "he never spends any, the old rat."

'Abd al Ya'uk rose, trembling, his hand on his dagger hilt.

"Rat?" he gasped.

But the King was happy and full of wine.

"A rat," he said, comfortably sure of the description. "Does he not remind you of a rat, Commander? An old one, in some unmentionable place, blowing bubbles!" And he laughed, a long reedy cackle. He must remember to order lots more of this new sweet, there was only one left in the box now.

"I have been insulted!" cried 'Abd al Ya'uk, in a high voice.

"Let it be!" snapped Slave-of-the-Sun. "Let it be, in the name of god! Are we all lunatics? We must arm and fight!"

"I will not," declared the King, "have any fighting if the Romans come here. Although they live a long way from us, they are, I understand, men of culture. If they come out of that awful country to the north they will be tired and we should be ready to entertain them. They may desire a treaty with us. But if anyone fights them, then I shall go at once to Sa'ada and I shall not return until the fighting is over. That must be clearly understood by all."

"But—but——" stammered 'Abd al Ya'uk, in a fury. "Do you not understand? They do not come in peace— they come to attack us, to seize our city, to make you their prisoner, to enslave your people, to seize all our wealth and our land! I tell you, if they come, we must fight! We must slay them, we must drag their vaunting General to Taslal and slit his throat beneath the Cube!"

"Like Slave-of-the-Sun, here," said the King, "a great, bellowing bull, that nobody wants to eat."

They glared at him, both now on their feet, in frustrated rage. There he sat, his empty cup on the floor before him, his filmy eyes gazing at them, an inane smile on his face. As they both opened their mouths to speak a servant called loudly from the doorway.

"A messenger for His Honour, Slave-of-the-Sun!"

The messenger strode into the room, a tall man, the dust of his journey still upon him.

"Excellency!" he cried. "They are come, the men of Room! They are encamped at the Green Mountain!"

"Poor fellows!" said the King.

Slave-of-the-Sun swung angrily away from him towards the messenger.

"How many?" he snapped.

"A *gom* from the east of two hundred camelmen came by night, surprising us and taking two of our number. Then, as I left to bring you this news, just after the light, we saw a further *gom*, of the same number, riding in from the north."

"Were they tired after their journey?" asked the King.

"No, by the Moon! They were like lions!"

"I must go!" cried Slave-of-the-Sun. "The young men must arm and mount and we must hold them in the narrow gorge!"

"If there is any fighting." said the King as the others hurried from the room, "I go to Sa'ada. That must be most clearly understood."

*   *   *

They had come to Nejran, with the first of the late summer rains, Valens, Sabinus and their four hundred men. They had ridden hard and far, for fifty nights of marching. Behind them, over five hundred miles of desert, the Legion followed them, towards the Green Mountain. And their fate marched with them, for to whomever they came, whether in friendship or in enmity, they brought sorrow. Sa'ab sat in his tent, uncomforted, shamed by his own people.

On the sixth day after Valens and his two hundred had left by the eastern route, the camp awoke to uproar. Sa'ab stood outside his tent, his hoarse voice raised in a rattle of harsh, tearing consonants. Men shouted and ran hither and thither and the women wailed. For, in the night, Lilleth had disappeared.

Aretas sat in his tent, his head in his hands, tears on his cheeks. Why had she done this foolishness? If she had asked, if she had come to him, would he not have taken her to Nejran? There might be friends in that city. The wind had blown strongly in the night, covering all tracks sufficiently to forbid a swift pursuit. Three camels were missing and two of Sa'ab's men—the dastards.

"I am shamed before my guests!" cried Sa'ab. "Who now will free me from blame? Speak, *ya* Hassan! Speak! Who has done this thing?"

Hassan, a tall, lightly-bearded man, stood before him, his eyes on the ground.

"It was my brother, *ya 'aqil*, my own brother, Talib. Last night he saddled the three beasts by the tent, saying he would depart at midnight and bring back my cousin, who is with our camels in the *khala*. How should I have known? Did I not ask him who rode the other beasts? He said one was for Hamed, the slave, and the other I knew well, my cousin's *naga*, the strongest she-camel we have. He said he would lead her, empty saddled."

"God blacken his face!" rasped Sa'ab. "Empty saddled? I myself have seen the tracks—a child could tell she was burdened and lightly ridden! As I am a man, I will strike off his head!"

"She is ridden, without doubt, honoured one, the weight falling a little to one side, where the water girbies have been slung. But consider, Sheikh Sa'ab"—he raised his eyes and met the chief's bloodshot gaze—"what man would carry off from her tent a woman against her will?

The custom—it is not possible. And would she not cry out? I have known Talib all his life and he does not want for wives. And if he is *mujennan*, djinn-haunted, and has raped this woman from the camp, where will he live, with every man's hand against him? Talib would take a gift, he is a man of secrets, a father of cunning. Thus has he done, as the woman herself desired."

"What woman would desire to ride into the *khala* with that baboon? He is misshapen, bandy-legged and *awwar*, blind of an eye. He is a djinn! No, he has seized this woman, the daughter of my guest, and has carried her off."

Hassan considered, speaking his thoughts aloud:

"Yet they rode to the north—not towards near water. Did not Talib offer himself to Jareiba, as a guide to the Roomi men? And Jareiba would have none of him. Now they have gone to the north, whence she came."

Sa'ab came to Aretas, in the late evening. He stood in the tent door and beat on his bare breast with the clenched fist of his right hand, his eyes downcast.

"A shame on me!" he groaned. "A shame on me!"

But Aretas led him in, comforting him, his arm about his shoulders.

"The trackers have returned," said Sa'ab. "To the north the tracks lead, marching fast. Then they turn west and that will be towards the water of Sabakha, a far journey. Thence, who knows?"

"I pray you," said Aretas, "have no fears for the child. She has been strange, these past days, since she fled from us in the tent. She has answered me only, she has not spoken other words to me. She is wilful and has gone back to her own people. Do not distress yourself, old

104

friend. To-night the second Roman *gom* departs and, in sixteen days, the General, Gallus, and I leave by the western route. You shall see, I assure you, by then will Talib have returned here, bearing a letter from my little dear one. She has gone north, back to her own folk, to Miriam, who nursed her, and the people of the valley."

But the days passed and no swift rider brought a letter to Aretas. The last evening came and the Prince stared across the sands, so vast, so perilous. A horn sounded and the men stood ready by their couched beasts. Here marched the proud Eagle, to be borne up and on, surrounded by its fierce guards. Here strutted Clemens, here came Gallus; and here, from his tent came old Sa'ab, humbly, his eyes downcast, leaning on his silver-bound spear. He would not take Aretas' proffered hand. Gallus came to him and spoke to him through his interpreter.

"Farewell, King Sabus; we were dead men and you gave us life!"

"It is nothing. It is the custom of our people."

"Will you take no gift before we part?"

"The gift of friendship and the promise of return."

"When Nejran is ours, we will send you word!"

"Oh, Red-of-Eye——"

"We will return some day with Caesar's thanks, for you are a King and a great man!"

"I am a King and in all my land there was none greater. But I am shamed—I am shamed——" And the tears fell down his cheeks as he turned from them.

They mounted their roaring camels. The sun sank, a fiery globe and was gone. Night closed in on them as they marched, a shadowy column, soundless, swift-striding, dimly lit by a quarter-moon.

Twenty-three nights of marching to their south, Valens and his two hundred rode in a long caravan, head to tail, steering a slow, erratic course among high dunes. They had been mounted since early afternoon and had entered the dune country a little before nightfall. Things had gone well with them on their march; there had been good grazing, better than Jareiba anticipated, and they were ahead of their time-table by two days. Somewhere beyond this rolling country of high, red sandhills, lay water, which they should reach before dawn.

Riding thus hour after hour, vision limited by the dim light, one knee across the hard wooden pummel, the practised body swaying with the uneven motion of the climbing and descending camel, the world lost its realities. Thought rose in the mind, now clear and bright, now fading to the edge of dream. The misty slope of a dune might bring its vision—a face perhaps, eyes pensive, lips serene—things known long ago. Each man became a double entity. The tireless, supple body responded to movement, changing its balance, now tensed and upright as the camel stumbled, now harmonious, yielding, a part of the patient strength beneath. The mind travelled other roads, with no continuity in its journeying. It passed memories. In the strange borderland of sleep it met with fantasies. It came close to sleep, longing for those still waters. Time moved with the swelling night wind, a river of air among the dunes, now a faint, uncertain breath, now a whisper in the ear, sighing: "*Khala—khala—khala—* emptiness—emptiness——"

Emptiness, emptiness, thought Valens. The heart is empty and we wander in a barren place. I am changed, he thought, I am Valens no more. There was a girl once, long ago, who fulfilled a dream. She is gone and the dream is left to me, to dream for ever.

A long dim valley between the dunes, the quarter-moon glowing, the stars afire. Jareiba carried his spear across his back. He rode stooping in the saddle, tireless, patient with the world. The silver binding of his spearhead caught the cold, distant lights. Valens did not need to press his mount nor to hold it back. It followed Jareiba's blindly, never altering its long, slow pace. They passed up a valley and turned, climbing, their beasts slithering on the sloping face of a dune. Valens looked back. The shadowy line of riders followed, silently over the stone-less ground. They passed through a narrow passage, deep between high sand walls, into the darkness, the moon obscured. They rode out into the moonlight over bare gravel and then turned right again, into the sand valleys of the dunes and turned and twisted among them.

Jareiba grunted in his beard and pulled his mount to a halt. The men behind pulled up, woken from their half sleep. The camels moaned, checked suddenly in their night-long striding. Jareiba dismounted and led his camel up the slope of a dune to the crest. He unslung his spear and took it in his hand. Then he turned and came down to them.

"It is there," he said to Valens, in a low voice. "Beyond this dune to the right, a little way. But there are others before us. Let us wait till morning."

The word passed down the column, the men dismounted and tied the head ropes to their belts.

"How many, Jareiba?" asked Valens.

"Three, three," he whispered, kneeling, peering at tracks in the sand. "Three fast beasts. Here, see the forefoot track, deep impressed and the nail not dragged as she stepped forward, a ridden beast, urged on."

Valens turned to the soldier beside him.

"Ten men," he whispered, "the first ten men hand over their camels and come with me."

"Armour?"

"No, sword and shield—leave all else."

They crept through the dunes behind Jareiba. He had left his spear standing in the ground and held his broad dagger, drawn, in his hand. They moved swiftly, stooped low. Then Jareiba stood still, stretching his left hand behind him to draw Valens forward. He did not speak.

A gravel plain lay before them and, beyond, the crescent moon. Some thirty paces from them a small fire glowed, a single flame trembling in the wind, which brought the scent of its burning to them. Two dark figures lay stretched on either side of the fire and, facing them, a hooded figure sat, stooped over the flame, crooning to itself, a high voice, singing a lullaby of cadences.

> "There lived a man, there lived a man,
>   Bin Do, Bin Do, Bin Doa, Bin Do,
>   He saw a lass, he saw a lass,
>   Bin Do, Bin Do, Bin Doa, Bin Do,
>   He came to her, he came to her,
>   Bin Do, Bin Do, Bin Doa, Bin Do——"

Valens unsheathed his sword and stepped past Jareiba into the moonlight. He shook his shield, gaining a grip for his left hand. He advanced towards the fire, but the singing figure paid him no heed. It bent over the small flame and, delicately, adjusted the position of the few sticks.

"The lass was fat, the lass was fat,
   Bin Do, Bin Do, Bin Doa, Bin Do,
He bedded her down, he bedded her down——"

"*Koom!* Stand!" said Valens.

The two sleeping figures sprang to their feet, dazed and knife in hand. The singer looked up calmly. Then she turned to one of the suddenly awoken men.

"You were right, Talib," she said. "They are here!"

Valens stood still, infinitely startled, for a moment uncomprehending. Then he turned to the soldier who had followed him.

"Let the men lead their beasts here," he said.

The Arabs began to exchange the interminable greetings of the desert. Dawn was breaking, an orange line, low over the dunes. From the dark bushes beyond the fire which marked the water-hole, a ring dove murmured. Lilleth stood up and stretched her arms above her head. She yawned, and let her arms fall to her sides, a movement of infinite fatigue. She looked up at Valens and smiled.

"You will not know me when the sun has risen," she said. "I am black as Talib, here."

The men watered their camels and freed them to wander and to graze. The burden of the sun lay on them. The rising wind whipped the dunes and filled the air with grit. They sought what shelter they could find, lying under the low bushes, their backs to the wind, their heads covered. Sleep claimed them, if such desertion by the spirit of the suffering body can be called by so sweet a name. As the sun inclined they woke, parched, shaking the sand from their garments, clearing it delicately from the corners of their eyes. In twos and threes they sought the water, rinsing their mouths, sipping it from their hands, holding their water skins deep in the warm seepage to fill them. They walked out among the bushes, where their camels stood, grazing and chewing the cud. The shadows lengthened, a cooling breeze came to them from the west and died. They mounted, with an easy spring, to the pummel, their camels roaring, lurching to their spread feet, eager for the road. They rode out, away from the water, heading to the south, two hundred lean and supple men, burnt black with the sun, full bearded, inured to hardship, skilful riders of the desert plain. In the last sunlight, their shadows stretched from their feet, forming a shadow company among the high, red dunes.

They spread out across the level gravel beyond the bushes of the water-hole, knees bent to the pummels, eyes expressionless as they stared out, in the fading light, on desolation. Night deepened, isolating each from his companions, bringing to each once more his lonely world of thoughts and fancies.

Valens was aware of her, riding beside him. He had learned from Jareiba what she had done. He had spoken no word to her. She had no place here, in this marching group of warriors. She should have stayed in Sa'ab's camp. She should never have been, to steal his heart under the moon, to haunt his night marching with her image among the dunes.

"Antonius——"

"You should not have done this."

Why had he answered her? Why had she done this mad thing? He was bewitched, they were all bewitched. When they rode out to the east from Yathrib, the world had tilted, they were cast out of the country of nature and sanity into empty, haunted places.

"Speak to me, Antonius."

Before them, dark shadows, Jareiba, Talib and the slave Hamed rode, the first two side by side, the other a little apart. The murmur of their voices came back to him. Behind them, spread in small groups, the soldiers rode and one sang a few notes of a song. Why should he not speak to her, tell her what she had done? He turned his head. She rode close to him, he could touch her shoulder if he wished.

"You have disobeyed your father," he said; "you have shamed the old chief, who would have cared for you." He hesitated. All this she knew. He glanced at her again. Her face was placid, contented, a smile on her lips and the light of a star deep in her eyes.

"What should I have done?" she asked, suddenly serious, turning to him in her saddle.

What should she have done? Exasperation nearly overcame him.

"You do not know what you should have done?" He used a familiar expression of the Arabs: "I take refuge in God! You should have travelled with your father, you should have gone back to your people of the valley, you should have stayed with Sa'ab, you should have done all or any of these things but you should not be here! This— this is a *Gom*, a force of warriors, a war party, and you have no place here. You should be somewhere else, a hundred other places, but you should not be here!"

"But I am here," she sighed.

He struck his left palm with the hard fist of his right hand. And she was here! Was it not plain to her, to him, to the sand and the moon and the stars that here she should not be?

"Hush! Antonius!"

"And call me Antonius no more! I am Valens, a Centurion!"

"I cannot pronounce 'Waleins'. I can call you Centurion, if you wish, but others might answer and there would be confusion."

They rode for some time in silence. Then suddenly she was close to him, her hand on his arm, leaning towards him, her face grave.

"Must I tell you why I am here?" she asked, in a low voice.

"You have told me," replied Valens, miserably. "You are here and that, to a woman, is the whole matter."

"No. No, Antonius, it is not the whole matter. You took something from me—I offered it, it was freely given. But you took it. You cannot give it back. I shall not claim anything from you. You shall not be ashamed through me. I will ride apart from you. I will camp apart from you and Talib will see to my wants. But because of the gift you took from me, you must bear with me a little. It will only be for a little while."

The burning days and the long nights of marching followed. The moon waxed to its full and waned. They rode together. They did not camp apart.

One night in the dark of the moon, there was excited talk among the guides and Jareiba hurried to Valens and pointed to the east. There, so small that an unpractised eye would not have seen it, was a red spark in the night, the glow of a distant fire.

Valens turned to Lilleth, when Jareiba had gone.

"Do you see it?" he asked. "The Green Mountain! Our pilgrimage is nearly ended."

She nodded her head. She could not speak for the moment. The march was ending. All things ended that ever were begun. The sadness of finality was in her heart. There came the last ride, the last cup, the last sleep. He took her hand, understanding her.

"Nothing endures," he said.

"Our love endures. Love must endure! For as long as we can think, so long will our love endure! And that will be for ever."

"Do the dead think?" He wondered. "When we fled together through the sand from the twisted mountains, I thought I saw dead men marching with us. But it was thirst casting phantoms before my eyes and the dead had forgotten us long ago."

"I saw them too," she whispered, "like shadows in the night."

A deep foreboding came upon him, stronger, far, than he had felt the night of his dream at Yathrib. That had been the shadow of physical disaster—this was a foreboding of the spirit.

"So may we be," he said, "this Legion, you and I. In some distant time a traveller may see us, as he sits by his fire, like shadows on the sand of his imagination, drifting by him in the night."

"Would he see us, you and I?"

"The shimmer of your dark hair."

"Then we would live again!"

"For a moment, while he wondered, but only as an echo of his thoughts."

CHAPTER 8

Pray for Me

. . . the King had fled. . . . At the first assault. . . .

PRISCUS, the *Pilus Prior* Centurion, who commanded the
First Cohort of the Legion, was a man of prodigious
strength, a black-haired Hercules. His curling, spade-
shaped beard spread on his chest obscuring, when he wore
armour, the many brazen medallions which commemorated
his battles and campaigns. Thick black curls covered his
head and hung above his brow. A broad nose, crooked
and battered, jutted from his hairy face and his luminous,
brown eyes were hard and questing in their expression.

He had ridden into camp the night before with two
hundred men by the western route and a further two
hundred of his Cohort had just arrived on the edge of the
Green Mountain. He reclined on a couch of sacks, in
the shelter of a grass-and-thorn hut. On his right, Sabinus
sat on the ground, his back against a camel saddle. Before
them Valens stood, a twinkle of humour in his eyes, as he
finished his report.

"And so," he said, "that is the way of things in the
Wadi Nejran. The Arabs hold the gorge with some three
hundred young warriors under Salih, the King's son. Their
Amir, Slave-of-the-Sun has now some nine thousand men
in the city, of whom some five thousand have horses.

The King has gone to Sa'ada and Slave-of-the-Sun and an old jeweller are in command."

"And all this you have from the maid?" asked Priscus.

"Yes, from her." Valens no longer smiled. He looked out through the door of the shelter to the high, sandstone mountains which hid from them the city and the valley of Nejran. Somewhere there, Lilleth lived in peril of her life.

"You sent her in?" asked Priscus.

"No!" said Valens, with sudden vehemence. No, he had not sent her in. She had gone, without his knowledge, taking the guide, Talib, with her. A masquerade—Talib as a desert man and she as his wife. She had left a letter for him, that was all.

"No one will regard us," she had written, "a poor *badu* and his woman among the poor of Nejran. I will send news to you first by Hamid and then by the hand of others, whom Talib knows. You will be proud of me. I will be like my father, one of you, and the General will smile when we meet. I will not have men say that I am weak."

"No," repeated Valens, "I did not send her in."

They were silent. Priscus—indeed all the Legion—had felt sorrow for Aretas'. daughter, driven out into the gipsy life of march and bivouac. A lone girl, with no part to play, in this game of hazard. Now she had found a part to play, a part for one hardened by life and skilled in trickery. If her enemies found her out—Priscus shook his head. She was gone from them, only her star and her wits could help her now. And here, in this camp, there was urgent work to do. The gorge must be taken and held and a war camp built beyond it, in the valley. He looked up at Valens.

"Now, Valens," he said, "it is you and I for the gorge to-morrow, at the first light. Our war camp cannot be here—it must be within the valley. This camp must be contracted—that is for you, Sabinus, and the pioneers. We will hold this water and the grazing and we must find horses and pasture them here, for our march to the south. Now let us all sleep, for there will be little rest to-night or to-morrow."

He lay back and was at once asleep.

Sabinus and Valens walked out into the evening. The light lay red on the strangely shaped mountains, which guard Nejran. A flight of duck circled high above the gorge. Sabinus laid a hand on Valens' shoulder.

"Good fortune, to-morrow," he said. "Go now, friend, and sleep, I pray you. In these three days you have tired as if you marched to Rome and back each night."

"No, only to Nejran," said Valens smiling.

"Nejran or Rome, they are all as distant by the light of a tallow candle."

*   *   *

They lay that early morning in the darkness, the thin crescent of the moon sinking in the western sky, their jerkins worn over their armour, their helmets covered, their shields boss-downwards. Before them the crest of a drift dune showed black against the starry sky. Priscus heaved his huge body sideways on his elbows, close to Valens.

"Near time to strike," he whispered.

From beyond the dune, sounding perilously close in the still night, a voice began to chant a high, quavering invocation.

"They now assemble for their devotions," whispered

Valens. "They will turn towards the sacred stone with their backs to us."

Priscus' enormous hand closed on the shaft of his javelin. He did not need to turn—every eye was on him, every left knee was thrust forward in the sand, every right hand gripped a javelin and pressed downwards on its knuckles, in readiness to spring.

Slowly Priscus lifted his knee beneath him, his face low to the ground. Valens heard him breathe in deeply, filling the great bellows of his lungs. Then, like a leopard, he sprang forward.

Javelins struck the Arabs down. Straight Roman swords flashed and stabbed among them. Some fled to the shelter of the forts, to be later smoked from them, in their burning. Priscus and his four hundred stirred the water of the stream to yellow foam in their headlong rush through the gorge. Young Salih, the King's son, withstood them, his curved scimitar upraised; he fell, torn with wounds, rolling in the reddened water. The Romans were out and beyond the gorge, swiftly pursuing, slaughtering, till a horn sounded and they came back, grinning in their beards. They had not lost a man. By the forts and in the water of the gorge, close on two hundred of the Arabs lay dead or dying, and a score of bound prisoners awaited Valens' prying questions. When the first fugitive staggered through the gate of Nejran, the first line of palisades stood thick before the Roman camp inside the valley.

After two nights, no Arab approached the camp by the gorge. They prided themselves on their stealth, but here, in the warriors of the Legion, they met masters in nightcraft. The Romans had no bows, since they depended on auxiliaries for archers and here there were none. But they were expert, deadly with the long sling. And the few Arabs who approached by night found themselves among cunning trip-ropes and beset by outliers. The Roman horns, marking the watch hours, sounded faintly and eerily in the still city.

Word came to Valens one morning, brought from Lilleth by a bedouin, who craved permission to leave the valley and rejoin his kin. Valens read the letter to Priscus and his Centurions.

"At dawn (on the morrow) they will attack the camp," she had written. "They will ride out from the east gate, four thousand mounted men and they will fall upon you before sunrise."

"Does she write no more?" asked Priscus.

"Yes," replied Valens, "but it does not concern us." Nor did it concern them, for she wrote for him alone: "My heart, if I should not see you again in life, I will wait for you. Our lodging is determined for us under some star, near or distant. Pray for me."

Pray for her! Night and day the prayer was said.

So it happened that, as the great eastern gate opened at midnight and the young chivalry of Nejran rode out into the valley, the flaring light of torches illuminating the tall houses behind them, they met disaster. Great bronze darts flashed among them, tearing through them, casting them down; a rain of javelins struck them from left and right and devils clothed in iron rushed among them, tearing them from their saddles, butchering their plunging horses. They turned, stampeding back into the city, as the gate closed. And a cry went up from the city: "Treachery! There are spies among us!" And each man looked on his neighbour covertly, doubt in his heart.

On the third morning after the ambush by the gate, sharp watchers on the mountains overlooking the gorge espied afar off a glint of gold above a small caravan, moving slowly towards them from the desert, and the camp rejoiced. They greeted Gallus with '*Ave!*' as he rode through the narrow gorge, the Prince beside him, followed by the Eagle and Clemens and the staff. By nightfall the soldiers in camp numbered some sixteen hundred men.

The next day, early in the morning, Gallus rode out of camp, accompanied by a Cohort of the Legion on foot, and made his way through fields and plantations of date palms, towards the city. They halted some five hundred paces from the northern gate. The people of the city looked down on them from the wall and the roof-tops, wondering what this small force would do. Valens had seized a few horses from the countryside and he now rode forward, with two mounted soldiers, until a warning arrow stopped him at the stream. The horses dropped their heads to the water. Valens lifted his right hand in salute and waited for silence on the wall.

"Greeting from the Amir of the Romans!" he called. "I desire speech with Slave-of-the-Sun, commander of the city and with the people of Nejran!"

There was a stir among the people on the wall and some shouting. Then, on the roof of the bastion, there appeared a powerful, broad-shouldered figure and a deep voice rang out across the stream.

"I am Slave-of-the-Sun! What do you desire?"

"That you should leave the city gate and come to me, with such escort and company as you may wish, to meet our Amir and his counsellors so that there may be talk between you of peace!"

There was a murmuring among the people. Three men were in earnest conversation with Slave-of-the-Sun and one, who held his sleeve, pointed with vehement gestures towards the centre of the Roman line, where Gallus stood dismounted. Then Slave-of-the-Sun turned and shouted again from the battlements.

"*Marhabba!* It is welcome! Await us there and we will cross the water to you."

At a signal from Valens, Gallus came forward, accompanied by the Prince, Clemens and Priscus and joined Valens by the stream. Clemens examined the city, with professional interest. The mud-brick wall on its foundation of limestone blocks presented a small obstacle to Roman eyes.

"Weak defences," he said to Gallus, "and the stream is shallow now, although it bore a light flood last night. It is no moat."

"No," said Gallus; "a morning's work to take the city and an easy afternoon to sack it. We shall have men enough for the task, in five days' time—a half of the Legion and all our heavy engines. Ah! Here they come."

Slave-of-the-Sun was not with them. They rode out of the half-open gateway, some twenty mounted men, splashed across the stream and dismounted. Six of them, only, advanced towards the waiting Romans, the morning wind stirring their embroidered head cloths and their thin, camel-hair cloaks. Their leader, a tall, hawk-faced fellow, handsome, with a pointed, oiled beard, halted some two paces from the Romans. He stared haughtily at them, his lips smiling, but not his eyes.

"*As salaam 'aleikum!* Peace upon you!" he said. "To whom do I speak? Who speaks our tongue?"

"I," said Valens. "Our Amir desires to enter the city in peace. He brings greetings from the Caesar of Rome to the King of Nejran. He had hoped to speak with the commander of the city."

"The Amir Slave-of-the-Sun does not speak to such as you; he has sent me as his deputy. I am J'abil, a Captain of a thousand." He raised his thin eyebrows. "Caesar sends strange greetings!" he said, his eyes roving over the Roman group with contempt. He turned directly to Gallus.

"We have nought to do with Caesar—you are not welcome here!" He gestured to the north, a graceful movement of long fingers and sparkling rings: "Go back to the kennel whence you came!" He snapped out the words.

Valens turned to interpret, but Gallus silenced him with a wave of his hand.

"I understood," he said, "but tell him that we do not return. If I do not enter Nejran in peace, I will break down the wall of the city and put it to the sword!"

Valens translated, urbanely, grading his voice to Gallus' level tones. J'abil turned to his counsellors, but one pushed past him, a grey-bearded man, alert of eye, and quick of speech. He turned to Prince Aretas.

"Are you," he asked, "the Prince Aretas of Nabataea?"

"I am," he replied.

"Then this is for you!"

He was too quick for them. They had only a glimpse of the tiger-light in his eyes as he sprang and stabbed twice from the opening of his cloak, upwards, his body pressed against the Prince—and Clemens' sword smashed through between his grinning teeth. The Prince fell. For a moment the Arab hung suspended on the steel, the sword point projecting from his neck. Then Clemens lowered his arm and cleared his sword with a vicious kick. The Arabs stepped backwards from them, silent, shocked by the violence of Clemens' thrust and the power of his arm. Then they ran for their horses and were gone in a wild scurry, over the stream and through the clanging gate.

They carried Aretas' dead body back with them in silence to their camp and they buried him deep in the rocky ground and placed a cairn of stones above his head. The camp was quiet that night. There was no laughter in the shelters, when the day's work ended and the men had eaten their evening meal. The silence boded ill for the people of Nejran, for these were ill men to offend and did not bear with treachery. They knew little of Aretas or who he was, but he had been their friend, a kindly man, and he had marched with them through the wilderness. Only he and the restless nomads, in all this wide land had befriended them. They would remember how he had died, when their foes fell down and begged for mercy at the sword point. There would be none.

"To be struck down thus in our midst, when we talk of peace!" exclaimed Priscus. "May the gods rot me with worms, if I leave one alive among them who can sire a child!"

Time seemed doubled to their impatient minds, until the watchers called and their comrades of the Fifth Cohort rode into camp.

"All in position by the first light," said Gallus. "The engines will breach the wall to the east of the north gate.

The Second Cohort will force the breach and the Third will take the wall. The Fourth and Fifth with me, in reserve. You, Priscus, with the First Cohort, will watch the east gate, for it is from there they will make a mounted sortie."

In the night the great engines rolled out of camp on their solid wheels, their teams beside them. The surveyors and pioneers watched them go, while the five Cohorts spread out towards their dawn positions.

*   *   *

It seemed to Lilleth so short a time from their invisibility to their discovery. No one had paid them heed—Talib, crooked and one-eyed and she, hooded, a humble bedouin wife, in her flapping trousers and her shapeless blue smock. Then Talib saw the man, as they stood outside the cook shops, at the corner of the street of copper-smiths. He was a tall fellow, in a ragged sheep-skin coat and loin cloth, his filthy hair hanging to his shoulders, and Talib snarled and crouched, his knife drawn. People seized on Talib and held him till the city guards came. It seemed that Talib, some years ago, had taken life and the tall man claimed him as a long-sought enemy, for trial before the Judges. She remained mute, but with no way of escape.

Then they turned on her. 'Black as Talib', she had said to Valens, in jest. But her face was ivory, youthful and delicate, and her breasts—for they tore her smock also—as white as snow under the moon.

"To the Amir!" they cried. "To Slave-of-the-Sun!"

They did not strike her, then. They struck Talib with the heavy butts of their spears, all the way to Slave-of-the-Sun's reception-room, where he sat among his counsellors. Then they struck him down to the floor, for good measure.

123

Talib lay there, moaning, his body conquered, but they heaved him to his feet by his hair, before Slave-of-the-Sun.

"Who is this woman?" bellowed the Amir, when matters had been explained.

"My wife!" gasped Talib. "Before god, my wife!"

They tore his clothing from his chest and one drew a knife and twisted the blade in his ribs.

"Speak truth!" said old 'Abd al Ya'uk, leaning forward. "Speak truth, or you will rue it! Who is this woman?"

"My wife," he sobbed. "She is my wife——"

"I am not his wife," said Lilleth. "Let him be."

Talib lay where they had let him fall. They looked on her in silence, while 'Abd al Ya'uk shuffled up to her and gazed into her face. Then he turned to Slave-of-the-Sun, his red-rimmed eyes wide.

"This," he declared, "is the daughter of Prince Aretas! None but she! Many years ago, I visited the Prince in the Valley of the Green Doves and there I met her mother, when the Prince was young: and, before the gods, here stands the same woman! This is the daughter—I am never mistaken, in a woman or in a mare!"

"It is true," said Lilleth, firmly. "I am the daughter of the Prince. Do with me as you will—but you shall release this poor man, Talib. He has done no wrong. You shall release him and let him go."

"She gives us orders!" exclaimed Slave-of-the-Sun. "I must think what shall be done with you. Know you that the dog, your father, is dead?"

Her dark eyes flashed with contempt.

"I saw him treacherously slain!" she said.

'Abd al Ya'uk looked up at her, red murder in his eyes.

"It is long years." he said, "since human blood flowed

at Taslal. You give us orders——" He laughed. "'You shall let him go!'" he mimicked her; he turned to the counsellors.

"Let her be taken, with her servant, to the Pit, this night. If she lives by morning, let her throat be slit beneath the Cube!"

The guards hustled them down corridors and endless stairs, not disdaining, now, to strike her with their spears, if she tripped or hesitated. They passed a guard-room, where oil lamps burned and a door opened on to a narrow street; then downstairs again into a passage, where the air was dank and heavy and all was dark. There they opened a door she could not see and a foul stench, such as she had not known before, enveloped them, as they were cast down steps and the door closed on them, in a pit of darkness.

For a long time she lay, bruised and barely conscious of her body. Then, not far from her, she heard the rustle and slither of a snake and sprang to her feet in terror.

You can imprison bodies. You cannot imprison minds, they can only be killed. And you can kill the mind of a desert man with four walls and a roof. The desert man is born under the stars and bred under the sun. All the wide vault of heaven is his roof-tree. But even the deep valleys of the mountains disturb the balance of his mind. His mind begins to panic like a trapped animal, to run from side to side. Here, in the dark Pit, Talib's mind could not live.

She heard him muttering, she heard his hands beat upon a wall. They had disarmed him, but they had not troubled her and she held a slim dagger in her hand, breathing lightly, stepping away from Talib, until her left hand felt the wall by the steps down which they had been thrown. Even then she pressed her shoulder against the wall, away from Talib—Talib who raved and sobbed, beating against the walls which held him, running hither and thither, falling in the darkness, trapped and demented.

At last he fell and was silent, exhausted, for a long time. Then he began to speak again, a low murmur of sound. He moved and found a wall. At once he struck against it, the evil thing, holding him here in the dark, and his voice rose, horrible, cracked, a scream of mad rage.

Then the door opened. Two men stood on the top of the steps, one with a flaring torch, one with a scimitar. They looked down at her and then at Talib, who groped his way towards them. The armed man spoke:

"She is to be kept," he said. He came down the steps. "Come," he said to his companion, "it is the man we have to slay."

Lilleth pressed her hands into her mouth and her knife, on its cord, hung down hidden by her smock. The man with the torch seized Talib's long hair and raised him with one hand. She closed her eyes tight, tight. She heard the chopping sound. She heard the body fall and then the head. When she opened her eyes, darkness pressed upon them.

For a long time she leant against the wall, aghast, her hands thrust between her lips. She sank down by the steps and her left hand sought something which pressed against her thigh. She felt the thing with her fingers, smooth and domed, and one finger slipped into an open gap and she knew what she had found. Talib was not the first to have his head chopped from his body in the Pit. As she snatched her hand away, for a moment her mind

126

reeled on the edge of the precipice of insanity. Then she was suddenly calm, her mind clear, mistress of all the horror which had so suddenly sprung upon her.

She rose to her feet, thinking, thinking, her limbs supple beneath her. Swiftly she undid the side laces of her smock, shook herself from it and rolled it round her left forearm, a tight cushion. She crept up the steps in the darkness and found the door, searching for the hinge. She waited there, her knife in her hand.

She leant against the wall by the hinge, her eyes open in the darkness. Then, at last, she heard a shuffle of feet by the door and the drawing of the wooden bolt. Yes, she thought, her dark brows frowning, I was sure of it! They would not leave a woman alone—even in a charnel house, her last hours in the world.

He opened the door and held his torch aloft, looking down, searching for her in the Pit. She struck the narrow blade into his throat and caught the torch as he fell, gurgling, down the steps.

For a moment she stood, the torch above her, looking down. They lay there, the unfortunates, some still with a horrid appearance of humanity, some long since bones and dust. Then she threw the torch down and stepped into the dark corridor.

She found the stair and mounted it, her left hand on the damp wall. She turned and mounted the next flight— and cowered sideways. Something had passed her on the stair! A ghost? Ghosts would throng here, on this road to death. Then she felt it again, a light breeze blowing from above her, cold on her naked shoulder. She mounted the stair again and, on the top step, she paused.

One oil lamp still burned on a small tripod, in the

guard-room. Beside it, a man reclined, his head resting on the ledge of a closed window, asleep. Beyond him, the door to the street was open and, at the end of the street, sunlight blazed on a wall. She crept towards the man. She stooped close above him. Her knife shone, raised, and flickered as she drove it down. She ran through the open door and, as she did so, a vast tumult came to her ears and the sunlit wall before her crumbled at a great blow and fell into the street.

*   *   *

Gallus sat his horse on a small rise of ground some six hundred paces from the city wall. To his right the Second and Third Cohorts stood, in the three lines of their formation, the siege catapults massed between them, facing the north gate. Behind them and to the left, the two reserve Cohorts waited, one behind the other, the Eagle and its guards between them. To his left, the First Cohort was drawn up in three lines, just beyond arrow-shot of the east gate.

He saw the throwing arm of the first catapult jerk up and forwards. The stone ball flew true, grazing the battlements of the bastion, mangling the warriors on its roof. At once the air was full of the sound of rushing stones. Stripped naked, protected from arrows and sling stones by tough hide mats hung above them, the crews laboured at their engines, pounding at the wall by the bastion, jarring it, breaking it down, their huge, rounded stones hurtling through it and over it into the city, while the Arabs scattered away from this chosen target, to left and right.

Behind the east gate Slave-of-the-Sun, his long curved sword drawn, wrenched back his silver-studded reins and turned to the wild stampede of horsemen behind him, his

128

grey mare plunging, fighting against the bit. In the open square, four thousand chosen horsemen, men and youths, the long sleeves of their Yemen cloaks pulled back and tied behind them, head cloths knotted below their chins, waited, their horses kicking and rearing, for the signal of the opening gate.

"I will lead you," cried Slave-of-the-Sun, "and let none turn back or turn aside! Shall the sons of the sun turn back?"

A wild yell answered him, the gate swung wide, and in a cloud of dust they poured through it, a long, undisciplined rabble of fighting and plunging horses. A cry hailed them from the city. These were the chivalry of Nejran, and dark eyes, full of yearning, watched them from the latticed windows of many a tall house, as they stampeded in a cloud of upthrown sand. Then they sprang out of the sand cloud they had made and hurled themselves forward, in a mad, loose-reined gallop, slashing the water of the stream to white foam, and charged down upon the First Cohort. With a smack and a hiss the six ballistae of the Cohort struck out at them, the heavy sinew-driven darts tearing through them; but they came on, through a hail of javelins, on to the Roman line, staggering it backwards, slashing, hacking with their swords, men and horses filled with a wild, triumphant madness. They pressed against the Romans, beards flecked with foam, their horses rearing up against the wall of shields with bloody nostrils. Then, the first shock of the charge held and checked, the Cohort began to move against them, at first step by step, then more swiftly, stabbing, leaping the fallen horses, tearing the men from their saddles, forcing them back towards the stream and the wall, while choking dust rose high above the slaughter and the men of Nejran cursed and slashed and died. The chivalry broke before the Cohort. Slave-of-the-Sun turned his horse, but there was no way of escape through his cursing, milling followers. In a moment he was seized and, dead of five sword thrusts, trampled under foot.

The guards in the gateway threw their shoulders against the great doors; but their own cavalry cut them down, forcing their horses through into the city, away from the terrible Roman swords. And the Cohort was behind them, leaping after them, through the gate, up the steps to the bastion, hurling the Arab defenders from the walls.

The wall by the north bastion was now a mound of rubble and up and over the mound advanced the *testudo* of the Second Cohort, some four hundred close-packed men, the leading shields held before them, the others locked as a roof above their heads. As they forced the breach, the Third Cohort sprang in, while the *testudo* split suddenly into leaping groups of men.

"Let all the Cohorts advance!" said Gallus, standing in the breach.

The war-horns blew, the blare of the *cornu* and the *tuba's* call, a terrible whooping sound, such as a huntsman might use, urging his hounds on to a kill. They sprang in. Gallus looked down upon the slaughter below him, a hard smile on his lips. Here was revenge for lies and bloody treachery! The sandy streets, where scented youths had lately walked hand in hand, were slaughter-houses before midday.

Valens had asked leave to advance with the Third Cohort. Now he stood in the centre square of the town. He could not search every street and every house. Here he hoped that, if she lived, she might find him.   The tumult of a raped and looted city filled the air and the thick, acrid smell of burning houses drifted through the streets.   Smoke thickened with the lessening cries.   Somewhere behind him he heard a Centurion's voice, sharply ordering, restraining his men.   From the roof of a many-storied house a flame rose, at first a flickering in the bright sunlight, then, as the roof beams sagged and the flat roof split, a red banner of fire.   The upper storey belched flame and smoke, the wall split, and the side of the house fell down-wards, a torrent of stone, on to the high, sunlit wall of a garden.

He looked away, across the square to the west.   He could not see her.   He did not see her, staggering from a narrow street, unable to cry his name, until she was in the dust, her arms about him, her face pressed against his knees.

The sun inclined.   The horns sounded and the panting, satiated soldiers stood still and laughed wordlessly at each other through snarling lips.   Dark-eyed ladies crouched weeping in shuttered rooms, and their children were wide-eyed and silent.   Gallus sat in a green garden, where a fountain played; and Nejran of the scents and flowers, city of poets and of love songs on cool evenings, the city of the Cube—and of the Pit—lay crushed in the hand of Rome.

CHAPTER 9

Queen of the Night

. . . in the country of the Agrani.

NONE of them had yet seen Gallus moved or excited. They had seen him as the resourceful commander in council, the skilled General in war and the kindly comrade in adversity. But his smile was rare, his laugh reserved.

They wondered, those who saw him now, standing in the garden laughing, animated, his servants agog for orders and scurrying to carry them out. He had been shaved and his chin shone smooth and pink, in contrast to the deep tan of his forehead and his cheeks. His curling, golden hair had been barbered and it glinted with a pomade of fine oil. He wore a laundered tunic, which hung to mid-calf, with the thin, purple stripe of the Equestrian Order. Gone were the sword belt, the dagger, the jerkin, the cuirass—all were cast aside with the dust and heat of past days. To-day—he clapped his hands for joy at some new idea, a boy again, entranced in the anticipation of a delightful escapade!

First three couches must be made, the carpenters must turn to at once, there was no time to lose. Let the couches be draped with the richest cloths and brocades and provided with sumptuously covered cushions. A table must be made too—if there was none in Nejran. A table in a house nearby, with a sawn elephant's tusk as a single leg? Splendid! It must be brought at once. The carving table —let it be made to the order of the steward. There must be a profusion of lamps, napkins, flowers in abundance and garlands.

Clemens was delighted. He, too, laughed—a staccato, barking noise. He would see to the servants and by dinner their precision would be perfect. Not only the servants— he would arrange for the flowers also. Surprisingly, they discovered, in this grim old fighter, a passionate lover of flowers, his pale face lit by some inner glow, as he lifted them to the light, his vast, horny hands gentle with their stalks and petals. He spread them on the grass before him in the garden and gave his orders—of this sort, none, it had a sour smell. Of this and this and this, there could not be too many, in their delicate coats of mauve, scarlet and blue. Of this—he breathed through his great, hooked nose—bring all that are in Nejran, the beautiful white lilies, with the scent of a rose! Let them be kept shaded and in water, until he ordered them to be paraded.

Priscus—the very man for the wine! Priscus squared his shoulders. There was a thin, white wine, very sweet and clear and he would have it brought at once. There was also a dark, spiced wine, a powerful wine, one which a prudent man would temper with water. There was no snow—alas! But did not Gallus think that it might be wise to have other drinks, as well as wine? Gallus frowned. Yes, it had slipped his mind, there was that possibility. Priscus suggested a syrup of raisins, judiciously watered. Capital! And a cool drink from crushed limes, flavoured with pounded ginger, such as the Prince had given them at Raudha? Gallus struck his thigh in delight—

133

the very thing, of course, and the praise to Priscus who had remembered!

Valens must find the entertainers. There must be musicians and singers and Valens must rehearse them at once and be sure that they twisted no phrases and that all, *all* were performers of respect. There must be nothing lewd, nothing which savoured of the cook-shop or the camp. There must be jugglers and acrobats, men expert in illusions; and clowns. Valens must scour the city and assemble them under a master-entertainer, who would ensure the smoothness of the programme and who would answer for its propriety.

Clemens spoke up, from among his flowers. Let there be a Roman song or two! To be sure, soldiers were not entertainers; but Lucius of the Ninth Cohort had a fine voice and could sing the country songs of Tuscany. He had asked to be allowed to sing.

Fat Serenus, jocund and rubicund, thrust himself forward. He had composed an ode for the occasion! In the Latin tongue, of course, but he had added a few oriental phrases, some innocent native quips, such as he had picked up in the course of a hard life. But he would reserve this gem until the evening, he would not tell them of it now. Let it come to their ears with freshness, a surprise! Clemens rose from among the flowers and confronted him. Everything must be rehearsed—it was the Praefectus' order. Let Serenus, therefore, rehearse this ode of his and let him do so forthwith! Serenus obligingly recited the first six lines and Gallus, with a guffaw of laughter, counselled him to be silent, if he valued his head.

In Serenus they discovered, not unexpectedly, a genius for the kitchen. He had turned to with his staff, they had

134

rounded up all the merchants of provisions, the bakers and the confectioners. Serenus had even sampled Tahir's famous sweet, to his confusion. He had found hunters, skilled with the sling, the bow and the net and they had returned well laden. Let the Praefectus see if he approved the menu: there would be snails, very small, but of a delicate flavour and, with them, a sauce of vinegar, raw egg and cream. There would be minnows, baked dry and brittle, with slices of lime and the larger, barbel-bearing fish of the perennial stream, their muddy flavour eclipsed with pepper, vinegar, wine and a touch of a leaf, like thyme. There would be radishes, too, but they were poor roots and green salads were not grown here. Let that pass. There would be slivers of a rich cheese, and eggs, hard boiled and shelled, stuffed with all manner of pepper and spices. And for all these, a strong, white wine, tempered with honey.

There would be roast wild duck—duck, he had said, no tough old drake among them. They would be lightly roasted and the little ones, the teal, hardly roasted at all, but thrust into a burning oven to seal in their goodness and their flavour and served at once, with a lime sauce. Great partridges—the hunters had brought them in, and Gallus admired the plumage of the first greater red-legged partridge he had seen. Wild guinea-fowl, with flesh white as marble, well roasted under strips of burnt mutton fat, since there was no bacon here. For them, a sauce made from white wine. For the principal dish there was a choice—fat lambs? A gazelle? No—he had chosen. There would be three great wild turkeys—more delicious than any turkey from a farm—roasted and stuffed with rock pigeons, with chopped hare which had been cooked in a marinade of red wine and oil and a wheaten sauce, mint flavoured. For all this another white wine—Priscus had found it—thin and a little sweet, but it could be spiced to suit the taste.

Then, the dessert—a great variety of sweets. Tahir had worked all day yesterday on his new one and had eliminated its bubble-forming constituents. It was truly delicious! There were raisins, small but of an excellent flavour and other choice of dried fruits. There were fruits preserved in honey. And the cakes! He himself had made some—little honey cakes, such as a man might nibble under the vines on a cool day, the juicy grapes to his hand. Serenus' eyes were suffused as he thought of them. And other cakes, pasties, pastries and tarts—a profusion, a cornucopia of the baker's subtle art.

And with the dessert a full-bodied, red wine, pure or judiciously watered. A wine to match the garlands, a fit wine for night-long carousal, until the nerveless hand released the cup and the garlanded brow bounced gently off the marble floor.

"There will be no carousal," said Gallus.

"No," sighed Serenus, "that is what I feared."

Then Gallus summoned them all to conference, under the tree by the fountain. There must be a gown. No ordinary gown would do—it must be the most beautiful gown in Nejran and that would be the most beautiful in all Arabia. It must be the most beautiful in the world, so said Priscus, his eyes wide at the thought! When he tried to imagine the most beautiful gown in the world, he could think of nothing.

A gown, a belt and a diadem, said Gallus. The merchants came and laid their wares before him. He sat on the grass, lifting this one, putting that one aside, asking hard questions of the merchants, through his interpreter. Whence came this cloth? This colour—would the sun fade it? And these pearls—they were well matched in colour, but their grading was faulty. This, now—ah! They all echoed his cry, as he knelt and laid it out before him. This was the gown, a faint and glowing green, slim-waisted, trimmed with little pearls, a simple thing, but very lovely. Yes, thought Priscus, that is the most beautiful gown in the world.

A belt for the gown must be found. Clemens held one up, a belt of cunningly twisted gold ropes, its buckle studded with gems. And here was one which Valens showed—a barbaric affair of jointed, golden plates, heart-shaped and a cornelian glowing dully from the centre of each heart. Gallus looked on them frowning, puzzled, deep in thought. Then he saw it, among the pile of treasure—a belt of delicate filigree work, cunningly jointed, gemless, no more than a thin mist of silver. He held it in his hands against the green gown. He laid it in a circle on the grass. Was it small enough? He smiled. He put it as far about him as it would go. He laughed and jumped to his feet—yes, the gown and the belt, both would do. They could never be good enough, but they would do.

And now, the diadem—he had already chosen it. He unwrapped it from its silk coverings and held it up, for all to see, a crown of crescent moons in silver, very light and, in the arms of each crescent, a round moonstone, clear and faintly blue, glowing with a pale, mysterious light. They were silent. He wrapped it again and laid it on the table, between the couches.

There was one thing more: let the carpenters come in. Here, beyond the fountain, at the far end of the garden under an almond tree, a pavilion must be built. The chief carpenter knelt down, while Serenus sketched it with the point of his knife, a frame of scented wood, covered in thick white silk, with many hanging lamps, a soft carpet and a mirror of polished silver. The carpenter smiled and rose. He had found the wood. The work would be done at once; Clemens had petals prepared for the carpet, fresh and soft and there were dainty sandals, of gold and silver and many colours, to be placed round the walls in the pavilion, so that there could be the excitement of a choice. And now they could leave the garden for a while —Clemens to his flowers, Valens to the couches, Serenus to the kitchen, his mouth full of Tahir's sweets, and Gallus to rest a little, lying down in the shade of a tree, sleeping as his head touched the pillow, just as if nothing were to happen that night at all! And Priscus, rumpling his strong black beard, wondering at the treasures he had seen.

The sun sank below the mountains, in a clear sky. Far away to the south, the horizon flickered, reflecting the lightnings of a distant storm. A cool breeze stirred the leaves of the almond tree above the white pavilion and the garden glowed, a place of many lights.

Valens climbed the narrow, winding stair. At the top, there was a door and, on either side of it stood two armed men, in helmet, mail, dagger belt with brass-studded, hanging straps, great half-cylinder shields on their left arms. They grinned when they saw him. Yes, the lady had slept silently all the night. She had eaten a light meal at midday. She was now stirring in her room.

Valens opened the door and closed it behind him. She ran to him across the room.

"Antonius! Why have you not come before? Oh, I have slept and slept."

He held her away from him, his face stern.

"I bring a message from the Praefectus!" he declared.

She looked up at him in mock humility.

"Let me hear His Excellency's words," she said.

"You are commanded to appear before the General at once. There must be no delay! He awaits you in the garden of his house."

"To appear before him!" The mock humility was gone. Here was genuine alarm. How could she appear before him—before anyone, in this white petticoat? There, on the window-ledge, lay another garment, a woollen military cloak, which she had cast from her when she woke. And her hair! She raised her arms and felt it. I must look like the rag doll Miriam made for me, she thought.

"But what can I wear?" she cried.

"Nothing!"

"Antonius! Nothing?" And she sat down on the couch and laughed hysterically.

Valens laughed too and his blue eyes sparkled.

"Come!" he ordered, taking her hand and drawing her to her feet. "Come! The General awaits you, pacing in his garden!"

"But this—this is an under-garment!" She pulled against him as he led her firmly to the door. "It is an under-garment, Antonius, I cannot go to the General——"

"Peace, woman!" he commanded her. "Under or over, it is all the same to him!"

"But, Antonius—my hair! Only a moment for my hair!"

They passed the sentries. She tripped on the stair, but he held her up and hurried her on.

"And my slippers," she wailed. "I have no slippers on—and this one shift—oh!"

"To the General! Careful now, it is dark here and—ah! Here are the lights!"

Lights! Flaring torches at the door to the garden—she pulled him back, frantic now and angry.

"I cannot come like this—this is not like you, Antonius! I will not be pulled thus, half dressed through the streets! I must have my cloak, at the least, if I have no gown to wear——"

"Have no fear, Lilleth," he said, turning to her; and she was shocked into silence by the gentleness in his blue eyes and by the love in them. He laughed, a laugh of sheer delight, and led her into the garden.

They stood in a group under the hanging lights, by the couches, Gallus, Clemens, Serenus, Priscus and two others, Pudens and Artorius, Centurions of the First Cohort, so that their number, when they dined, should be nine, the number of the Muses.

Then Gallus came forward and took her hand. He led her across the garden towards the white pavilion, glowing under the almond tree and, at the door, he turned to her.

"You will honour us?" he said. "You will dine with us? We are rough soldiers making war, which is our trade. But within this pavilion are such things as we have prepared for your adornment. If you enter, you will understand and we will await you."

She stared back at him, uncomprehending. He had

140

spoken with such humility. She lifted the curtain of the door and stood for a moment, looking in on the lights and treasures. Then she entered the pavilion and the curtain fell behind her.

They waited with impatience.

"Women take much pleasure," barked Clemens, "in the donning of new raiment!"

"Yes, yes," growled Priscus, "yes, they prink."

"Prink!" Serenus looked at him with contempt. "Prink! What a word!"

But within the pavilion, Lilleth did not "prink". She sat on the little stool they had provided, in her white petticoat, the green gown and the misty silver belt on her knees and the tears ran from her open eyes down her cheeks. They had done all this for her! How they must have planned and thought, these rough men. The little petals so evenly spread on the soft carpet at her feet—which hard-muscled hand had laid them down? The silver mirror and the lights, placed with such care and understanding. "I will be like my father," she had written to Valens, "one of you." She could never be one of them, she knew full well, but she had tried to serve them and her father's cause. Who had chosen the gown—and the belt, so perfectly its match? And who had arranged these coloured slippers, so many pairs, so that she could have the joy of a choice, to put colour in her cheeks, before she stepped out into the lighted garden? She must hurry, hurry, she must not keep such kindliness waiting. But the tears fell and fell and would not be checked.

At last the curtain was lifted. She came towards them and they waited for her in silence, for, however beautiful the gown, this was a loveliness they had not planned.

Gallus led her to the couches.

"We will dine in the Roman manner," he said to her; "Valens, you must explain. The Princess on my left here, on the right of the centre couch. I here and thus closest to you, to my joy and honour. Clemens beside you and beside him, Priscus—you must excuse Priscus—his father was a bear from Germany. Beside me Serenus, who is responsible for the feast; if you do not like any of the dishes, tell me at once, and I will put my knife into him. Beyond him Sabinus—that is right; we have put him and Valens as far from you as we can, Valens at the foot of the third couch, for they are too handsome. These are Pudens and Artorius—they are handsome too, so you need pay them no attention."

So he jested, while Valens translated and she laughed, her delight growing, shy of them in this strange, intimate setting.

"And now," said Gallus, "we shall be garlanded; but before we dine, there is a ceremony to be performed."

He took the diadem from its silk wrapping. Very gently, he placed it on her dark hair. Her eyes opened wide with wonder and she looked across to Valens, her lips trembling.

"Why—why does he crown me?" she asked in a low voice.

Valens did not hear her. He gazed at her, enchanted, but in the enchantment there was fear. She was Lilleth, the devoted to the moon, the Queen of the Night. To-night was dark, only stars in the clear sky; but she had paled suddenly, her eyes on his, and the silver crescents in the diadem shone white on her brow and the moonstones in their arms held the pale glow of a dying moon. Did a

142

shadow lean above her? He shivered suddenly and a little cry of fear escaped her lips as she saw the fear in his eyes.

At once they were solicitous. What ailed her? Had Valens offended? Come! Let the servers serve and the carver be prepared to carve. If Valens had offended, she must excuse them, not him. He was not of the Legion and talked too much with nomad barbarians and the riff-raff of bazaars. Come, she must try the snails—the more she ate, the easier it would be for Serenus to buckle his belt in the morning! And the little fish? They were hot and delicious. She laughed again. The shadow at the feast had gone. They all laughed, relieved. She must be kept from whatever had alarmed her.

Valens looked at her again, covertly, watching her sip the strong, white wine, laughing at Gallus and Clemens, a healthy, merry girl, her shyness and her fear departed. What had it been that startled them—him and Lilleth—when Gallus had crowned her with the diadem of silver moons and moonstone stars? She was so lovely—was that the reason for his fear? She had been the Queen of the Night for a moment—and Queens are jealous of each other.

Gallus was talking to him now, as the servants cleared away the first service and bore the wild turkeys to the carving table.

"Tell her, Valens, that it was Clemens who arranged the flowers!"

He told her and Clemens laughed, barking his embarrassment.

"But it was the General who chose your gown and the belt," said Valens.

"And the crown?" she asked. "Did you choose nothing, Antonius?"

"Antonius!" They all caught the word. So Valens was Antonius, was he? The gay spark. Serenus leered at him and turned to her, craning past Gallus and waving a partridge leg.

"Valens!" he said, "*Gul* Valens!"

She tried to say it: "Waleinis—Waaleinis——"

"Hence Antonius," said Gallus. "When you ride long in company, even with a shut box like Valens there, you need a name, if only to keep him away. You know what the soldiers call him?"

Yes, Gallus would know that—the badger, that was it, because he kept his counsel, deep in his own earth. Not a very clever or a very polite nickname. Did Valens know the word for "badger"? Valens did not but he would find out. Let a servant of the house be summoned. How could one explain a badger, if there was such an animal in Arabia? Valens would try—see, it ate frogs and worms and its hide was like armour to the knife. It was grey and black in colour, lived in a hole and waddled about by night.

"Ah!" cried the servant. "A *gufus!*"

"*Gufus?*" She clapped her hands with delight. Antonius was called *gufus* among them! There had been one nicknamed *gufus* in Ar Raudha—a foul old man, who never washed.

"But no!" she cried, suddenly serious. "I will not call you *gufus*—you eat snails, it is true, '*Audu billahi!* You are black and white, but you are no *gufus*."

Priscus, catching a murmured remark from Serenus, suddenly laughed and choked. He rose and staggered away into the darkness. Gallus' hand was on her arm. Let her have no fear, Priscus had only swallowed his

144

beard, a common trick with him. He would return. In the meantime let them all talk, to drown the volcanic noises from the shrubbery. Ah! Here he was, returning —that thing in the middle of his beard was his nose, soon he would grow hair on that and disappear altogether. Poor Priscus!

"Ask her, does she speak the Coptic tongue," said Serenus. "A little."

"Then Serenus does not!" snapped Clemens. "Do you, Serenus?"

"Oh no, not a word!" said Serenus. "But I learned once a little love song in that tongue——"

"Then you will keep it to yourself," growled Priscus. "A love song! With your paunch you could not get your arms round a maid!"

"That you shall not translate," said Gallus firmly. "You shall tell her that Serenus is an unseemly old man and that Priscus is nothing but beef and beard—tell her that, Valens, and let them bring the third service."

They brought in the honey-pickled fruits, the cakes and the sweets and the dark, red wine. The performers entered. She laughed with delight at the clowns and the tumblers and they, in the shadow of they knew not what fate of service and slavery under these new masters, saw the dancing light of enjoyment in her eyes and played as they had never played before, to her and her alone, for her joy and her beauty. The singers chanted their nasal songs and she listened, serious, disguising her dislike. But Priscus bristled.

"It is like a cat!" he said; and, startlingly, he burst into an imitation of a cat fight. His beard writhed, as he yowled and screeched. Even the astounded singers

145

laughed, and Lilleth wiped her eyes and held a hand to her side, laughing until it hurt her. Priscus had produced the best turn of the evening!

"Take him out and poison him!" said Gallus.

"Enough!" shouted Serenus. "Have you seen Priscus lay an egg? Then you have seen nothing! Priscus, lay an egg!"

Priscus was ready to oblige. He sat on the grass and clucked, a doubtful wonder in his eyes. He was going to lay an egg! But no; he was not so sure—he glanced behind him—nothing there! He clucked again, determined, his eyes glowing with inner triumph, his clucking changing from confidence to frenzied certainty. Then he suddenly spread out his arms and sank low to the ground—and there it was, a hard-boiled egg, stuffed with spices, while he squarked in ecstasy! Well done, Priscus!

"He can imitate bears mating, too," volunteered Serenus.

"Bring wine for the Princess," said Clemens, "she is in distress!"

All laughter has an end. They stood again and bowed to her, grinning broadly, thanking her with their eyes for her joy and her loveliness. Gallus went with her to the garden door and she turned and thanked him.

"Tell her, it is from us that thanks are due," he said. "We thank her for her kindness in making merry with us and for her beauty. She is one with us, now, the emissary of her King." He smiled. "One day we may crown her again—the Queen of Arabia the Happy!"

She climbed the stair and one of the sentries turned and opened the door of her chamber. She went to the window and looked out on the sleeping town. She was tired now. She turned from the window and crossed the room. A small table stood near her couch and on it a single oil lamp burned. She lifted the diadem from her head and put it on the table. She looked at it, her eyes widening, taking a step away from it. All night she had worn it, a crown of crescent moons, the symbol which, with her name, she should never wear.

CHAPTER 10

Kingdoms in the South

. . . utterly unfit for war. . . .

SOME one hundred and twenty miles south from Nejran, as an eagle might fly in straight, stooping flight, the morning sun shone on a valley of blue, sparkling water. The great dam of Marib, of vast stones, bound by bars of copper, stretching across the three-mile wide valley, was an unknown wonder of the world, one of the outstanding achievements of antiquity. Below the dam, the city stood on its orchard-covered hills, the capital city of the ancient Kingdom of Sheba and, to its south, glinted the golden Temple of the Sun.

Shamsi, Queen of Sheba, sat on her throne of gold and ivory, in the Hall of Audience. On her left stood her priests and counsellors, leaning on their silver spears, greybearded, ancient men of wisdom, masters of magic. On her right stood her Amirs, the Captains of thousands, golden-hilted swords gleaming through their thin camelhair cloaks, their head cloths bound with ropes of gold and silver. Between them, the floor of black marble stretched, from the Queen's golden sandals to the pillared entrance which the Queen faced.

She sat erect, one hand resting on the arm of the throne, the other holding her heavy ivory sceptre. She had

148

passed the bloom of her youth, but there was beauty in
the perfect oval of her face and in the soft curve of her lips.
There was no colour of blood under her pale brown cheeks.
A thin circle of gold crowned her greying black hair.
Above her head a blue panoply stirred gently in the breeze
from the entrance and above it, on the ceiling, glowed a
great golden sun.

She looked now down the line of her Amirs, her eyes
calm and expressionless. She knew them all. Some
were gallant and impetuous; some were arrogant and
boastful; many were cowardly and corrupt. And none
was wise. She looked at the priests and counsellors, so
grey and pompous on her left. Some were versed in
ancient magic—old Abd an Nejum, there, sold love
philters—but the priests had no philosophy and the counsellors no wisdom. Long ago Sheba had owned all the
land, from the sea in the south to the gulf in the north. In
those distant times, the young Queen Bilqis had gone to
treat with Solomon the Wise. This throne of gold and
ivory upon which she sat, had been the throne of Bilqis—
the djinns and spirits of the air had seized on it in the dark
of the moon, their grey talons stretching from the shadows,
their wings rustling like the wings of bats. They had
carried it through the air, high over the mountains, to
Solomon, who ruled them with his magic ring. But now
—Sheba was pressed down from the north by revolt, held
from the sea in the south by Qataban, while the rising
power of the Empire of Himyar loomed over her from the
mountains of the Yemen. The ancient circlet crowned
her head; the ancient sceptre was cold in her hand. She
was a tired, ageing woman and Sheba's sun sank behind
the world, after its thousand years of glory.

From the court outside a brazen trumpet sounded. The herald turned in the entrance. Four men suddenly appeared, swiftly mounting the steps between the pillars, their white head cloths bound with golden cords, their cloaks of camel hair gold embroidered. They strode into the room, the herald leading them, up the long black marble floor, until they stood before her, touching heart and head with jewelled fingers.

"The Emissaries of Il Shara, Priest-King of Qataban!" cried the herald.

"Who speaks for Il Shara?"

"I!" He took a short pace forward, a forceful, strongly built man, thick-bearded, small-eyed, arrogant. "Hear the words of Il Shara, *Mukerrib* of Qataban: Know you that Nejran has fallen to Rome and to Rome's captive state of Nabataea. None know now whither Rome directs her thrust. Let Sheba, therefore, join with Qataban in strong alliance. Let us stand side by side and hold, with our swords, our cities, our trade and the temples of our gods!"

The Queen sighed wearily.

"Know you," she asked, "that this Roman *Gom* is but a scant four thousand men?"

"Yet they are strong, Majesty, and of a strong race. We have heard that they broke down the wall of Nejran in a short morning!"

"If they are so strong, why do you not treat with them? If they should weaken you——" She smiled. If Qataban were weak, there might be peace on her southern border.

"This Roman *Gom* is dangerous, Majesty," persisted the Emissary. "It may well be that it will first attack you here."

She saw her Amirs fidgeting and heard the shuffle of

their feet. They were all against her. She wished to go herself to Nejran, for she had heard much of Rome. With her warriors and the Roman force, she might have struck south to the sea or west at the pride of grasping Himyar, those overweening people whose King called himself *Tobba*, the Compeller of Obedience! And no lasting friendship could ever be made between Sheba and Qataban—the border between them reeked with ancient blood. But all her Counsellors were against her. Let them take this offer of peace from Il Shara and, the Roman force defeated, let them turn, united, against Himyar. If her Counsellors had the true wisdom of their forebears, they would stretch out their hands to Rome and her son might live to rule all Arabia and Sheba's ancient glory would blaze again.

The Emissary turned slightly towards the line of the Amirs.

"Thus says Il Shara, the Priest-King," he cried: "Open your southern border! I have summoned my warrior tribes and the land shakes to their tread—open your borders to them, call your men to arms and let us meet where the deep river flows from your land! There let us fall upon the Romans and hang their heads here, in the Temple of the Sun! Then, among the bodies of our foes, we will make a treaty of peace between us for ever and Himyar will wither in the cold winds of the mountains!"

"And what of Ma'in?"

There was a murmur in the room. The Counsellors looked at each other and smiled. The question was timely. Long ago, two thousand years ago and longer, to the beginning of time, Ma'in had ruled Arabia, under their Grand Council of Kings. Now Ma'in lived oppressed by

Qataban, a remnant only, but untamed. If Qataban moved all their forces to the north, would Ma'in not rebel? But the Emissary was unmoved. He held up his hand, a gesture commanding attention and silence.

"Ma'in marches with us," he said; "even now they gather from all their hills and plains. The Beni Hilal, of ancient fame, are also among us. We are united as never before and thus united we stretch out our hands to Sheba and her sons in lasting peace and friendship."

All this, she thought, for a Roman *Gom*. The frontier guards could have dealt with it.

"Your Majesty!" cried one of the Amirs. "See how the land unites! Ma'in marches with Qataban and all the deep wadis ring with songs of war! See these men, how they gather their strength under the great Il Shara! And we—what do we do? Let us join with Qataban and sweep these Romans into the sands, as a broom sweeps date stones from a room!"

All this she had heard before. Her Amirs believed in the friendship of Qataban. She looked at the polished mirror of the black floor and her white sceptre drooped a little in her hand. This black floor, also, carried a tradition of her ancient race—when they told Solomon that Queen Bilqis had the body of a woman and goat's legs! He had built a black marble floor in the reception-room of his palace, flooding it with a handsbreadth of water, so that, as she came to meet him, she lifted the skirt of her gown and he, looking down from his throne, had seen the reflection of her graceful limbs. Since then, to commemorate their meeting, the floor of the Audience Chamber here at Marib had also been black.

The black floor, the crown, the sceptre—all remained.

But the greatness had gone. From Qataban and Himyar there was no help. There could be nothing but enmity from them and they would eat into her kingdom from either side, until all the glory was dust, the history became old tales of long ago and the people serfs. She looked up at the Emissary, the proud man, and at her restless Amirs.

"Let it be so," she said, wearily. "Let papers be prepared for our seal to all the Governors and Chiefs. Let the border be opened in welcome to Il Shara. The audience is ended."

They fell before her, the Amirs, kissing her knee and her hand and the hem of her gown, crying out in praise of her wisdom, and she smiled, a sad smile, for Rome might have been a friend and those of Qataban were all her foes.

She rose and walked down the long hall, bowing to right and left, the peacock fans a moving roof above her head. She paused on the steps, looking towards the Temple of the Sun. The breeze was cool within the sleeves of her gown. Suddenly she turned to her servants.

"Take away the fans," she said, "let me feel the warmth of the sun."

The Emissaries sped to the south on swift horses. They passed by night the frontier city between Sheba and Qataban, As Saqia, where one of the aquaducts from the dam of Marib ended in a deep cistern. From there they pressed on by camel, the tireless, swift *dhelul,* to the broad foothill country of the Wadi Harib; they rode hard to the city of Qohlan, in the Wadi Beihan and there they stayed, for the green banner of the Priest-King fluttered there, high above the citadel.

Il Shara was the very figure of a desert King. Tall and broad of shoulder, lean of flank and sinew, swift and graceful of movement, resonant of speech. His aquiline nose was strongly bridged, his nostrils delicately chiselled. Below his shaven upper lip, his mouth was thick-lipped and cruel, his chin-beard jutting, black and strong. Restless, fanatical, plagued with ambitious dreams, he was a dangerous man.

His large brown eyes lit with inner fires when the Emissaries told him of the success of their embassy at Sheba's court. The cruel line of his mouth hardened. He had fretted and his father and grandfather had fretted before him under the title of *Mukerrib*, Priest-King, or "he who brings closer" the people and the god. Long ago the Kings and Queens of Sheba had cast away this subservient title and had styled themselves *Mulk*, Absolute Monarchs. And now indeed, for the achievement of all his ambitions, the hour had struck. He might remain *Mukerrib* of Qataban, but he and his line would be, without doubt, *Mulk* of Sheba. Here, in his hand, was the paper. A truce and a lasting peace? He let the paper fall to the floor—for those before him shared his hatreds and his thoughts—and he spurned it with his hard, bare foot and laughed.

The border was open to him and his warriors. As Saqia, the frontier city of Sheba, which had changed hands so often in recent centuries, would change hands but once more. He would not even await the defeat of the Roman *gom*, before he seized it and enslaved its people. He would turn west into the hills, with all his armed thousands. For too long had Sheba lorded it above him on the road. Let Ithtar, the male Moon, come into his own and let

Shams, the lady sun, be truly and justly subservient to her husband in the heavens. And Shamsi, the Queen? He would not leave one of the royal line of Sheba to breed trouble and rebellion. There were but a score of persons of kingly blood—he would have them all and, when he had killed the son, then only would he end the shame of Shamsi, the mother. His hand fondled the hilt of his great scimitar.

His Amirs watched him, the triumph in his smile reflected in theirs. It was a moment over which to linger, to lick the lips. And one cried: "By Ithtar, the god, here Sheba dies!"

"Ay!" he said. "Ay! Here Sheba dies in very truth—let the drums beat!"

The drums beat from the citadel above Qohlan. From guard post to guard post up the mile-wide wadi of Beihan the hills echoed the beating of the drums. The echoes spread, far up the cragged gorges to the high plateau of Al Beidha, to the city of Yafa, down the great four thousand feet cliff of the Qor and on to Aden by the sea. They rumbled east, over the long eastern spur of the Qor hills. In town and village the heralds mounted and rode forth, calling on the tribes to arm and march, to assemble, sanctified for battle. And in the tall mountains of the Yemen, where Himyar ruled, they heard the dull throbbing of the drums by night, as it were the feet of an host of warriors, stamping and thudding as they danced round their camp-fires the dance of war.

All night, from the frontier city of As Saqia, they heard the drums and from the wall, far spread in the darkness, they saw the camp-fires of Qataban, flickering as the warriors tripped and stamped among them, in their wild dances.

155

Na'aman, the Governor of the city, sat alone in his belvedere, looking out on the night. He was of the royal house of Sheba, a cousin of the Queen. He looked out on the throbbing night, doubt and fear in his heart. He was a young man, beloved of Queen Shamsi for his gallantry, a loyal servant of his Queen. He mistrusted these sleek Amirs from Marib, soft-bodied from their city lives, soft-headed in their trust of Qataban. He frowned and struck the table by his side. A treaty of friendship with the Priest-King? He had been shocked when they brought him the order. To throw wide the southern border, so long contested, to Il Shara and his savage hosts! For centuries this border had rocked with feud and war, nor did a moon pass without killing. Now they opened the door wide—and for what? A tiny foreign *gom* of four thousand weary men! A *gom* the outlying tribes could crush, a *gom* he could ride down and scatter with the frontier horsemen. He feared Il Shara. A violent and treacherous man, a fanatic, a professed enemy of Sheba—who could trust such an ally? And with him he brought the warriors of ancient embittered Ma'in in their thousands. Why should Ma'in leave their last lands of Yeshbum and Khora, if not to slit Sheban throats, Sheba who had usurped the power and the wealth of Ma'in a thousand years ago? For each year of that thousand years, a thousand years of hatred burned in Ma'ini hearts.

His thoughts turned to his young wife, Leila, and their baby son, who slept in an upper room below him, guards at their door. Leila, so beautiful and so gentle, herself of the royal line. When Il Shara's thousands poured into the city to-morrow, they would hold Leila and her baby in the compass of their cruel hands. These hundreds of fires spread across the plain, were but the first small sparks of Il Shara's fiery host. He did not sleep that night.

All day the wild men of the south moved into the city. Il Shara entered before noon, riding in the company of his Amirs, his eyes alert, a sneer on his face. Half-naked, blue-painted savages, their broad daggers brandished, tripped and stamped in a wild dance before him through the streets, the dust rising thick about them. He did not halt and he sent no message of greeting to the Governor of the city; he was eager, so his men said, to reach the river and prepare his camp. His warriors, with their spears and double-headed axes, filled the streets, a sullen light in their eyes.

That night, wherever they looked from the city walls, they saw fires, and all around, from field and palm garden, from hill and desert, rose a throbbing, stuttering murmur from the drums of Qataban.

Na'aman slept lightly, fully clothed, his sword by his side. At midnight he awoke, a sudden awakening, a clear brightness of the mind. The drumming had ceased and, from somewhere in the dark city, came a cry, a scream of fear cut short.

He sprang from his couch and called loudly for his guards down the dark stairway. His voice echoed, as in an empty house. He was familiar with the stairs and he did not need to touch the wall as he descended. His naked feet were soundless on the stone. He reached the stair foot and stumbled, nearly falling, knowing the thing he had met with in the dark—a man's body, sprawled across the way. Then a light flared on the far wall of the corridor and three men appeared, one with a torch held high and two with drawn swords. They paused a half step, surprised on seeing

157

him. Then they came towards him again, but slowly, mincingly, the torch-bearer behind them, their curved hack-swords raised, ready for the cut.

No word was spoken. He stepped over the fallen man, drawing his knife with his left hand, his sword in his right. He ran towards them on light, strong feet. They hesitated —and, in that moment of hesitation, he sprang. The corridor was narrow and the cutting sword, with its heavy blade and its single edge, does not lend itself to the parry and riposte of scientific sword-play. He flung his sword, hilt foremost, in the face of one assailant and closed with him, swinging him away from the wall, feeling with his right hand for an opening through the frame of the ribs, thrusting with his dagger deep, deep and then, with a quick twist and thrust, he hurled the twitching corpse at its comrade, thrusting past the body with a long, upwards stroke. The torch-bearer turned to flee—but Na'aman desired, above all things at that moment, the torch. His spring was swift and his dagger-thrust a part of it. He held the torch in his right hand, its light flaring on the three men he had killed and, dimly, on the still body of his murdered servant, at the stair's foot.

In a moment he was at the door of Leila's room and there he paused, listening, struggling with fear. Only through her could they hurt him, or through the child. Then, drawing a breath, he threw open the door—and cried out with joy! Leila lay there sleeping, the child beside her. She woke as he had woken, when the drums were silent, clear-eyed, mistress of herself. She understood, in a moment, what must be done—the escape into the courtyard by a rope of mat and linen, hastily contrived. The un-haltering and saddling of a donkey. The faithful servants, in the women's quarters, bringing out their oldest and most tattered clothes. And the baby quiet, contented to be borne out of the courtyard door in its mother's lap, after that last whispered word and kiss.

Then the action for which he had longed! The tumultuous city which must be regained, the clash of arms, the hiss of the sped arrow, the whip-crack of the sling. Uproar ruled the city, in every quarter. Morning broke on the flames of burning houses turned to choking, all-pervading smoke. Qataban paid for its treachery, gaining only a smouldering ruin, from which the poor fled towards the hills and to which none would turn again. And, in the narrow streets, corpses lay sprawled, blocking every alley, every stair, while to and fro the uneven battle raged as dawn broke and daylight came.

No one looked at her, in her tattered rags of poverty. She rode, sitting sideways in the donkey, the child contented in her lap. She passed the encampments of Il Shara's warriors, but none gave her more than a glance, a poor townswoman, carrying her child to safety in some hovel in the hills. She looked back towards the city, its houses flaming, the smoke rising from its fiery torture in the early morning light. She remembered his face, its gentleness, as he placed their baby in her arms and bid her go to Marib, to the Queen; she remembered his voice and his words—"Farewell my love!" She was not to hear it again. For all his strength and daring, he could not prevail. By mid-morning, he and his men were dead and Il Shara held the empty, smoking city. And, obeying Na'aman's last order, as the remnant fled towards Sheba, they broke the walls of the water cisterns and smashed the aqueduct which fed them and which gave the city its name, and left behind them a burnt, useless thing, a place where only ghosts could live.

*　　*　　*

Far away, among the tall mountains, they brought the news, which the war drums had foretold, to the *Tobba* of Himyar. The Tobba was the mountain King. From his great Keep of Reidan, near the town of Zafar, he ruled all the highlands of the Yemen and his dominion stretched across the sea to Axum, in the land of the blacks. From his high mountain throne, he looked down on the warring kingdoms, Sheba, Qataban and, far away, the new Kingdom of Hadhramaut. He would have them, each and all. When that time came, he would stretch out to the southern ports and all the golden road would be his.

The great *Tobba*, the "Compeller of Obedience", King of Axum, Himyar and Master of Reidan, held court in a long room. All down the room, on either side, the light flooded in through rose-shaped windows, set high in the walls, of purest alabaster. He sat at the end of the room, facing the door, leaning back against black cushions. From the left side of his immense white turban hung a broad strip of tasselled, crimson silk, the *Imama*, the emblem of his kingship. His hawk-like face was sallow brown. The centre of his upper lip was shaven and, from its sides, hung long, black moustaches, joining his long pointed beard. His large eyes were almond-shaped, faintly aslant above his high cheek-bones and they glowed dully, for he had chewed the leaves of *qat*, a sleep-destroying narcotic, for many hours. Over a high-laced black smock he wore a full-sleeved, dark-red gown, belted with a broad belt of gold.

Beside him, his back in a corner of the room, sat his secretary, cross-legged, a sheet of papyrus rested in the palm

160

of his left hand, his wooden pen poised in his right and, before him, a golden bowl, half-full of bright red sand.

Down either side of the room sat his counsellors, old and young, their white turbans shining with the pale glow from the windows, shadowing their dark faces. They waited now to hear him speak, while he considered what he should say, his ringed hand caressing the tip of his beard.

"Now," he said, "I shall tell you how all these things shall be. First, there will be war, bitter and unceasing, between Sheba and Qataban. You, Amir Salih, will prepare a host at San'a and all the Governors and chiefs shall send men to join you according to their means and power. When Qataban press Sheba back into her stronghold, I myself will lead you into Marib and I shall be King of Sheba. And that time is near at hand. For too long have I and my fathers looked down from the mountain-tops on that golden river which flows northwards from the sea."

There was a murmur of approval from the seated men. He spoke again, his hands outspread, weighing, in each, a rival kingdom.

"Il Shara is rich and strong when he goes thus to war, his tribes united. But for how long can he sustain his thousands? For how long can he keep them from their feuds? And it may well be that from the Roman *gom* he will suffer loss. They are small in number, but they have some skill in war, as we have seen. Then there are the cities and the mountains of Sheba, they must be conquered and held and at Saqia he unsheathed the sword too soon. Sheba is old and dying. I shall wait until Il Shara's hand reaches out to take her crown and then I shall bend down from the mountains and thus"—and he made a little sideways chopping gesture with his stiff right hand—"thus I will take off that proud woman's head with the golden circlet on her brow!"

One of the younger men laughed and turned to the King, an eager, unbearded face.

"It is your hour, Majesty!" he cried.

"Yes," said the Tobba. "It is my hour."

He turned to his secretary.

"Now write thus," he ordered. "To his High Name the Governor of the city of Sa'ada, greetings: take of the Amirs and chiefs of your Province one hundred and of gold and provender a great store and ride to Nejran to seek audience with the Amir of the Roman *gom*. Greet him in my name, and, through him, the *Tobba* of Rome. Offer him all he desires in the furtherance of his enterprise against Qataban. Discover his designs. Should his thrust be directed towards us in the high Yemen, accompany him in all friendship to Sa'ada, and there accomplish his destruction. Should he desire Sheba, council him first to strike at Qataban, who is the stronger. For that enterprise offer him guides, as far as the river and no farther. When he does battle with Il Shara, send word at once of his fortunes to San'a, where I shall be. I wait to move down on Sheba, to its conquest. When the Roman *gom* is dead, seize Nejran in my name."

He turned again to the seated men.

"How like you that, my uncle?" he asked.

An old man nodded his head.

"It is well," he answered, in a high, quavering voice, "but there will be much expenditure of treasure in entertainment and assistance to these Romans. There will be presents and provender—and all to men who will see but a few suns more. Now there is an old merchant who has

162

sought refuge in Sa'ada, one 'Abd al Ya'uk, of Nejran. Before the Romans took the city, he sent all his treasures, of vast value, to Sa'ada. Four hundred camels carried his jewels alone, rubies and *mas*, the hard, glittering stones of the east. One must consider the matter of this old merchant 'Abd al Ya'uk."

"Then," said the *Tobba*, turning to his secretary, "you shall add this to the letter: You shall take the old Nejrani merchant 'Abd al Ya'uk and he will make a full accounting of all his possessions to you and of their disposition. Those which he has in other places, he will send for, until you hold all that he has. Then you shall strike off his head and send it, with all his treasures, to me at the Keep of Reidan. For he is very rich and has lived too long."

"That is one of the most satisfactory letters," quavered the old uncle, "that I have ever had the fortune to hear!"

CHAPTER II

Awake in the Dawning

. . . a fertile country, peaceably disposed.

THE poor do not make war. When armies meet in a city and the dust of battle rises in the streets, the poor flee away; or they hide deep in cellars or behind barred doors from the fury of the warriors. Then, when all is still again, when the fires smoulder and the blood has dried, the poor return to the streets, fearful, yet hopeful and wondering. Merchants do not make war. They hide their possessions and fly from the slaughter; but, once they are beyond the echoing walls, they stop and look back towards the city and in a little while they too return, even if all their treasures have been lost. For, to those who have only life to lose, to-morrow always brings hope.

Nejran lived again, under its new masters. Each street returned to the trade of its name. Near the north gate, the long street of the copper smiths rang all day with the music of little hammers. In the dark shadows of the booths hung copper trays and vessels, shining with a deep, red fire. One turned sharply from this street to the wide shops of the leather workers, an airy, dusty thoroughfare, broad enough for four horsemen to ride abreast. Here they hammered and stretched the tough hides. Here one could purchase saddle pads, water skins, sandals, bags fringed with cowrie shells, sheep-skin coats and soft cloaks of delicate lamb skins, justly matched.

As one continued between the booths, the street turned and changed its name. It became the street of the cook shops, odorous with the steam of hot spices. Here was sustenance to suit the purse of poor or rich. Hard cakes of coarsely ground millet flour, each a bellyful, or, by order, a sheep roasted whole, stuffed with succulent fowl and the rarest spices of the eastern seas, basket-covered from the flies and the gaze of poverty, to be borne swiftly, in hot perfection, to your own house. This street opened into the great caravanserai, the central city square. Here, under thatched shelters the men of the road ate and talked and slept. You might meet with strange people—a Greek sculptor on his way to the Court of Himyar, a tall brown man of Hind beyond the sea, a blue-painted savage from the south, with his lithe step and his contemptuous eyes. By day and by night the caravanserai was ever astir, save in that last hour before the dawn, when all things must sleep. Here stood mules from Abyssinia, flicking their long ears at the flies, and the little country donkeys, patient and enduring, their pack saddles before them, and horses, drooping their lovely heads, their beauty lost in immobility. Here knelt long lines of camels, the white camels of Nejran, the red camels of the desert and the great, black camels of the high mountains, chewing the cud, grumbling and complaining. And this central square filled to overflowing every seventh day with country folk, their goods and stock, from all the long valley and the hills beyond, who came to barter and to gossip.

The narrow streets spread out from the central square like the threads of a spider's web. In this one, in dark, smoking caves beneath the houses, smiths struck at red-hot metal, bellows groaned and sighed, sparks flew and charcoal flamed, white and roaring, casting vulcanic shadows on the walls. In another, under tall houses, shone the many lamps of the jewellers. Here, ready for the discerning purchaser, were treasures of eastern art, the rich, hot jewels of India, the cool carved jade of China. A man might linger in the street of the jewellers for many hours, entranced by the beauty of ring and necklace and precious ornament, going deep into these street-side caves of Aladdin, where they smoothed the moonstones and cornelians of the mountains, set the purer gems of distant countries, turned gold and silver wire into miracles of filigree.

Here, in a winding alley, dwelt the fruit sellers and the merchants of spices, an alley of small shops, haunted by strange, sharp odours. Then the street of the basket-makers, a broad, short thoroughfare, whose wares were spread before the feet of passers-by, from strong, heavy panniers to delicate trays for ornament, intricately woven in yellow, red and blue. One stepped over and past these lovely things into the street of the confectioners, murmur-ous with its hordes of flies, colourful and scented with its long trays of sweets—round sweets, heart-shaped sweets, red and green and sugar-white, rich with protruding dates and raisins—and here, at the end of the street, is Tahir's shop, the envy of his rivals. There is always a crowd before Tahir's shop, yet he makes but one sweet now—a sugary, red confection, with a subtle flower scent. He calls it, quite simply, *Haluat al Mulk*, The Sweet of Kings!

Then there is the street of the potters with their mur-muring wheels and of the vendors of honey—the amber-brown honey of the coasts, the clear, dark honey of Jardan (beloved by Pliny the elder), and gourds of thick, white honey from the Yemen. And beyond, street after street with a jumble of merchandise, golden stools and vessels from Sheba, boxes of scented woods, carved tusks from Axum, ivory trees from China, cloths, silks, earthenware lamps, cowrie shells, ostrich feathers, whips of rhinocerous hide and the flaring skins of leopards. A city of merchants, a city of treasures by day, when light and shade struck their sharp contrasts on the walls and corners of the streets. By night a city of darkness and peace, a lighted lattice here and there and a voice, perhaps, muffled and distant, singing, in soft cadencies, of love.

"Which is the sweetest, Antonius, a love song at night or the song of the man who draws water, early in the morning?"

"A love song at night."

"No; for my heart, the morning song! When morning comes, water rises from the wells, the dove murmurs to his mate, the beasts are tended, the fields are tilled; the hunter takes his bow, the traveller sets forth, ships sail and captains scan the sea and the eagle soars to greet the sun!"

"And trumpets sound and the soldier must mount and ride."

Yes, they must mount and ride—but whither? To their south, the stone cities of the Yemen stood high above the mists of morning. Must the Legion make vast engines to batter at their granite walls? Must they climb those dizzy cliffs and force the iron-bound gates of those fantastic strongholds, perched above the clouds? Or must they follow the desert way south towards the sea, braving again the sun and the burning sands?

The two plans lay before Gallus and he sat alone, in his private chamber, hearing—but unconscious of the sound —the slow, distant cadencies of a song. There was no rest for him here, in this city of treasures. He must choose, he must make the throw—south into the Yemen mountains, or east of south, through Qataban to the sea.

To capture and destroy Sa'ada; to strike at Marib and to hold Sheba in his grip; thence, through the mountains to San'a and Zafar, to destroy the growing Empire of Himyar—this was the first plan. To assault and break down city after city—it could be done in a year. Valens, for all its difficulty, favoured this plan. It was, indeed, a Roman plan, a sure and progressive advance from strong-hold to stronghold, always with one foot secure, a slow concentration of force at the heart of an enemy state. It was the long plan, the sure plan, well-ordered progress through fertile country, opening the Tobba's dungeons, making allies of his disaffected tribes. And—this was the crux of the plan—from Marib they would hold the centre of the incense road, the great trade route, and could turn its course across the high plateau of the northern Yemen, to a port on the Red Sea. Cut off, thus, from the fountain of their riches, the merchants of the Hejaz would come to terms.

And the other plan? Ah! It drew his heart and his mind, this plan of daring and genius! It was the swift lunge, the thrust to the sea. He had lost men by desert marching and by sickness, that was true. But he had succeeded, marvellously, in capturing Nejran, a rich oasis, impregnable now, a fit capital for the new Province of Arabia. Why tire themselves besieging mountain cities? The whole strength of the country lay in this one road, running far south to Dhufar, where the incense grew, and to the ports on the southern sea. Once he held the ports and the road, he held all Arabia. No—the bold stroke, that was the one he would make, to the south through foothill country, mountains to his west, desert to his east and the road straight before him—the caravan road—to the southern sea. Here it was, plain to see among the later pages—"to strike at Qataban through As Saqia, Athrula, Qohlan, Nisab—what names! to Azzan and the gates of the sea."

He rose and strode to the open window, his strong hands on his hips, his shoulders squared, his step as buoyant as his heart. Yes—daring, simple, the plan for a small force, the swift masterstroke! He looked down on the city, its orchards astir in the light dawn breeze. He heard a ring-dove murmur to its mate. He heard the creaking of a well-wheel, water splashing in a garden and the sound of a man singing, as he drew water, early in the morning. And a trumpet sounded, high and loud, calling, "Awake! Awake, soldiers! Awake in the dawning, for you must mount and ride!"

They waited that afternoon to hear their leader's orders, in the long reception-room of the palace. Gallus had summoned the senior staff officers, Clemens, Serenus and their lieutenants, Valens and the *Primi Ordines*, Centurions of the First and Centurions commanding the other Cohorts of the Legion. They stood before him, round the long room, divided into groups. He sat at the head of the room, his writers beside him, his papers arranged before him.

They regarded him, their faces expressionless, their minds alert. There was no question of his power. He was Caesar's lieutenant, the *Praefectus Legionis*; but, to them, he was more—the inspired leader, loved and respected, in whose strong hands they laid their lives and honour, grateful to him for his acceptance of their trust. Gallus knew these men; he was one of them. They were of the rank most famed in war, most trusted by the great commanders. Fearless, hard-headed, in the prime of their powers, they were in no way military automatons. Their minds were trained to grasp unmapped distances, to weigh political forces. They could order and control now a hundred, now many thousand men. They could command armies of savage tribes, administer civilized cities. The hard backbone of the Legion, they were also the backbone of the growing Empire of Rome.

"We go from here to the southern sea," said Gallus.

No one moved. No one answered him. Only their eyes showed a sudden softening of relief. So—he had made his choice of the two alternatives, well known to them all. It had been his to make, but its burden had lain on them all, in some degree, while they wondered which course he would favour. Now that he had chosen, it remained only to prove his wisdom by their actions.

He turned to Valens, his pale blue eyes kindly and a slight smile on his lips. Once again he had chosen against Valens' advice, but they knew each other better now and there would be no more arguments—no need to tell Valens to stop thinking and go to bed!

"Give us some information, as briefly as you can," he said.

Valens was ready but, although his face remained unmoved as he bent over the table before him, his heart was sick. One cannot always throw dice with the gods and win, he thought. Now, once again, we take a pace with the left foot—absurd superstition—but the slow and certain course lay the other way and this which had been chosen seemed once more a tilting of the world, to cast them into the deserts of peril and uncertainty. He turned to the assembled men.

"From here we march for seven days, until we come to a river——"

"A river!" Here was something new in Arabia!

"It is a perennial stream, no more, flowing from the basin of the lands called Jauf al Yemen. We must carry three days water supply in skins. Tribes are assembling at the river, under a leader Il Shara, a Priest-King of the moon-worshippers. He will oppose our march. It is reported that he has already some twenty thousand men under him, a force which daily increases. Beyond the river, to the west, lies the country of the Sabaeans. Our route leads to the south, through desert country, to the city of Ithtar the god."

"Will that be defended?" asked Clemens.

"Not in any strength. Once Il Shara is defeated, the south is open to us. He is the King of Qataban, the southern kingdom, and is at war with the Sabaeans."

"Proceed—proceed——" said Gallus.

"The city of Ithtar the god is rich in stores of grain and fodder. From there it is a day's hard marching to the city of Qohlan, where there are also granaries. Thence two days over high dunes and dead lava flow to Mariba, a hill city. From there, one may reach the first incense groves in two days and it is three days' march to the sea."

"There will be no need to adopt peculiar ways of marching," said Gallus. "We shall march in column, in the usual manner, in four days' time. I will leave a small garrison of sick men here, under you, Lucius, to order the city and the valley. You will supervise the native administrators, who seem peaceable and intelligent men. All questions about the march should be put directly to the staffs concerned. That is all."

They turned to leave the room, but Gallus detained Valens with a hand on his shoulder.

"I am guilty!" he exclaimed, when the others had departed. "For the second time I have offended and discarded your advice. It is the swift conclusion of our affairs which tempts me and I have made up my mind. But now tell me, what is the nature of this country, between the river where they will give us battle and the sea?"

Valens had interrogated many merchants and caravaneers in the city and he could visualize the country, through which passed the great trade route, they had described. He pointed with an outstretched arm through the wide window to the mountains in the south, now turning fiery red as the sun sank.

"Those mountains," he said, "stretch from here south to the sea and drain to our left, the east, into the great central desert of Arabia. Our route lies across the mouths of the wadis, where they run from the hills into the sands. The trade route, except when the wadis flood for a few hours after rain, is dry. For their caravans, the people have built water cisterns, in which they trap the flood water. There are wells, also, both within and without the cities. Thus caravans of three thousand camels may pass comfortably through the wilderness. But——"

He paused. He had no wish to appear to argue with Gallus, Gallus nodded his head.

"But they may destroy the cisterns," he said; "that was in your mind? And it is true. Cisterns may be destroyed and wells filled in. How much can we depend on flood waters after rain?"

"They come by chance, Praefectus."

"I see."

Gallus was silent, deep in thought. They come by chance—even so he had come here, by good fortune only. But all life was chance, chance to be born, chance to die. One made a decision, one chose a road and thereafter one must contend with chance. He had made his decision— the bold stroke—he had made up his mind. For the sake of swift victory, they must take this risk of broken cisterns, blocked wells and dry wadi beds.

"Now these tribes which oppose us," he asked, "from whence do they come?"

"From the Yam. . . ."

(The men of the Beni Yam had come in from the edge of the great desert. They were rich in stock of she camels. Big-bodied, heavy of beard, armed with bows and slings, they rode eastwards, five thousand strong through the night. . . .)

"The Balharith. . . ."

(Camel-men, with long spears and wicker shields, their hair cloth-bound, they sang as they rode north over the plain, songs with a rhythm matching the camels' pace— "Oh, we graze the she camel on the sweet spring grasses and in winter she carries us two and two to war." . . .)

". . . and the Musabein. . . ."

(They came on foot and on camels with their allies of the 'Abid, armed with axe and spear, dressed in long-skirted cloaks, their hair bound brigand-wise, their beards

173

combed and oiled, from their rallying point of Jebel Reidan, and their foes of the Beni Hilal followed after them. . . .)

". . . and the Kings of Ma'in and the Awalek. . . ."

(Hair oiled and cut to shoulder height, lithe bodies shining and blue with indigo and oil, long curved daggers and ragged beards, spears and slings—a bitter-hearted, ancient race—they ran northward swift-footed from the mountain of the Nisiyin. "Oh, you great pointed mountain," they chanted, "veiled in lightning and my eyes beholding you! . . ." Drums beating, voices chanting, swift feet running in the night, in the deep darkness of the gorges, over dizzy mountain tracks above the thunder clouds, across the waterless plains—a great host of warriors moving through the land, to join Il Shara at his river camp, where the camp-fires, in their thousands, lit the world!)

Gallus was silent for a long while. Then he turned with a gesture of dismissal.

"We shall see," he said, "we shall see. We must join battle in the early morning—to slay twenty thousand men may take all day. . . ."

But after Valens had gone, after a light supper, Gallus still pondered on the choice he had made. Yes, twenty thousand men could be slain easily enough, if there was time and the place was suitable. But if the rains fell unchancily, if the wells were blocked, if the cisterns were broken—he shivered in the cool night breeze.

He looked up at the tall houses. From one near at hand came a murmur of voices, then a staccato sentence, then a murmur again and the closing of a door. That was Clemens working late into the night, a patient, thorough commander, who left nothing to chance. Fat Serenus would be sleeping, after a heavy supper. For all his jocular vulgarity, and the attentions he lavished on his stomach, Serenus' staff was brilliantly organized and its work well done.

Farther away, a light glowed through a closed lattice in a small house, above the street of jewellers. In that street he had found a crown for a lady. He smiled, remembering her merry laughter and forgetting the fear in her eyes when he had placed the crown on her dark hair. It was right that she should live above the street of the jewellers. But it was not right that her lamp should burn at this late hour; she should be sleeping.

Gallus opened the garden door and walked out into the street, the guards at the door following him. Their feet made no sound in the dust and the city was dark and silent. He came out of the narrow, winding street into the small square behind the south bastion. The sentry by the stairway drew back as he passed. He mounted the winding steps to the guard-room door. From here he could see the sentry on the flat roof above him, his helmet glinting in the starlight, a motionless, watchful figure. Within the guard-room a horn lantern cast a yellow light. A trumpeter stood ready to leave the door, his curved horn on his shoulder. A sentry seated by a table stretched out his hand to the guard-room water clock and turned it. 'Second watch," he said, as the trumpeter mounted the stair to the roof. The call echoed through the sleeping city.

Gallus descended, walking once again through the narrow chasms of the streets, pausing to look up at the sky, entering a garden, climbing stairs where sentries stepped from his way without challenge, standing for long minutes looking at rows of sleeping soldiers, covered in their scarlet woollen cloaks, their heads pillowed on kit-bundles, their armour and their arms beside them. He came out into the centre square; even the men of the road slept now, their fires extinguished, in the deep sleep which comes before the dawn. He climbed the stairs of the gateway bastions. In each guard-room was the same picture—the yellow horn lantern, the watchful sentry, the sleeping men and the water clock, which ruled the night. He mounted again the stairs of the south bastion. The trumpeter was ready, the long straight *tuba* in his hand. The inner guard leant forward to the table and turned the water clock. "Awake!" he said. And from the roof the high call echoed through the city, rousing them up, scattering their dreams—"Awake! Awake, soldiers! Awake in the dawning, for you must mount and ride!"

CHAPTER 12

The Vultures Gather

. . . in six days march he came to a river. There the barbarians were assembled for battle. . . .

THEY marched to the southward in column, through empty, hilly country, treeless and barren. Herds of *reem*, the tall, white gazelle of the desert, scattered to the east from their path. The ibex, the wild goat of the rocks, looked down on them, curved horns laid back, blunt muzzles questing the air. Among caves and fissures in the rocky hills, the mountain leopard crouched, shoulders hunched, lips twitching to a snarl, as here and there in their long column a weapon or a shield boss flashed in the sunlight. From craggy eminencies, belly down on warm rock, the red lynx stared down on them, with his expressionless eyes of moonstone blue. Above them, invisible in the depths of blue sky, sailing on spread pinions, the vultures marked them, seeing them dwarfed in the vast expanse of hill and desert, a thin sand cloud, the dust of their marching, streaming from them to the dead lands in the east.

They had assembled at dawn before the east gate of the city, for the ancient ceremony of choice, Gallus and the Herald ranged beside the Eagle and its guards, confronting them. Three times the Herald had cried, "Will you march to war?" And three times they had answered with a joyful shout, their right arms raised in salute. Then, vaulting to the saddle, the mounted men had ridden away down the long valley, splashing through the waters of the gorge, turning to the south.

They marched at a good pace, the mounted pioneers and the native guides, sharp eyes alert, horses swift and sure-footed in the rocky terrain, leading them, followed by a lightly-armed Cohort of infantry. These spied out the easiest route and could hold any savage enemy they might encounter among the tumbled hills. Far behind this light screen rode Publius Sabinus with the mounted wing at its full strength of six score men. Then came Gallus, with his escort and the senior commanders, the eagle and its fierce guards, the forest of sparkling standards, the trumpeters with curved *cornu* and coach-horn *tuba* and then the eight Cohorts of infantry, their kit bundles slung on sticks, their slim javelins sparkling behind heavy, half-cylinder shields. Behind these plodded the long baggage train of camels and, far to the rear, a single Cohort marched, unburdened, ready for war. And in the uncharted waste through which they journeyed, no human eye saw the pageant of their marching.

They halted at midday, finding what shelter they could under stunted thorns or in the shadows of rocks. They marched again and camped within a wall of palisades at sunset, with thirty thousand paces between them and Nejran.

They broke camp before dawn, marching without rest all that day, through barren country. Throughout the afternoon the hills to their west were overcast with dust and mist, a thickening in the air, behind which thunder

178

rolled and, that evening, fortune favoured them. The dry watercourses flooded into violent spate, cutting their long column into three and trumpets sounded 'halt', while they struggled among the rolling boulders of the torrents, refilling shrunken water skins and watering their beasts. Then they marched on by night, when the violence of the flood was spent, under a heavy sky and a light rain, which cleared at the rising of the morning star.

They rested that morning in a wide valley of thorn and acacia, adjusting the loads, drying their kit in the sun, tending the sick, who were few. At evening they marched once more and, as night fell, the full moon rose, shining down upon them, turning the red desert into a silver sea, lighting their way until the morning. In the first sunlight, guides led them among rocky, wind-worn hills to a chain of rain pools, blue and clear, where scarlet dragon flies flashed in the sun.

This day they shortened the hours of their marching. They had travelled wide to the eastward of the caravan road, which led south, through mountains, to Marib, the capital of Sheba. Moving thus through barren country they might have escaped observation for a day more, but they had not done so. The mounted men scouting ahead of them reported fresh camel tracks across their front, riding camels making a fast pace to the south and Valens had seen, far to the east of their route, three horsemen, their silver-bound spears glinting, riding hard up a long valley into the hills. They marched that afternoon, the long column of infantry and baggage train contracted to the four columns of the *agmen quadratum* formation, the baggage interspersed between the Cohorts; and they camped early in the evening on high ground, behind palisades and a rough breastwork of stones. When night fell, far away on a rocky bluff, they saw a pin-point of red fire.

Gallus sent for Valens and the commanders of the surveyors and pioneers.

"You will press on to-morrow," he ordered them, "and locate the enemy force. You should be near the river by midday. Site a war camp and prepare it for the baggage and the heavy engines. Send me word as soon as you have located enemy in any considerable numbers. You, Valens, endeavour to locate Il Shara's main camp and be prepared to lead me to some place from which I can examine his dispositions. When I hear that the main force is found, I will ride forward and join you with the *Primi Ordines* and the mounted wing. If you find enemy in any force advancing to meet us, send word at once."

A joyful spirit pervaded camp that night. Publius Sabinus had pitched the leather water troughs by the north wall and towards these Valens led his horse, through the roughly-marked camp roads. He led it past the baggage centre, hoping for a glimpse of Lilleth, whose place on the march was with Serenus; but in the ordered confusion among piles of grain sacks and *impedimenta*, where Serenus filled the air with his oaths and obscenities, he could not see her. He walked on, past the camp of the First Cohort, whose Armourer held court before the tents, splashing water sparingly on a revolving grindstone, his hairy chest bare in the firelight.

"Come on!" roared the Armourer. "Forward, soldiers of the First! A bright, sharp shaft of iron for the moon-priest's ugly guts!"

The long troughs shone wetly in the moonlight. Most

of the Legion's horses had already watered, but he recognized the grey mare he had chosen for Lilleth in a waiting group and then he saw her standing a little apart, where a chain of men passed full skins from the shadow of the wall to the watering point.

Valens had not seen her since the march from Nejran began. Now he would not see her again, until a battle had been lost and won. Once again he felt foreboding, a sinking of the heart. This love which they shared was an ephemeral thing, born of a dream, lived in emptiness, foredoomed to tragedy. She saw him then and came to him, a leather water trough, half filled and gurgling, between them. But she was in no mood for a lover's farewell.

"Antonius! I learnt a song to-day from my uncle!"

"Your uncle! Has that pig Serenus——!"

"My uncle Serenus is not a pig—and hold your horse in until the Amir here gives the order."

"What song did Serenus teach you?"

She laughed.

"One day I will sing it to you. And Uncle Serenus has promised that I shall see the battle, from a seat high above it, as if I were the King of Rome, watching a fight in an arena!"

Valens threw his reins to one of the waiting men.

"I will find Serenus!" he cried. "I will speak to the Praefectus! A fight in the arena, did he say, the fat sow? And what song is this he has taught you?"

She laughed merrily, teasing him, leaning towards him across the trough.

"It is a very sweet song, Antonius. It is about a little pig which couldn't see its tail——"

"That one!"

Valens strode away towards the centre of the camp. But Serenus skipped nimbly behind a pile of sacks, a broad grin on his face.

"Has she sung it to you?" he asked. "No? She sings it beautifully—but when you have had your battle we will both sing it to you, she down one ear softly and I down the other very loudly. I will teach her the one about the mule which wanted twins——"

Valens laughed. But he stretched his hand across the sacks and took Serenus' hand in his, his eyes suddenly earnest and pleading.

"Have a care for her," he said; "you will guard her, Serenus?"

"With my life." And Serenus' eyes were hard and unsmiling.

*　　*　　*

Moonlight and dawnlight cast their faint, opposing shadows as Valens and the horsemen clattered out of camp, their javelins across their knees, their shields slung on their left shoulders. The native guides were cautious now but, over the hard gravel between the hills and round the rocky spurs which stretched across their way from the west, they made good progress. At about mid-morning a scout far to the right signalled to them and they halted. But it was not an enemy which he had found; it was a friend. There, on the crest, surrounded by a stone-and-plaster wall, were the ruins of houses, a small settlement, deserted, perhaps because of war or plague, long ago. Below the houses lay an oblong sheet of water, dammed at its lower end, deep and clear, the village water cistern. And Valens, lifting his eyes from the water, saw, far away, a long cloud of smoke rising in the air from behind a rocky spur. The man beside him had seen it too. He heard him draw his breath sharply between his teeth. Valens turned to him.

"To the Praefectus!" he said, "ride like the wind!" And pebbles flew and rattled as the horse sprang down the slope.

The ground round the ruined settlement was irregular in shape and contour, but it was suitable for a defensive camp. The surveyors dismounted and ran out with their coloured flags and measuring ropes and the pioneers unslung their short crowbars and shafted their picks. Valens, sitting loosely in his saddle, had let his horse drink and then rode down the slope and across the plain. He reached the foot of the long spur of rock unmolested and halted, examining the bare slope before him. Here were two strange things: smoke, by day, in such volume and no enemy on this spur to watch for their approach. Along the face of rock, nothing moved but the little lizards, scuttling in the shadows or basking, with twitching tails, in the sun. He rode on, up the steep rock, and nearing the crest dismounted, haltering his horse to a small, deeply-rooted bush of thorn. He made his way to a boulder, a block of stone balanced on the ridge of the spur and, moving cautiously forward in its shadow, he looked down on the plain beyond. There below him, about a thousand paces from the foot of the spur on which he stood, the river, a greenish-yellow flood, ran between its rocky banks. On the far bank, spread wide and stretching back across the plain, smoke rose and blew westwards into the hills, the smoke of hundreds upon hundreds of camp-fires— Il Shara's river camp!

Here was the explanation of the things which had puzzled him. No doubt scouts among the hills watched the movements of the Legion. But here, secure in their vast numbers, the Arabs had no cares until the day of battle. To-morrow, or when it came to them, they would destroy the Roman *gom*. To-day Il Shara had slaughtered for them and they sat round their fires, feasting before battle. Not one of all those warriors paid heed to the lonely figure of the man by the boulder, looking down on them.

Valens looked with narrowing eyes at the river. It varied in width from ten to thirty paces between its green banks, in its deepest part not above the shoulder. Almost opposite him it shoaled and there a man could walk across, the water below his knees. But the banks were high and steep on both sides, an ample channel for violent thunder floods. Between the spur and the river, the ground was uneven, rock-strewn gravel. He looked to his left. There the spur on which he stood dropped steeply to the plain. The river ran out into the distance in winding, diminishing flow, until it disappeared from view behind an outjutting berg.

He returned down the hill, led his horse to level ground and mounted, riding east to round the end of the spur. He pulled his horse in when he could again see the river. The smoke was diminishing now. He smiled, imagining Il Shara's feast. The stew-pots would still be bubbling, but the fierce fires spread on flat rocks had died down, the ashes were being kicked away, and goat carcasses, split and flattened, were hissing as they roasted.

He turned his horse again and rode slowly back towards the camp, until he reached a hillock of scattered stones. There he dismounted, stretching his long legs before him

184

as he sat down, his back against the shadowed side of a rock, and waited, his eyes on the bare slope of ground to his north.

He had not long to wait. With a sparkle of sunlight on weapons, helmets and flexible breastplates, they came in sight, Gallus and his escort, the *Primi Ordines* and the mounted wing, riding towards the spur at a brisk canter, and he mounted and rode to join them.

*   *   *

All night Valens had lain on the spur, watching Il Shara's camp, its thousands of camp-fires aglow under the moon. Not a man of the Arab host had moved across the river. From the wide plain beyond the river came the night-long thudding of drums, while the Arabs danced their wild war dances or sang the long, boasting epics of their race. In the early morning before dawn, a Cohort of men occupied the spur and he gathered his few scouts and guides and mounted his horse, riding back to meet the advancing Legion.

The Legion, its baggage and its heavy engines disposed in the fortified camp, moved forward in the battle formation of the 'Triple Shield', in three lines, each three ranks deep, one behind the other and they moved slowly, for with them the sixty dart-throwing ballistae rolled, on their solid wooden wheels.

Gallus marched between the first and second lines and, on his right, surrounded by its devoted guards, the Eagle flashed on its tall white staff, borne aloft by the *aquilifer*, a terrifying figure in his bear mask covered helmet, the long shining claws crossed over his armoured breast.

They turned when they had passed the foot of the spur, moving directly to their right, their formation unvaried,

on to the plain between the spur and the river and from the
Arab host rose a roar of derision and rage. Then they
halted and turned, closing their ranks, to face Il Shara and
his army.

Il Shara had ordered his battle array since the dawn.
He sat his horse now, in the centre of his forces, his green
banner fluttering above him, among his own warriors of
Harib and Beihan. He rode a strong, grey mare of the
Beihan breed and his thick lips curled in scorn as he watched
the movements of the Legion and he laughed, deep in his
chest. His chiefs and Amirs were gathered about him,
gentling their curveting horses. His own warriors of the
two wadis numbered a full ten thousand men, a shouting,
milling crowd on foot and camel-back, whose leaders
moved up and down before them, marshalling them,
restraining their hot impatience to attack. To his left,
facing the right of the Legion, fifteen thousand of Ma'in
and the Awalek, leaped and danced, shaking silver-bound
spears, flashing broad daggers in the sun, while poets
moved among them, exhorting them, reminding them of
ancient glories, in couplet after ragged couplet. They
crowded in on each other now, towards the centre, each
man thrusting himself forward to find a place opposite
the tiny Roman army. But it was to the far right of his
line that Il Shara looked. There, where the river banks
were low and the stream shoaling, he had placed his hammer
blow, always decisive in the open battles he had fought,
a herd of camel-men, armed with long spears and wicker
shields, six thousand strong! One-half of that number,
unaided, could stamp flat this impertinence from
Rome!

The Cohort on the spur had now joined the Legion.

A *cornu* sounded the advance and in their three lines they marched slowly towards the river, the mounted wing in the rear. A hundred and fifty paces from the river bank they halted, in perfect order.

"Ballistae to the left front!" ordered Clemens. They trundled the machines forward, massing them in line on the left of the Fourth Cohort. There was less shouting now from the Arab host confronting them and among those surrounding Il Shara ran a murmur of speculation—these lines of helmeted men, was it fear which made them so silent? They were so few in number it would be hard to find blood for the spear before they were overwhelmed! And what were these wooden frames rolling out to the front? They were soon to know.

There was a rattle of sixty whip-lash cracks and a rushing hiss in the air as the great darts hurtled upwards, flashed turning in the air, and fell, amid cries of astonishment and horror, on the centre of the Arab line. The first shower had hardly struck them before the next was on its way. All round Il Shara, men and horses lay screaming, pierced and mangled by these terrible missiles, which could strike a horse from its feet and pin it struggling to the hard earth. For a moment he glanced back over his shoulder and, as he did so, a dart flashed by him, four feet of neck and shaft, with heavy, brazen head, hissing in the air, and struck a mounted man through the abdomen and through the horse's loins beneath, skewering horse and man together, in kicking, bloody confusion. He turned from the sight, his eyes afire with anger as he drove his horse forward.

"Attack!" he cried. "*Hajoom! Hajoom!* To each who brings me a Roman head, five handfuls of gold, I, Il Shara swear it!"

"*Hajoom! Hajoom!*" The deep-chested roar rolled from wing to wing of the Arab host. The great mass of warriors surged forward, slipping down the steep bank, wading and splashing across the flood, leaping forward from the river, battle-axes and spears alight in the sun, eyes wild, teeth bared in rage and blood lust, the banners of their tribal gods stiffening in the wind above them. And, launched in thundering, wide-legged gallop, the camel herd surged forward at the left of the Roman line.

"Leave the machines!" called Repetinus. "Quickly, now, into the ranks with you!"

The Fourth, Seventh and Tenth Cohorts, who held the left of the three Roman lines, wheeled back to face the camel charge, in Triple Shield formation. Through a shower of javelins, the thundering mass of great beasts crashed into the Fourth, their snarling heads held high and burst through them into the javelin storm of the Seventh. The Seventh held them for a moment, bending before the heavy momentum of the herd, staggered backward by its weight. Then the Cohort split and the stampede broke through them and bore down upon the Tenth Cohort, who hurled their javelins and sprang forward in the attack. The front of the Tenth held. The disrupted Cohorts raged among the camel-men, plunging their swords into the beasts' throats and bellies, tearing riders from their saddles, thrusting them through and trampling them underfoot. Il Shara's hammer blow was spent. The camels crashed into each other, reared up on fallen, struggling bodies, slithered wide-legged in a confusion of terror. Crushed in the mêlée, their riders were powerless. Those who could turned their beasts towards the river, urging them back with blows of their spear butts. But the mounted wing was ready. The high, rippling call of the *lituus* sounded. Sabinus and his men gripped their spears and charged. Il Shara's men had no defence, their backs turned, their camels in full, lumbering flight. They could only crouch, terrified, gripping their saddle pommels, waiting to be struck down. And the Roman horsemen thrust them through, tumbled them to the ground, cleared their points, and plunged them in again.

On the centre and right of the Legion, Qataban and Ma'in hurled themselves in their shouting thousands, with stabbing spear, axe and sword, the weight of their massed bodies pressing the First, Second and Third Cohorts back towards the second line. Gallus slipped from his horse and drew his sword. He had seen the camel charge checked by the Tenth Cohort. It would now, for a time, be a matter of disciplined fighting, of drill and swordplay. His guards and messengers stood beside him, ready to carry his orders when the time came. In a choking cloud, the dust rose among them and hung above them in the hot air.

High on the spur, Serenus settled his fat back comfortably against a rock and smiled.

"Now I will show you a battle," he said. "Caesar himself never had a better view and it is distant enough. A distant view of a battle is the one I like best. You need fear nothing."

It was distant from them, a pageant of a battle. The cries of the Arab host as they rushed on the Legion, the rolling shout of "*Hajoom! Hajoom!*" had lost their volume and terror high up here on the spur. But, even so, her heart stood still and her mouth was suddenly dry as she looked down on that vast host of warriors, the sun sparkling on their upraised weapons, pouring forward to envelop the Roman force. She held her breath.

"There is a great deal in fighting a battle, you know," said Serenus cheerfully. She glanced at him and away again, a mounting terror in her heart. His voice had been cheerful. But his eyes were hard and narrowed and in their brown depths hot coals burned. His left hand lay clenched on his knee, the knuckles white with the strength of his grip. Then, as she looked down again on the plain, the thundering camel herd struck the Roman left and, on the centre and right, the charging warriors hurled themselves in deadly fury on their prey—and an upthrust explosion of sand enveloped the tiny, shining Legion and hid it from her sight.

She looked across the desert to the east, a wide, red plain, spreading to the far edge of the world, fading in a mist of rose. She could not look down again. But her heart cried within her: "Look down! Look down, for he is there—you cannot let him go, you cannot let your love die without a look!"

"Why did I come here?" she whispered. "Oh! Why did I come here?" And the cries from the slaughter below her gave her no answer.

The warriors of Qataban and Ma'in raged impotently, thrust by the weight of their numbers upon the thirsty, stabbing Roman swords. Surging, crushed together, they had no room to thrust the spear or swing the battle-axe. Pace by pace the Legion moved backward, clearing their front of the slain. Choking in the dust of the battle Gallus turned to the messenger beside him.

"Tell them it is time!" he shouted.

The right of the Legion began to swing back more

swiftly towards the spur. Suddenly, on Gallus' order, the rear line of Cohorts broke from the formation and ran out to the left and fell upon the Arab right flank in a steady, thrusting advance. The warriors of Ma'in, exulting in the swift backward movement of their foes, hurled themselves forward into the opening trap, while others, sensing a momentary advantage, surged to their support.

Il Shara, riding with his standard-bearer and the remnant of his Amirs and chiefs behind the centre of his army, saw the danger but he was powerless to control his men. "The right!" he shouted. "The right!" But his voice was lost in the turmoil and the right of his army was swept back in confusion, unable to understand this sudden swinging of the front of battle. The Tenth Cohort, on the left of the suddenly extended Roman front, began now to wheel inwards, and the Legion became a closing semi-circle of iron-clad, bloodthirsty men.

Il Shara turned his horse towards the river, driving his heels into its flanks.

"Away!" he cried. "Away to the city!" and he galloped for the river bank, his standard-bearer a stride behind him. But there was no escape for his warriors, in the tightening iron trap.

"Aaah!" said Serenus.

She turned, startled by the savagery in his voice. And she cried out, her eyes wide, uncomprehending. The scene below which had so terrified her, had utterly changed. Ragged edges of the Arab host now streamed back towards the river, in the loose panic of flight. But all round the milling thousands of its main body helmets shone, a thin constricting band of iron—and suddenly the dusty air was rent by a terrible sound, the hoarse, strident whooping of the *tubas*! The ring of iron gripped and gripped, tightening on the mass of warriors, merciless, squeezing their life's blood from them. And the iron band closed and closed until, as the sun inclined towards the mountains, the shouting and the helpless cries for mercy died away and ceased and the slaughter was complete.

High on the spur Lilleth lay, small and crumpled among the rocks, while Serenus tried, in a foolish way, to comfort her, patting her shoulder with a fat hand.

"There, there," he said. "It was only a battle, you know—a battle, that's all!"

But below, on the corpse-strewn battleground, there was little rest for the victors. Gallus stood among the heaps of gashed bodies, his Centurions before him, their right arms blood-stained from wrist to shoulder, their faces and beards caked with sweat and dust.

"We must pursue!" he said. "You, Sabinus, send word to break camp at once and join us here with all speed. Valens, how far is this city of Aska?"

"Saqia, Praefectus; marching from here at sunset, we should reach it by midday and the mounted men before the dawn."

"That is excellent—they must have no time to reform or to garrison their cities and oppose our march. We must go with all speed to the south. Let the men wash in the river and rest themselves till sunset. We will march in column for the sake of speed. No halt from here to Aska!"

The men went down to the river. They threw their

arms and their armour down on the banks and pulled off
their sweat-soaked tunics. Stripped naked they waded
into the warm, swifty-running water, washing the blood
from them, splashing the water over their heads, plunging
in the pools and lying on their backs in the shallows,
letting the water swirl and ripple over their weary bodies.
Gallus, too, stripped with his men, revelling in this mercy of
the gods. He lay on his back on the shoal gravel of the
stream bed, looking up at the sky, his body rested, his
mind afire with impatience.

Then he saw them, tiny dots in the blue of the heaven,
circling down, down, their eyes on the dead—the gathering of the vultures. The first comers swooped low on
widespread wings, long as a man, croaking as they settled
to their feast, while from the depths of the sky others came,
circling and stooping down to the carnage by the river.
Not often, in that bare land, did ten thousand warriors lie
dead, heaped together in one place. There would be
plenty for all. And, in the hills above the river, hyenas
padded from their foul dens, their huge shoulders crouched,
scenting the tainted wind, as the sun went down.

That night the moon rose on the marching Legion.
From here to the sea was none to oppose them. At last
their feet were on the road which led to Ophir and the
cities of gold. They were the victors of battle, the con-
querors of the south! Yet they marched stooping, weary,
their arms and bundles a heavy, dragging burden, their
minds a mist of pain and fatigue, in the torture of chafed
skin and sleepless, burning eyes. And they trod a road
of death, strewn with dead animals and dying men, the
rout of Il Shara's army.

How long, how long the night! Would the stars stand

still for ever and the sun forget to rise? Men weary from wounds, heat and lack of sleep, stumbling on through the night on a road marked by the bodies of dead and dying enemy. A dead road under the moon, a road of pain. The endless road of disillusion, long as the span of a man's life, which is as long as the history of the world. A road of sad dreams. The golden incense road.

CHAPTER 13

The Guttering Candle

. . . he took the city of Aska, which had been forsaken by its King.

It was dark when Valens and his small party of horsemen came to the palm gardens, north of the city of As Saqia. To their east, the morning star rose, haloed, on the far rim of the world. They had followed the dim-lit road without difficulty, its sandy stretches deeply trodden and, where it led over rock, worn and polished by the feet of countless camels, which had passed along it in the millennia of its history. For this was the oldest road in the world.

They had ridden fast and hard through the night. They checked their pace among the palms, picking their way past low walls and over irrigation channels until, surprisingly, the city wall loomed above them, raised high upon its debris of antiquity.

They dismounted in silence, gathering together on the edge of a palm grove, drawn each to the other by something daunting in the dark wall before them, its angle sharply turned to the double bastion of a gateway.

In the nearer tower, three high loopholes glowed, a dull, smoky red. From the gateway, in a cave of darkness overhung by a curtain wall, came the rhythmic creaking of an iron hinge. From within the city rose a low wailing sound, not loud nor high, a moaning cry of sorrow, now faint and trembling, now crying with words which had no meaning for a listener, now rising to a long sighing wail of desolation. There was no other sound from the dark city. Looking up at those walls as the star rose and dawn glowed in the east, each of them felt a stirring of the hair and the cold breath of terror on their backs.

He had seen it before his neighbour gripped his arm and pointed, a still figure leaning in an embrasure of the battlements above him. Its left hand hung down stiffly and a faint breath of morning wind stirred the long, linen sleeve. It was quite still, unnatural in its rigidity. They watched it, this lonely guardian of the wall. In the spreading light, it took face and form and figure, head twisted towards them, mouth agape, eyes open and sightless in the dreadful stare of sudden death. Then as the first sunlight glowed upon the wall, it moved, drooping, flacid with the touch of heat, leaning far out, slipping forward until it fell, with a dull rattle and thud, in the sand below. And, standing there on the edge of the palm grove, they breathed in deeply and looked at each other.

Valens shook his shoulders. "Three with me," he said. "The rest wait here."

The gateway was open, the broken door swinging rhythmically on an iron hinge. They stepped through, their javelins ready, poised in their hands. In the guard-room on their right, smoke rose from the timbers of a fallen ceiling and, far up in the dark interior of the tower, a dull, red glow of smoky fire waxed and waned. In the other guard-room, a body sprawled on a broken bench, an arrow in its back.

196

They came out of the shadow of the gateway into the sunlit square beyond and paused, drawing back a half-step, their breath sharp-drawn in astonishment and horror. Piled on one another, corpses lay heaped against the walls. But they were not the corpses of warriors. Women and children had been herded here and slain. Old and young they lay, gashed and torn by scimitar and spear. Il Shara had ordered the extermination of the royal line. Who could tell where, among the multitudes of Sheba, flowed the blood of ancient Kings? And if a base-born infant or two or a grandmother here and there were cut down, who could raise a cry? So they had herded them here, the weak and the innocent.

Valens and his men had no knowledge of the ancient hatreds which had been unloosed in As Saqia. The native guides, from peaceful Nejran, looked round them silent with horror, aghast at this evidence of Qatabanian violence and treachery. And the moaning which had frozen their hearts in the dawn rose again, a fitting lamentation, an eerie coronach in the still city.

"One lives in that house . . ." said a soldier. They looked at each other. Someone must mount the stair to the abode of grief. And it was Valens, the Centurion, who must go.

He climbed the winding stair, an Arab guide following him, and entered a dark room, the sunlight striking a pattern through closed lattices. He strode to the nearest window and opened it and the light flooded in. On a couch outstretched, its arms to its sides, lay the body of a young man. The handsome face, eyes closed, was marble-pale, beautiful with the beauty of emptiness. Beside the couch, a young woman knelt, sitting back on her heels, her eyes on the dead man's face and from her lips came again the ghostly, moaning cry.

"Cease, woman!" said Valens, his voice husky, in a dry throat.

She turned her head and stared at him and he drew back; for her eyes were dead, unseeing, the eyes of a body deserted by its soul. Then in an even, expressionless voice she spoke.

"Who bars my keening? Who bids me cease to mourn? Let death songs be sung, let there be weeping for Na'aman the bold, and for all the children of Sheba."

The Arab guide started forward, staring at the corpse and turned to Valens.

"It is Na'aman bin Itiamara!" he exclaimed. "He who was Governor of this city, a cousin of the Queen!"

The woman held up her hand, an imperious gesture.

"Wake not my love!" she whispered. She put a finger to her lips, turning towards the body on the couch. "He sleeps after the grievous battle, he must rest."

She took the cold, pale face in her hands and raised it, pillowing it on her right arm, a twisted smile of pain on her gentle lips.

"Let him rest," she said softly.

"How did he die?" asked Valens. For he must know, he must unriddle the mystery of this dead city.

She turned to him, letting the dead man's head fall back upon the pillow, her eyes alight with fires of madness and anger.

"How did he die? In battle with you, foul dog of Qataban! His child you shall not have, he is safe from your red hands. Treacherous, slaughterous son of *Iblis*, accursed of all gods, may devils take you in their grey arms by night and cast you forth beyond the moon!"

"We are not of Qataban," said Valens, gently.

For a moment her eyes wavered, the light dying in them and she shook her head slowly, a hopeless, weary movement.

"Then, if you are not of Qataban," she said, staring away from him blindly, across the room into the dead world of her heart, "weep for Na'aman, sing dirges for Na'aman the brave, for he is dead. Let the grey dove mourn him in the dawn, let the passer-by cast a stone of remembrance upon his cairn, let the stars weep dew for Na'aman, my love, and for lost Sheba and her children; for the lamps grow dim as the world turns from glory and Sheba's candle gutters in a little room."

Valens took a pace forward and, stooping, laid a hand on her shoulder.

"We are not enemies," he said. "Come, let us help you bury the Prince. We mourn his death with you and are strangers only, come from afar."

But she turned to the corpse again, moving her shoulder away from his hand, her eyes once more on the pale, dead face.

"No," she murmured, a child again, fretful, wishing to be alone. "No; leave me, let me mourn for my love."

He came out into the sunlit square, his face white and strained. In the house he had left the sighing moan began again. His men waited for him to speak, their eyes restless, their javelins tight gripped. But he could find no words for a moment. Did they bring this with them, too, the Legion of Rome? No, this slaughter of the children was not from them; but it was part of the nightmare in which they wandered, cast here when the world tilted and they marched into an accursed land,

"This is some devilry of civil war," he exclaimed. "The moon-priest, whom we conquered, struck here, treacherously, on a city not his own and there in the house a woman mourns for her dead mate. Come, let us search for water. Keep close, for who knows what may lurk in such a place?"

They walked through the narrow, winding streets. Everywhere they looked the dead lay, in dark booths, sprawled across the steps of battered doorways, heaped at street corners, and above the city carrion hawks circled, whistling, while from their path cumbrous vultures rose, on wide, slow-thrusting wings. They turned at last into sunlight again and there before them, framed between houses, stood the delicate pillars of a temple and, beside the pillars, the white stone wall of a cistern. But its stones were broken down and they passed between them on to the dry cistern floor. Climbing steps, they found an aqueduct, a ditch of stone and plaster, two spans wide. No water flowed in it. They followed it until it traversed the city wall by a gate to the west. Thence it stretched out across the plain, a long white ribbon in the sun. Were there no wells? They climbed to a house-top, high above the city, searching for a well-head within the walls or in the fields beyond, but they could see none. An Arabian city without wells—it was not possible! They rejoined their companions by the north gate and mounted, spread out widely among the fields and palm gardens but, in all that oasis, no well was to be found. Too often in past centuries had the city changed hands. Now, by the Queen's command, the wells had been filled in and only the aqueduct remained, so that, if her enemies seized it once more, she could expel them by the lowering of a sluice gate. Valens and his men could not know this, they could only marvel at this waterless oasis, blooming in the waste, fed by a single vein of life from the mountains in the west. The city had been well named, 'The Aqueduct', for without the aqueduct, there would be no city.

He gathered his men and, leaving some to watch for the Legion, rode up the line of the dry water channel. At intervals it opened into cisterns, from whose deep sluices water could be loosed to feed the city's fields and orchards. In some of these, in corners where the sun had not yet dried it, a dampness remained, but there was no water. They passed over the plain into the foothills. There were no cisterns now, only the white plaster channel, leading up into the mountains. It led them to the mouth of a wide, rocky gorge and, turning sharply under an overhanging crag, Valens cried out and urged his horse forward, for here water flowed in the wadi bed and, at the next bend, he came in sight of its source, where the wall of the aqueduct had been broken down and clear water gushed out from it, cascading over the rocks below, sparkling in the bright sunlight of midday. He turned to give orders to his men and the horses whinnied deeply in their chests as they dropped their heads to the stream.

*   *   *

Il Shara and the remnant of his army had not halted in As Saqia, the city he had slain. In some of the water channels, pools lay, drying in the sun and here they had watered their beasts. Then they had ridden on, a swiftly-moving party of some three hundred on horses and camels, forcing their beasts forward through the night. In the darkness before moonrise, thoughts flickered in his mind.

At first they flashed like summer lightning, leaving a deeper blackness behind them, unrelated one to another in origin, scattering his purpose. Then they began to join, to gleam together, to bend and shape themselves to his will. And his will gathered them together into a single plan, a fanatic design. He unrolled, in his mind, a map of his dominions. From 'Amd to Ma'in and the sea; to Aden and the narrow straits of Bab al Mandeb, north to the high plateau and the desert road.

He could not remain at As Saqia, because the aqueduct no longer watered it and there were no wells. Thus had Sheba done to him and thus would he revenge himself on Rome. Cisterns can be destroyed. Wells can be filled in. And without cisterns and wells the great caravan road became a road no longer, but a desert, a wilderness uninhabitable by man.

In the morning they halted by a small, unwalled settlement, a cook-shop village, where a traveller might snatch a meal, or sip a bowl of camel's milk, while his caravan passed by. Here, in the shadows of a palm grove, he spread out his plans before his weary followers. And, a short while after, the wailing villagers had left their dwelling-place, carrying what they could on their shoulders, and with their few beasts, looking back on a broken rain-water cistern and on the sandy hollows which had been their wells.

A violent storm of activity seized upon Il Shara and his followers. They struck at two more settlements near at hand. They split into two parties, one riding south down the road, the other, on horseback, forcing their pace into the hills. They met again at evening, with a tale to relate of destruction and misery over their fires. Full-fed, they rode south again at midnight and morning found them riding through the gates of the city of Ithtar the god, the green banner fluttering above them, while Il Shara called loudly for Salim, the Governor, to come to him now, in the central market square.

Il Shara raged, his fierce eyes aflame, his cruel lips curved in the curve of a scimitar.

"You shall do as I say," he said, his voice hoarse with anger, "you shall do as my other cities and towns have done. Here, in *Ithtar ila*, my city of Ithtar the god, let there be swift obedience, or I shall punish with the sword's edge! I go from here south down the road to Qohlan, and you, Salim, will lead your people forth into the hills. Let none remain! Break down the cisterns, destroy the wells, burn the granaries, destroy your city I say!"

Salim, the Governor, fell to his knees, his hands raised in supplication.

"But, sire, consider—I will lead the people forth, I will burn the grain, I will block the wells, all this I will do. But the temple of the god and its water—how can we stretch out our hands against the god, in his own city?"

"Better the sand should drink it, old fool, than the gullets of Rome—it shall be broken down! From here to As Saqia the land is dry and burnt. Come!" he called to his Amirs and servants. "To horse! To horse! We can delay no longer!"

Salim watched the cavalcade canter through the gateway, under the green standard of the Priest-King. The suppliant look faded from his eyes and, in its place, first anger lightened and then a narrowing of contempt. He fingered his ragged fringe of grey beard, his head low on his broad shoulders, his squat body bent forward from the hips. He turned slowly to face the dejected group of men behind him.

"To the *mijlis*," he said, "let there be a council."

They felt no comfort in the long chamber, met together to consider the destruction of their city. They sat in silence, waiting for Salim to speak and he leant back against the wall, examining their faces one by one, his dark eyes crafty, weighing their hearts and their thoughts. These men had no desire to flit with their families, among the inhospitable rocks. There sat old Mola, fat and lecherous —how would he fare in the hard, nomad life of a fugitive? Would he go hunting, bow in hand, to feed his nine wives and his forty or so children? Only a few moons ago, the whole city had laughed, when two of Mola's wives bore each twin daughters on the same night—an explosion of female children, whom he had buried at once, of course, since they were uneconomical.[1]

"How say you, Mola," he asked, leaning forward, leering at him; "will you skip upon the mountains like the ibex?"

They laughed, nervously, and old Mola groaned, scratching his ribs, with stiff fingers.

"And you," continued Salim, turning to a frail old greybeard at the far end of the room, who sat far back against the wall, in an effort to efface his presence, "you, Thabit, will a rock content your skinny shanks, in the autumn rains?"

"I am no baboon!" quavered Thabit.

"Where goes Il Shara now?" asked one of them.

"South, to destroy all the cities of the plain," replied

[1] A practice condemned in the Koran.

Salim. "To Qohlan, Merkha, Nisab and Mariba and thence east to Yeshbum and Azzan, Hadhina, Jardan and 'Amd, so that these Romans may find no water in all the land and will die!"

They looked on one another with horror and, too long pent-up, talk burst from them and filled the room, while Salim leant back against the wall and listened, a smile growing on his face.

"Ferid, the Ma'ini, will never leave Mariba!"

"Would he slay us all—where will the folk bide? Whither will caravans now march?"

"Is our wealth to be thrown to the dogs, while the trade turns west to Himyar?"

"The Romans do not cast the people out into the *khala*—Nejran is prosperous again, so it is said—who is the enemy, Il Shara or the Roman King?—to destroy and to leave all here! From whence shall we find provender when the Romans have gone, shall we beg from Shemsi of Sheba, shall we crawl to the *Tobba* on our knees, with empty bellies? It is madness, and if the Romans come not, shall we destroy our nest and fly away only to return and rebuild it, a laughing-stock of the world?"

"Peace!" shouted Salim, his voice vibrant in the noisy room. "Let Il Shara's will be done—if, indeed, the Romans come thus far. Let guards be posted night and day at the gates and watchmen on the towers. But our obedience shall be tempered with wisdom. The grain shall be hidden, buried deep in the sand and the sand stamped down. And the water—how may a city be rebuilt, once the water is lost? Il Shara rides in haste, he has not pondered these matters as I have done. If the Romans should come I will parley with their leader. We shall give them camping ground without the walls. No door shall open to them and they will pass us by."

They all smiled now, a happy gathering. They would obey the King's command, but with foresight for the future, with wise heads, firmly planted on their shoulders. They broke again into excited talk, nodding their heads together. Il Shara had been hasty, there were many things of which he had not thought. Assuredly he would praise them for their wisdom, when his caravans once again found rest here on the long road to the north! And a seed of knowledge opened in each man's heart, that Il Shara would not return, that his star had set and he would be King no more.

*   *   *

Shemsi, Queen of Sheba, sat in her private chamber, clothed in a long gown of scarlet wool, her greying hair in two plaits on her shoulders. She wore no golden diadem. Her lips trembled and she looked on the messenger before her through a growing mist of the tears she could not check.

"And Na'aman, the Prince, my cousin?" she asked.

"He is dead, Majesty."

Yes, she had known. He would not leave his post, a loyal servant and a man she had loved.

"Say on," she said.

"They held the gate and the wall by morning and in the city they killed and burned. Then, when the Prince was dead, they slew the women and the children——"

"The children. . . ."

"It was the Priest-King's order, Majesty, for he seeks the destruction of your royal line. But, when the tide of war turned full against our Prince, he bade them loose the water. Thus was the cistern destroyed, so that all of

Qataban left the city and joined Il Shara by the river. All this I had from a dying man within the walls. When I came, with my *gom* to its relief, I found the city dead. I laid the Prince on a couch in a house above the north gate and, until the road turns, I broke the aqueduct and the field cisterns. Thence I came to bring these fell tidings to Your Majesty."

"And is there more?"

The messenger's eyes gleamed, his speech grew quick, his voice strong.

"Qataban lies slain by the river, praise the sun! There, by day, the vultures gorge, by night hyenas prowl among the dead. And Il Shara, with a remnant, rides to the south on loosened rein!"

But the Queen could not flash her eyes and praise the sun. She could not see, for her tears. She sat still, her head bent, her hands clasped together, for a long time, before she could find a voice in her throat.

"Let them close the sluice gate to As Saqia," she said, at last.

She heard the messenger leave the room. She heard a stir of men and horses in the courtyard below and the gate swing wide and a thudding of hooves on the road to the east.

He rode at a gallop down the broad, sandy path, his horse full stretched, its soft, chestnut coat shimmering and glinting in the sunlight. He swung it with his knees where the path turned round rocky hills, he pressed it forward up steep inclines, he held it, lightly, when it slipped, bounding on a downward slope. And, at last, in the full midday, he reined it in on its haunches by a great plaster cistern, built in a valley of the hills.

They had seen his flying figure afar off. Now they gathered by the cistern to meet him, the controllers of the sluice gates, expectant and alarmed.

"Let fall the sluice gate to As Saqia!" called the horseman. "It is the Queen's command!"

As Saqia! Here was news of tragedy! They ran to the wheels and levers. Slowly the great plug of stone fell down within its grooves. The hurrying waters gurgled and splashed as it fell, with a heavy crunch, into its bed. And the last of the water ran down the long aqueduct, shining in the sun.

*   *   *

They halted before the walls of As Saqia. They sat down or leant against the boles of palm trees, weary from the battle and their night-long marching. They looked longingly at the open gateway—could they not go in? There would be deep cisterns of water, under shady walls. There would be cool, shadowed rooms, dates and grain and, perhaps, a cup of wine for the tired soldier. There would be rest from heavy arms, peace from the chafing of burdens.

But there was some delay in entering the city. Gallus stood by the gate, the *Primi Ordines* had been summoned, and some of the advanced party of mounted men spoke earnestly and pointed to the hills in the west.

The long column bunched together among the palms. The baggage train spread out in the plantations, the camels lumbering forward, grumbling in their long necks, halting in scattered lines.

Then word passed among them, repeated by parched lips—no water in the city. There was no water here. They must march again, some way into the hills, where

208

water had been found. And there was no rest for them in the shade of the palms for, in expectation of finding water here, they had not spared the water skins. They looked away from the city, their eyes red-rimmed from lack of sleep. It was a long way over the plain to the hills there, trembling in the heat.

They reformed their ranks, lifting their burdens to their shoulders again, walking stiffly, on aching legs. They set off across the plain, a straggling column, those who had horses leading them; and the horses drooped their heads, stumbling on the uneven ground, their flanks heaving with short drawn breath.

The sun inclined to the west and struck full in their faces. They marched across the plain into the barren foothills, seeing only the ground before their feet. They climbed, gasping, over the rocks and shuffled wearily in the deep gravel of the hollows. They checked and stumbled forward and checked again as their long column lost its intervals and bunched and spread. Intolerable hours passed. At last, they entered a rocky gorge, finding some shade from the sun in its winding course and, in the evening, the leading men struggled through loose gravel in a bend of the river bed and saw above them a cascade of clear water, falling from the rocks.

They were constricted by the steep sides of the gorge. Far back, camels loaded with skins lumbered up towards the water. By the cascade, Serenus, stick in hand like a drill-master, ordered the marshalling of the skins, some full, some half full, many dry and empty. The camels trod and fouled the trickle of the stream in their passing, but the men came forward, crowded in this straightened place and knelt where the water flowed, throwing it up into their faces, taking long draughts from their cupped hands.

Valens watched them, sitting above them on a spur of rock. Their faces were drawn with fatigue, their beards grey with dust. Among them, unnoticed, in her blue trousers and shapeless smock, Lilleth knelt down beside the water, lifting it to her lips, splashing it on her pale face, sitting back on her heels and looking at it, as it ran past her knees over the pebbles, her shoulders drooping, her eyes dark and haunted.

"Now let those empty skins soak awhile," said Serenus, "and bring forward any that have water. Let them be filled first."

And suddenly, from the stream bed, from the rocks above it, they all turned, startled, and looked upwards towards the cascade. For it had ceased to fall.

CHAPTER 14

Forward the Legion!

. . . thence he went to a city called Athrula. . . .

How far to the city of Ithtar the god? As the mind journeys, only a little way. As the bird flies, it is but a waft of wind under a pinion. For the torn foot, the aching shoulder, the swollen tongue, the way to Athrula leads through all the caverns of hell and back again.

They rested by the drying river bed till sunset. They straggled back, from the narrow gorge, the light swiftly failing, and reformed on the plain. Then they set off into the darkness and the road, from which one must not stray, stretched before them, shining under the stars. The leading men trudged beside their horses, no longer spying out the land. The long lines of camels plodded forward, patient, enduring, fortunate in their brainless nature, inured to hardship at the hand of man.

How far to the city, to the flooding cisterns, to a song in the still morning and a man drawing water from a well? A little way, a little way—two marches for strong soldiers, with their trumpets and horns, under a golden Eagle; two marches—and perhaps a little more—two days of easy pageantry, on the golden road! For between As Saqia and Athrula were settlements, halting places for rich caravans. Valens knew it all from hearsay, but he was afraid. He hurried on, striding through the night, his listless horse a burden on his arm until, after midnight, he saw the few palms and squat mud houses of a village and there, dark against the stars, stood the frame and wheel of a well-head. And it was as he had feared, for beneath the wheel was no well, but only a depression in the ground. It takes many days to sink a well. It takes a few hours to fill it with rocks and sand.

He walked on into the village and found the rain-water cistern—dry and its wall broken, tumbled in the dust. He walked slowly back towards the road. Life in this land depended on wells and cisterns; here was disaster for them all. Without wells and cisterns they could traverse the road in small parties with expert guides, or not at all. It was too far now to return to the flowing river, to reform there, to change this wild plan of marching to the sea. He had told Gallus—cisterns can be broken and wells can be destroyed. He had been right, the proof was here; and it brought no comfort, for right or wrong, unless they could find water, they would die.

No trumpet hailed the morning star. It rose, white and untrembling in the dry air. The eastern sky lightened and, its spears ready for the Legion, the sun sprang into the sky. At first it comforted with warm beams, brushing nightmares from lonely minds, bringing with it the courage of companionship. But this was its deceit; this was the way it opened hearts to its treacherous thrust. Better to march on staggering legs by night, when the mind can stray from the body in a dreamland free from pain, finding solace in separation, than by day, under the fierce heat, with cracked lips and swollen tongue. They halted. They sipped sparingly, enough only to keep them free from madness. They marched again, silent, bent low by their burdens and their miseries. They kept their eyes on the ground or on the backs of their companions. If they looked up, the sun was ready for them. It struck down at them, it stooped upon them, seizing the corners of the world in fiery hands, shaking it, tilting it this way and that, so that they reeled and fell.

To their west the hills drew back, under a mantle of hot haze. In the early afternoon the wind dropped and the haze spread out to them, stifling and heavy. Perspiration no longer cooled them. It lay on their cheeks and throats viscous, gritty with dust. Far to their left the sand stirred, at first a ghost-rustle on the surface, then a sudden hissing of hot air, whirling, rising up, expanding, a great pillar of revolving sand. As if awakened to a dance, other devils rose out of the desert, columns of whirling dust, their heads in the sky, bowing to each other, setting to their partners, making the wilderness a vast ballroom for a hellish minuet.

Lilleth, leaning on the fore-strap of a baggage camel, looked east into the desert and west to the hills. She let go of the strap and, swaying with sudden loss of balance, waited for Serenus. He came towards her, hanging heavily on a rope binding a pack of empty skins, his eyes on the ground before him, his fat cheeks sunken. She turned to walk beside him, touching his arm with her fingers, pointing to the western sky.

"There will be rain," she said. But he did not understand her. His mind was far away and here walked only a fat body, unfitted for its toil.

"Look!" she said. "It will rain!" And her tongue was heavy, slithering on the words.

He looked up and smiled, a vacuous smile which split his lip, so that the blood ran and he lifted the back of an unsteady hand to it.

"Only a little way . . ." he said, but his words were so thick that she could not understand them. He swayed against the camel with the effort of speech.

She felt a sudden horror of him, the poor stumbling body, mindless, hanging loosely on the rope. She had been right in what she said, there would be rain in the hills; it was an important matter. In an hour from now, rain would fall in the tall mountains, cold, cutting hail and the rain, sluicing down over their shoulders, torrents in the hills, fallen from the utter cold of the sky. She might lie down in them, drinking, breathing the rushing water. High spate in the hills, deep pools among the rocks and the rain beating perfume from the thirsty earth. She quickened her pace, leaving old Serenus, passing the heavily burdened Legionaries. They did not look at her as she passed up the columns of the Cohorts. Some looked to the right towards the darkened hills, yearning in their eyes. But they turned their eyes to the road again, their bearded faces grim and patient. She felt a passionate anger against them —did they not know that the road led nowhere, but that away there, in the high hills, rain would burst upon the land, bending the trees with its weight, flooding the steep glens with roaring water? She passed the ranks of the trumpeters as the first low murmur of thunder echoed in the distant mountains. She quickened her pace again at the sound, her feet tripping against each other, losing the ground, so that it seemed to rock unsteadily, jarring her bones, as she slipped and faltered. She passed the standards, sloped untidily on drooping shoulders, swaying against the darkening sky. The foolish men! Why should she march thus to die on the tortured earth? If they would not turn, she would leave them and run into the hills, swiftly, lightly, to where the torrents swirled and the deep pools overflowed with their mercy!

Then, suddenly, she shortened her stride. She hurried no more. Yes, there was the reason they did not turn from their road and run into the hills, there, marching in front of her, his powerful shoulders square, his strong, athletic body erect, his legs evenly striding and his head raised, alert, a figure of command—Gallus who led them and whom they must follow. Where he led, there was no turning aside. They must endure to the end. She understood, now, those patient, foolish men. And Gallus had made her one of them, Gallus who could play the father and the courtier and who could slaughter ten thousand men in a morning. Where he went she must go, they must all go and he walked easily, a swing in his gait, to the south, not to the west.

Thunder rocked the western mountains and, as the light died, lightning glowed through the thick sky. They halted when darkness fell, lying down on the track. Valens walked back down the long column, searching for his leader, a tall, erect figure, his long stride untiring. Gallus recognized him before he spoke and, rising, led him into the night, away from the men, far out into the sand. They ran their tongues over their lips, loosening their mouths for speech. Gallus gestured with a wave of his hand towards the Legion.

"That is the last water we have," he said, "they are sipping it now."

Valens nodded.

"At this pace," he said, "marching all night, we should be close to Athrula by morning."

"I would rest them more, if I dared." Gallus shook his head. "It is no time to rest, thirst gains apace and we must find water."

"It is that or death," answered Valens.

"You shall say that to none but me!" said Gallus, his voice hard. "A man must have hope. I shall tell them it is but a little way to water, I shall force that knowledge on them!"

"That is right," replied Valens, "all day I have told those who march with me that we must march and march or die. Now I have told them that this is the last halt and the water is before us."

"You have told them the truth!" Gallus smiled wryly. "For, if the land lacks water, the sea at least is before us."

Gallus pondered for a while, his head bent, his right heel digging a hole in the sand. Then he looked up at Valens and spoke again.

"If we find Athrula dry and destroyed," he asked, "is there hope in the hills?"

"There is hope from now on, Praefectus. It still rains there in the west; somewhere the wadis flood and flow. There is always hope."

There was always hope. The men rose unsteadily at the call of a horn, hitching up their heavy belts. They set off again into the night. On, on the Legion, it is but a little way to the city of the moon! The well ropes run, the wheels creak there by night and day, the palm gardens are flooded, the fat cisterns overflow, spilling their treasure unwanted in shady streets. There are pools, deep pools of water, where the tired body can sink down, down

216

into dark depths of peace. On! On! And the road so bright now, under the clearing heaven, that you cannot mistake the way!

Yet many did that night. It was easy to shut the eyes and wander into the desert and stumble on there, on and on until they fell and dreamed they still went on, until they dreamed no more; or until they woke and found themselves alone and far from the Legion and called and ran and went mad in the night. They leaned upon each other, or held themselves up by camel girths and the camels moaned, empty-bellied, and let their heads hang on their head ropes, pulling each other head to tail. Here and there in the long column, a camel would snap its head rope and kneel down, stretching out its long neck on the sand, looking its last on a hopeless world, with its dark, long-lashed eyes and die, splitting the baggage train. And a wind blew down from the hills with a scent of rain so that the beasts edged away from the road to the west, unguided, wandering from the road which you must hold and keep; for only it can lead you. And, one by one, the horses died.

The night was kind to Serenus. His mind, his spirit were steadfast, bearing him up, urging him on; but his heart could not endure and a deeper blackness than the night flooded the world of his visions. He fell, silently, on the sandy track and the long column passed him by to either side on soundless feet and the peace of the desert claimed him for its own.

It was right that they should walk side by side on the road to death. He had known it, always, that there was no other road for him, Valens, and the dark-haired girl. When their roads met, already they were deep within the land of fantasy. In that land no General ruled, for all their fates led them to a valley among twisted mountains, out into the uttermost deserts of the earth to a waterless road, the golden road which led to a city of the moon, in the land of Dream-no-more. And she walked now beside him, leaning on his arm, taking the rhythm of her stride from his, her eyes closed, towards the city.

Visions passed through her tired mind and in them always were pools and streams of water. The little stream that ran through the green valley of her childhood, far away. The pool, blue in the sunlight, deep and cool, wind from the hills warm on her naked body, stepping down slowly into crystal water. Water, water falling from swelling leather buckets, sparkling in the sun, splashing down into water channels, flowing out into shady gardens, under palms. The stream in the valley of Nejran, rippling over shining pebbles, minnows darting from her shadow. A blue pool in the hills and the Legion marching out to do battle by the river; the great, flowing river from Sheba's high mountain. The little stream running past her knees in the gorge and the cascade falling, falling, sparkling and splashing down the rocks and then—no more water. But under her shut eyes she saw it clearly, a dark pool, which was strange to her. She had not seen this pool before. A quarter moon glowed in its water and it reflected, faintly, the four slender pillars of a temple. If you moved a little way to the left, you could see the dim image of a kneeling ibex, carved from white marble, its head bowed low in worship and all about it in the water, the diamond points of stars. Clearly she saw it, very, very clearly. You knelt down by the pool, you put your hands into the water—and the stars reeled and the pillars bent and staggered, the marble ibex split into a thousand gleaming fragments and the pool had gone! She cried out, she caught at his hands, so that he turned and held her close to him, uncomprehending. And they both heard the sound, the thudding of a camel's feet, running in the night.

He turned his head and saw it and another, dark shadows, trotting with a lumbering, swinging gait, away from the road they marched on, to the east. And there another, a rope trailing from its pack saddle, striding away from the road into the desert. He turned, his arm round her shoulders and stepped off the road into the night. He had not gone far when he saw it, almost at his feet, a lake of rain-water in the sand and the camels, their necks stretched to it, drinking soundlessly, lifting their heads from the water against the stars.

They knelt together by the water, lifting it to their lips. But he could not stay with her and in a moment he had gone, striding back into the night. He ran towards the road, the wide desert spread before him, misty and uncertain of contour in the starlight, until he saw the line of men and camels, a dark shadow army, slowly moving past him, from right to left. He ran to them and tried to speak to the passing men, but their eyes were not on him. Their eyes were blind and their minds gazed inwards, each upon his soul and each toiled on a long and narrow road, that had no end but death. He pulled at their tunics but they shook him off or lost their unsteady balance and fell, cursing him with suddenly awakened eyes. He shouted and pleaded with them but they marched on. Forward, the Legion! Nor god, nor man, nor evil spirit from the night could turn them from their road. Forward the Legion!

The passing camels lifted their heads, edging their way off the road, and the rain pool hidden in the darkness split the column of the Legion, while, afar ahead, Gallus marched, his mind high above his tortured body, determined to endure.

A trumpeter, his long coach-horn slung across his back, staggered past him. Valens seized his arm, swinging him round with an iron grip, forcing him to halt, shaking him into consciousness, pointing to the east. The trumpeter swayed, his eyes stupid with thirst and pain. Then, suddenly, they flashed with fear. He grasped his trumpet and pressed the mouthpiece to his lips. A fierce, challenging call split the silence of the night. The passing men halted, unslinging their heavy shields, grasping their javelins, closing in on each other on stumbling feet. Valens stood listening, fear in his heart, until from far away he heard a high, rippling call in answer from the mounted wing.

They closed in, those who remained, from up and down the road, gathering to repel an attack out of the night. Gallus remained on the road, after he had heard the report. He would risk no more to-night. Before he marched off the road into pathless desert, he would wait for the dawn.

So the Legion waited, their ranks formed, their javelins ready, for their enemy the sun.

*   *   *

The sun rose out of the desert flaming, in triumph. They were but a remnant of a Legion, exhausted, by the treeless lake; and Gallus rumpled his straggle of golden beard, when they brought him the count. He looked back over the land to the north, his eyes hard. Close on a thousand men lost, paid over one by one on the road, to the gods of desolation. Six great engines gone astray, lashed to beasts wandering in the hills. Thirty-four ballistae, more than half their store of darts, all were lost, and Serenus no more, the greatest loss of all. And for the small number left to him, he had grain and dates for two days only, on short rations. For one of those two days they must rest here. They could not go back. They must go on to the south, to Athrula, chancing their fortune once more among empty cities and broken water cisterns.

"You say, Valens, that Athrula should be close to us now?"

"Very close, Praefectus."

"Take two men and ride out on camels until mid-afternoon. Return by sunset and report. You, Sabinus, take twelve men and ride into the hills. You Jucundus, take six men and twenty or thirty camels. Ride back down the road and bring in any men you find alive. I will consider your report, Valens, and yours, Sabinus, at sunset. Gather your men now, and ride."

It seemed incredible to Valens that they should have halted in the night so close to the city. He had ridden a bare three thousand paces by his reckoning, when he pulled his camel in, and dismounted, handing the head-rope to one of his men, and ran to the ridge before him, kneeling down in the cover of a rock. Below him stretched the palm gardens and fields of the oasis of Athrula. From the city, smoke rose peacefully in the air, from roof-top kitchens. A crowd of children played in the dust by the gate. As he watched, a horseman cantered slowly from the town, a landowner, no doubt, inspecting the morning work in his fields. A yoke of oxen lurched down a sand ramp and he saw fat water buckets rise from a well-head swinging, spilling a flashing cascade into a trough. He looked towards the city, standing on a mound above the palms. It was not a fortress. The wall was low, of mud brick and the bastions no more than loop-holed houses, while, within the city, in contrast to its poor defences, stood tall and beautiful houses, the homes of rich men. He contrasted the city with As Saqia, so strongly fortified, its walls of heavy stone, lowering over the plain. It must, he thought, be very many years since Athrula had been threatened by attack. Sheba barred her door. Qataban had no cares, his door was open, he could stay in or he could go out. The strong fellow! To-morrow Rome would march in on him.

*   *   *

Salim, the Governor of the city, stretched out his hand to the basket of fat, hot meat before him, turning the chunks over with greasy fingers, searching for the juiciest piece of fat he could find. The windows were shuttered against the night. Opposite him, also engaged in this hunt for fat, sat his old friend and counsellor, Salamah, a tall, horse-faced fellow, some seventy years of age, a successful dealer in camels. Just now his mouth and his hand were full and his eyes were on a piece of kidney fat which his host had overlooked. He almost choked in his eagerness.

"And then," said Salim, "when the watchman spies them, we will put on our best raiment and we will greet them with the *moqab*, the greeting ceremony. These Roomi men are men of culture, often I have heard it said. Their King is a djinn, so it is told, who married the sphinx of Egypt, a fabulous creature and she bare to him nought but he-goats, till he struck her down. They worship a golden bird, a phoenix, which they carry with them,

222

sitting on a pole. All this I have from a Greek trader, whom I met but yesterday, and who awaits news here of the road to the north."

Salamah belched heartily, seizing the kidney fat.

"And what else does he say?"

"He told me of their strange customs, how before they eat of anything, they lie down on beds and eat only lying on one side, since their stomachs are not as other men's, but only a single tube, passing down the body from right to left. They wear very long clothes of no shape, since their women have no skill with the needle. They are not of a natural race. Two shepherds, they say, married a she-wolf——"

"*'Audu billah!*"

"Yes, a she-wolf, on a mountain with seven horns. She gave birth to this djinn and thus, in some way I have not fully understood, founded the city of Room!"

"*Ajib!* Wonderful! And, the city founded, whence came the Roomi men to populate it?"

"*Billah*, from this same she-wolf! From where else, seeing that in all that land, only she was feminine? For she married the djinn, her son——"

"*Istaghfur Allah!*"

"Ay, so it is said, and bare ten thousand at a birth——"

"Ten thousand! But how long is her time of gestation?"

"That I do not know. Yet the Greek assured me that thus can one tell a Roomi—open the mouth; from the sides of the lower jaw, rise the two tearing teeth of a wolf!"

"Master!" a slave called from the doorway. "The men of Room are here!"

223

"It is well, it is well; bid the watchmen tell them to camp outside the city till morning, when we will go forth and greet them with the *moqab*."

"But, Master"—the slave wrung his hands in distress—"they are here indeed! They have thrown down the gate and slain the guards who opposed them and, even now, their camels kneel in the city square!"

CHAPTER 15

The Moon Girds on his Sword

. . . Mariba, in the country of the Rahmanitae, who are under Il Asarus.

ATHRULA had been built where the broad mouth of the Wadi Harib runs out from the massif of the Yemen mountains into the red sands of the great desert. Under all the land, at twenty fathoms depth, lay a copious supply of water, tapped by narrow-shafted wells. To the south from Athrula it is two days' hard marching, the desert to the left and the projecting spurs of the mountains on the right, until you reach the great Wadi Beihan, which runs north-east from the mountains and then turns east under the sands to join the vast seepage system of the Hadramaut.

South of Beihan, the main massif of the Yemen throws out a giant spur of mountains, rising to seven thousand feet, a jagged granite barrier, the Qor range, from which wadis drain north into the sands. It was here, in the angle formed by this eastward projecting spur, that the great caravans assembled, before commencing their three-thousand-mile journey to the north. In the gullies and foothills of this spur, lived the remnant of the nation of Ma'in, the oldest Kingdom in the world.

Farid bin Abd ar Rahman was Chief of the Chiefs of Ma'in. Like all his race he was small and perfect of body, dark brown in colour, a vigorous and a valorous man. Once his nation had ruled all Arabia, holding the road in their power from the southern sea to the Jordan and beyond. That was in ancient times, before ever a Pharaoh ruled in Egypt. They had traded with far Kingdoms in the dawn of Egyptian and Mesopotamian civilization. They had warred with Naram Sin of Akkad. They had sailed to Crete and had built there altars to the moon. They had been traders, seamen, warriors, owners of the world's only incense, a magic gum essential to all worship in the ancient world.

One thousand years before the Roman invasion, the Priest-Kings of Sheba had risen in revolt. Ma'in had been driven from Jauf al Yemen, where Sheba now ruled, into the Wadi Harib. There they had warred with Sheba for six hundred years, when Qataban arose and Ma'in, a remnant now, were driven south again into the sharp-pointed mountains of the Qor. A remnant they were indeed, in their numbers and possessions; but they were fierce, bitter-hearted, a vigorous people, who had no peace for Sheba and no subservience to Qataban.

Farid ruled as a Priest-Chief, elected from the sacred family of the ancient line by the leaders of the nation, themselves Priest-Chiefs of lesser degree. His power was in no way absolute. It depended much upon the fall of rain, increase of flocks, profitable trade and success in war; but, above all these things, it depended upon his own personality. Farid was wise and courageous, a counsellor and a warrior of repute. In his ten years of Chiefdom, few had opposed his will. He submitted to the boast of Qataban, that Ma'in was held subject, well knowing that, within his borders, none ruled but he. Under him Ma'in had enjoyed prosperity, in the narrow wadis of the Qor hills. They had strengthened their cities. In the foothill country and beyond, on the southern edge of the great desert, they had built cisterns and cunningly-sited aqueducts, so that the great caravans found ease and comfort here in their passing and rested after their arduous journeys from the sea.

But now, Farid's power hung in a precarious balance. Some four thousand of his warriors lay dead by Sheba's river and many thousands of others were scattered, fugitives in the unfriendly hills, returning one by one to swell the tale of disaster in their cities and towns. They had all voted for war by the side of Qataban and the Grand Council of Priest-Chiefs had placed the leadership of their host in Farid's hands. The tide had not yet set against him, but it would turn, when sorrow turned to bitterness and doubt. And his power to stem it, to preserve his chiefdom and his life, depended much on what happened now in the city of Mariba, where the Grand Council met and where Il Shara, spreading panic and destruction, was hourly expected.

A strange city, this mountain keep of Mariba. A dark red granite wall, seemingly grown from the contours of the rock, fenced the city about, with every artifice of masonry. Who had built this wall but the moon god himself? What human hand could have carved and raised these massive stones, the upper courses longer than a man, unmortared, the foundations huge cubes, hewn from the granite mountain and joined so closely that no knife point could be slipped between them? The city stood on a smooth slope of rock. From below, the walls curved upwards on either hand like a crescent moon, wide based, its horns drawn in together, looping the sharp peak of the mountain. Thus the city stood ringed by the moon god's own symbol, while high between the horns of the dark-red crescent a small temple stood, like a white star in the arms of a dark moon.

Within the crescent wall rose the city, tall, fantastic, a city of slender, coloured towers, with but one gateway, a double iron postern within the breasts of a double bastion. You called from without to the tower warden, the outer gate of iron rose in grooves, with a groaning of wheels and counterpoises. You rode under the hanging postern into a narrow, twisting passage. Above you in time of war and alarm, hot fires glowed and boiling oil spluttered and gurgled in delicately poised tanks. As you rode down this firelit passage, at every turn a loophole barred the way and, from its dark shadow, a strung arrow followed the quailing breast. From behind you the block of iron fell back into the rock, ringing like a monstrous gong, while, at the passage end, the inner postern rose before you and you looked into the city.

A long, straight flight of steps, cut into the rock, led from the gateway to the temple on the mountain peak. On either side of the steps, massive buildings stood, door-less, windowless, built of white marble blocks, the dwell-ings of the dead. At the top of this street of tombs, the temple stood, an oval pool of deep, clear water, reflecting four slender pillars, flanked by marble statues of the kneeling ibex. Within the shadowy temple court stood a low altar, carved with bulls' heads and sacred symbols of the moon. In the temple there were no inscriptions, for it was older than the art of writing.

On either side of the street of tombs, stretched the ways and byways of the city, narrow gorges under the tall houses, murmurous all night with the sound of running water, which flowed down from a spring, swelling beneath the temple floor. The water ran, in ever-dividing channels, to every part of the city. Beside the bastion of the gate it cut through the wall in a passage so narrow that a man must move through it sideways, his hands to his thighs, and the passage turned and twisted through twenty feet of wall thickness. Thence a deep plaster aqueduct carried it far out across the valley to a cistern, high above fields, terraced one below the other on the hillsides.

The Grand Council of Priest-Chiefs sat in the *diwan* of the palace in their full war-paint, their brown bodies, naked to the waist, rubbed with indigo and sesame oil, gleaming in the dark room like statues of living gun-metal. Here were no flowing robes, no embroidered head-cloths. Their long, straight hair was cut to shoulder height, bound with a single cord from which hung little beads of red cornelian. Barbaric silver bracelets decorated their upper arms. They sat erect against the wall of the room, body and knees bound tight with plaids of blue-stained linen, long-handled daggers, in broad, silver-mounted sheaths of crescent shape, gleaming in their leather belts, hilt and sheath tip together rising to the level of their breasts. They wore flounced, blue-stained loin cloths of knee length and their feet were bare. In this gathering, all were equal but one, Farid the Chief. He sat in no special place among them and he spoke now, swift of gesture, challenging of eye, his thick brows drawn together in a frown, his handsome, hook-nosed face alight with controlled anger. The others, listening to his words, were statue still, the whites of their eyes brilliant in their blue painted faces.

"Thus," he said, "by foolishness and cowardice were those of Ma'in cast away in the battle, and I, your Chief,

229

who never turned my face from the foe, fled into the hills, before the horns of Rome closed upon our people. Four days we wandered, a band of fugitives, until we came to As Saqia and saw that raped and murdered city. Thence, by way of the mountains once more, to Qohlan, in Wadi Beihan, and heard news from wandering men. The Roman *gom* is in Ithtarila, for in all the plain, only that city blooms. The road of the caravans is *khala*, empty. Thus has this devil done, this Il Shara of Qataban! Shall I say more? They lie deserted, the great cities, Qohlan, Merkha, Nisab, Jenadina—the snake finds there a home and the owl calls by night. The people are gone, to the hill springs, to the mountains, dying on the way. And now see here, this letter—read it Ruweis!" And he tossed the ragged papyrus to a young man across the room, who held it to the light from a loophole.

"And you of Ma'in," he read, "shall obey me, Il Shara, the Priest-King, as my other tribes have done. You shall break——"

"Mark that, 'my other tribes'," said Farid. He laughed savagely. "Is ancient Ma'in now but a serf of Qataban? Read on!"

"You shall break the walls of your cisterns and the spring of the moon in your city of Mariba shall be blocked——"

"Read no more!" cried a heavily-bearded man close to Farid. "This we may not suffer! Will he lay impious hands here on the temple of *Wadd*, the moon himself?" And he used the ancient name of the god, under which, in all the world, the god was known to Ma'in only.

"It is enough, in all truth," agreed Farid. "Now hearken—Il Shara is *mujennen*, djinn-haunted. Shall we close the gate, so that he goes otherwhere, destroying in his rage? Mark what he has done—our warriors slain in Jauf, the cities of the road destroyed, the rich made poor, the poor sent empty-bellied to the hills, the priests scattered, the tombs and the temples left unguarded. He will not turn on Rome again like a man, but the bitter rage of his defeat he wreaks upon his own people. Does he not deserve to die? I ask it now of this Grand Council—does Il Shara, the Priest-King deserve to die?"

It was a hard question. To slay a Priest-King of the moon, albeit he was not of Ma'in, and here, in a city of the moon. What evil gleam from the god might not steal out to haunt and destroy the very spirit of the slayer? What black curse might not thereafter lie on the tribe and the city where the fell blow was struck? A drum began to beat from the wall, its sound muffled in the *diwan*. Farid raised his hand, listening.

"He comes!" he exclaimed. "The Priest-King comes! What says the Grand Council?"

They were silent, not meeting those dark, challenging eyes. Farid looked at them, each in turn. No; no one would say the word. And in his heart he had known that it would be so. They heard the loud challenge of the tower warden. They heard the lifting and lowering of the posterns and the clatter of horses' hooves on the rocky street.

"Go down," said Farid to a guard standing by the door, "go down and welcome Il Shara to our gathering."

They sat round the room, Il Shara by Farid's right side, the blue men of Ma'in and the cloaked, brown men of Qataban in equality of numbers, evenly interspersed. Il Shara glanced about him, contemptuous of these primitive, ancient people, whom Qataban had cast back into the wild mountains of the Qor. He had cut short their windy compliments and greetings, his temper rising. He turned to Farid.

"Have you prepared the rubble and the plaster for the blocking of your springs?" he asked. "Why stand the cisterns, when I say they must fall?"

"We do not block these springs," answered Farid quietly, and the tension in the room was at once taut, a bow-string of danger.

Il Shara turned to face the Chief, his hand on the hilt of his dagger, below the fine camel-hair cloak. The handsome face before him was calm, the eyes watchful, the lips parted. Madness rose in Il Shara, a red, hissing fire, tearing at his bowels and his heart, sparking in the narrow slits of his eyes.

"You defy me?" he asked, his voice the rising whine of a tiger snarl.

Only those of Ma'in noticed the slight movement, the freeing of the plaid round Farid's knees; and all round the room the same slight movement rippled, a finger slipping the drawn plaid loose, while the body remained erect, unmoving.

"There is no defiance," said Farid, urbanely. "Here, in Mariba, I rule—not you."

The narrowed eyes before him opened wide and he sprang to his feet, twisting his body sideways as 'Il Shara's knife-point struck and broke on the wall behind him. But Farid's broad dagger remained undrawn, and, as all round the room knives flashed bare from their sheaths, his voice held them, strong and clear, so that each checked instinctive, impetuous action, and all froze, still as statues, arrested in their postures of attack and defence. Only

232

Il Shara moved, slowly drooping, his left hand rising to his forehead and his eyes.

"Let every knife be covered," ordered Farid. Slowly they sheathed their knives, their breath still held, their teeth still bared, their eyes wide, restless, quick-glancing to left and right.

"Let the men of Qataban stand up," said Farid, "and let all of Ma'in remain seated. There is no blood between us here, in this room. Take, then, your Priest-King and go from the city in peace. Let it be said that here none spoke and nought was done. For, of a truth, nothing happened here."

Yet something had happened in the room. Il Shara, as they led him away, his feet stumbling, his mind reeling, was King no more. His sceptre was already passing, as he went, to other hands, ready to receive it, of the royal line. And over his weakened kingdom a shadow lengthened from the west, the shadow of Himyar, spreading out from the high mountains over all the land from Sheba to Hadhramaut and the sea.

They heard the posterns rise and fall and they turned again to Farid the Chief. He sat pensive, his large, dark eyes untroubled. He looked up at them, his gaze wandering from face to face, wondering how much or how little he had gained in power over them, in the last few moments. For he was already quite sure of what must now be done. He had no doubt but that the Roman army would come here, to this city, a three-day march from Athrula and the first step between Athrula and the sea. He knew the power of the Roman *gom*. He knew how swiftly their heavy engines had breached the wall of Nejran. He knew, from witnesses, the size, weight and range of their heavy missiles. He had seen the power of their dart-throwing machines and their disciplined agility and strength at the river battle. Body to body he could never defeat them, however many warriors he assembled. But he knew also—he was sure—that the Romans could never breach the wall or the postern gates of Mariba.

They listened eagerly, as he unfolded his plans. The women, the children and the old men unfit for battle must go, with all the beasts of burden, to lodge in comfort in the settlements to the east. They would go with all their possessions. For the better defence of the wall here, he needed three hundred more warriors, the strongest men of the Ba Ras family, who were always ready for war. Let arrows and spears be brought to the city, a great store of arms and an abundance of grain, flour and oil. The Council nodded and agreed—all this was clearly necessary and should be done with speed and thoroughness.

"Let the wall of the field cistern be broken down," he continued. "We cannot altogether spill the water, for there are rock pools above it. Water lies there at this season, but the pools are shallow and difficult of access among the rocks. Let great stones be gathered on the battlements of the wall, and smooth stones for slings and let oil be kept heated on the bastions. Sharpen the spear, string the bow, lift up your hearts for war! Let hunters go forth into the hills with ropes and bring here six leopards, fully grown and unscarred, in perfect coat, and let us sacrifice them to great *Wadd*, the moon, in our high temple, that he may strengthen our hearts and hands in defence of his city, Mariba of the springs!"

CHAPTER 16

Fear Not

Having mastered it (Athrula) without a struggle, he placed there a garrison, arranged for supplies, and advanced to a city called Mariba. . . .

To return to Nejran would be an easy matter. Here at Athrula were granaries, stores of dates and oil, hides for water skins, horses, donkeys and herds of camels; and the chief of the city, Salim, terrified of his strange guests, driving himself and his people like slaves in the service of Rome. They could rest here, in Athrula, reorganize their depleted Cohorts and return to Nejran, thence west across the mountains to the sea and in ships to the world they longed for. But they would have failed.

They would have failed. How far from here to the first incense groves? (But a bare ten days' marching, *Sidi*, a short ten days!) And is the land rich? (Rich? Nay it is *khala*, an empty land, but when the caravans come through and water in the cities of the plain, bearing gold and ivory, silks and spices and all manner of wonders, then is the land rich!)

"Then let men be sent," said Gallus, "to spy out the land, while we make ready here to advance to the south or to retreat to the north."

They laboured, the remnant of a Legion, in familiar

235

tasks. They could forget the past. They could envisage the future as a journey, whither mattered not, which must be undertaken with food and water, carried on camel-back. That was all their problem and it could absorb the energies of mind and body, every day until sleep came. The horses and camels were collected, fed, and exercised. There were skins to be stretched and stitched, fresh sinew ropes to be dried and cured, cow hides to be stacked, grain, dates and oil to be estimated, set aside and portioned into loads.

For Valens and others were other tasks, no less absorbing. The spring to the saddle pommel, the camel lurching to its spread feet, the long night marching; questions, the search-ing eye, the bright-lit land, ridge to hollow, hollow to ridge again, dry peaks to the right of them, desolation on their left; a quiet, fireless camp at night and then a deserted, walled city, Qohlan, with its low tombs, its burial hill and its tall buildings and the high walls of Wadi Beihan, dim and shimmering in the heat of midday. And beyond, amid mountainous red dunes, the desert well of Adh Dhuma, so justly named, the Well of Thirst. There they met with nomads, who had cleared the well, dying as they worked, for only here could they find water. And from them they had more news of the south.

"We are of the Beni Hilal, the Sons of the Crescent, and enemies of Ma'in, as are all in the land. Farid, Chief of Ma'in, holds his keep of Mariba, in the Mountain of Springs. Il Shara, the Priest-King lies dead, slain by his cousin, who rules in his place."

Thence they travelled with caution, a small mounted party, away from the road. They passed by night over the bare pass of the Quarter Way, hiding by day among

236

boulders; then by the wall of Na'ab, a city of ghosts, the flames of burning Merkha a red glow to their east, until, at dawn, Valens crept forward, invisible among huge, tumbled rocks, and looked down on the valley and the strange city of Mariba of the springs. And below him, like jewels of sapphire in the early light, a series of linked, rock pools stretched down to a broken cistern.

As he watched, a party of horsemen cantered up to the single gateway of the city and entered between high, red granite bastions, disappearing in a dark passage and, behind them, an iron postern fell back into its groove with a deep clang, which echoed in the hills.

Intense excitement gripped him, as he lay among the boulders looking down. He shook with it, a tremor of his whole body, and his lips parted, his breath suddenly indrawn. It was like no city he had ever seen. Yet that was not, could not be the cause of this sudden awakening of every nerve, this fierce blending of eagerness and dread. For some time he lay, shaken by this disturbance of the spirit, gazing down on the city, its strong wall a crescent looped to the mountain peak and the white temple shining high above it, a star in the arms of a dark moon. It was a jewel of the mountains, not real, a thing of fantasy. But it was neither the jewel not its setting which held him here. Some call had come to him, when first he saw it, a call from infinitely far away, appealing, demanding that he should enter those gates of terror and climb those long steps to the white temple on the hill. And there, by the pool before the pillars, what was there for him? What could be there for Valens and the dark-haired girl, for whatever came to the one now, must also happen to the other. And, as he wondered, he felt peace and a knowledge, a certainty that

Q* 237

one day he would stand there by the pool, and he would know the reason why he must climb those long steps to the temple of the moon.

*   *   *

On only one man among them lay the burden of choice. Gallus moved his broad shoulders restlessly, when he heard Valens' report. How deep were the water pools, which they had seen? And between Athrula and Mariba, the one well only, the Well of Thirst? Four days the water above Mariba would suffice them; perhaps, with very careful supervision, six. The city wall—it was a strong obstacle, so Valens said. Their engines could not breach it nor, in this timberless land, could they build wooden towers to surmount it, nor could they raise banks from the hard granite of the hill. To assault the wall would be a matter of scaling ladders by night, of stealth, before a few daring men could make a lodgement on the battlements. The city must be assaulted from below for, behind the temple, was a sheer precipice of many hundred feet. The Legion was weak in numbers, a bare three thousand men, and he must leave some two hundred to hold Athrula, as a garrison in his rear. And, if he took Mariba, what then? He could, perhaps, treat with these curious, blue savages and he would hold the heart of the great road, the gathering place of the caravans.

If he attacked and failed to take Mariba, what then? He walked a little way, deep in thought. How did they fare, now, in Nejran, so far away? For, if Nejran fell, his retreat would be barred against him. He wondered if he should ask Valens, once again, to sum up the courses open to them and to recommend the one of his choice. Perhaps it was unnecessary—he was sure he knew what

238

Valens' answer would be, the safe, sound man! He would choose retreat to Nejran and he would give ample reasons for his choice. He walked back to the small group of Centurions who awaited him, to Clemens, erect and stiff as a javelin, Priscus, like a great, lumbering bear, Valens, tall and hard. He looked up at Valens, a twinkle in his pale blue eyes.

"Back to Nejran, eh?" he asked.

But Valens started, taking a half-pace backwards, alarmed.

"No!" he exclaimed. "No, Praefectus—to Mariba, that is the way we must go!"

They were all startled. His reply had been unhesitating, almost vehement, as if there were no other course but to plunge into danger and uncertainty. But Gallus was more than startled; he was amazed. For he knew men and he knew Valens very surely; he had long studied him. To go to Mariba was not Valens' choice—it was a choice he could never have made. With a sure road back to the north and, to the south, unknown hazards and a strong city, he knew Valens' choice without question; had he not written it, indeed, when they were in Nejran—to hold Nejran, to turn the river of trade across the Yemen to a port on the Red Sea? The twinkle died in his eyes. He looked at Valens searchingly. Then he beckoned to him and led him across the sand, far out of hearing of the others.

"Now you will tell me," he said, "why it is to Mariba we must go."

"Praefectus . . ." Valens' eyes were troubled in their depths. He looked back at Gallus' hard, searching glance. How could he explain this thing? There was no reason why they should go to Mariba, it was a stupid, foolhardy thing to do. They had neither the men nor the machines for that task, for the scaling of the wall, the bursting of the iron posterns. And once there, within the arms of the crescent what could they do, but climb those long steps to an empty temple on a hill?

"Why must we go to Mariba?"

"Praefectus, I spoke in error. There is no reason why we should go there. We should retreat to Nejran, reorganize and raise auxiliaries and strike at Sheba——"

"Turning the river of trade across the hills, west to the sea?"

"Yes; that is what we should do."

"Yet it is to Mariba we must go—you did not speak in error. You spoke from your heart and your heart is true and steadfast. When we return to the world, I will not forget you. You are wise, Valens, a man on whom even the great Augustus might safely lean. You do not speak in error. But here is the riddle: the mind says, 'Nejran and seize the road,' but the heart cries, 'Mariba!' Now, which is right?"

"We should retreat, Praefectus."

The pale eyes still held him, with their straight, searching gaze. Then they became of a sudden gentle, a sparkle of laughter deep in them.

"Come," said Gallus, "let us go back to the Centurions."

They waited for their General, their faces stern, impassive. The choice was his. When he had made it—whichever it was—the tension would be gone, they could set themselves to their tasks with ready hands.

"We will leave a garrison here and we will go to the south," announced Gallus, "to the south, to Mariba in the mountain of springs."

So Gallus chose, wondering at his choice. For him, it had been, perhaps, the natural choice, the onward thrust, the swift blow. Always, since they had met, he had chosen against the mind of Valens. And this time, again, he had chosen the way of Valens' heart, not of his mind.

The Centurions dispersed to their duties. Gallus remained, a smile on his lips, his eyes on the ground, relieved of the burden of decision. Others had much to do. He could relax, his work done.

But there was yet another task before Gallus that day. He stood in the evening in the city square, watching the off-loading of camels from a practice march and beside him, but turned towards him, her face flushed and her eyes alight, was Lilleth.

"I go," she said, with slow emphasis, "Mariba!"

"You stay Athrula," replied Gallus wearily. "This is *gom,* war-party, and I Amir—you stay Athrula!"

"I go Mariba!" she stamped her foot—the stupidity of the man!

"You stay Athrula—I go Mariba—I come Athrula—you, I go Mariba—oh!" and he ripped a fierce oath off his tongue. "What avails it?"

"I go Mariba?" It was a question now, a soft voice and gentle, pleading eyes. "I go Mariba?"

"You stay Athrula!" he exclaimed, loudly. Not all the trials of command could shake Gallus' patience. He was losing it now.

"Mariba?" she said.

Oh, after all, why not? Better to go to the place than to argue half the night. When he took Mariba, she might be of use to him. She had never troubled him, as her father had often done, with long talks of the future of

241

Nabataea—as if its future under Rome could be in doubt. She spoke this southern tongue—indeed every tongue from the Aramaic to the Sabaean. She was but a barbarian and, if harm came to her—and that was the cause of his annoyance. He should not care a jot for her and he cared a great deal, far too much for his peace of mind when it came to besieging cities, with a force one might leave to guard a river crossing but no more, so small it was. Yet, if disaster came to his main force, it would assuredly befall his little garrisons in Athrula and Nejran.

He called an interpreter to him.

"Ask her," he ordered, "why she desires to accompany me to the south?"

"She says," said the interpreter, "that she has sought the protection of the Eagle; that she is in her father's place and, were he here, he would have gone with you to the south. She considers Your Excellency as her father, she trusts Your Excellency and none other, she is Your Excellency's slave, she loves——"

"Enough! It shall be as she desires."

"Oh!" It was a cry of pure joy. She could hardly keep her feet from a little dance and she rose on her toes and clasped her hands, her eyes sparkling. He laughed too and the interpreter; they were a happy group now. He turned to the interpreter again.

"Tell the lady that I go now to make sport. There is a seer, a teller of fortunes who lives near the temple, whom Valens has found. He has had some success, so they tell me, with the men, and Valens now awaits me there. Say that I would be honoured by her company."

Most fortune-tellers like darkened rooms and mysterious surroundings for the practice of their art. But this old greybeard sat in the sunlight on a low wall, with three younger companions, where a water channel ran out towards the fields. He rose when Gallus and Lilleth came and bowed deeply, touching his forehead with both hands.

"What!" exclaimed Gallus. "No grotto, no hanging curtains, no stuffed serpents and philters?"

"He says," replied Valens, "that he works with the palm of the left hand, his eyes and a bowl of ink."

"Come, then; proceed!"

For a long time the old man looked at Gallus, his eyes expressionless and impersonal. Then he took his hand, not glancing at the palm, and closed his eyes. After a while he began to speak.

"He says he sees a hill of white stones and an old man who walks among the vines. He is white-bearded—so are most old men—but he limps on his left leg. His eyes are blue. He has a ring, a silver serpent, on his right hand and a white scar, a jagged line, across his forehead."

"Limps and a white scar?" said Gallus. "That is like my father; say on."

"On the hill is a small house, and two tall trees, of uneven height, such as he has never seen before."

"Even so it is! Two cypress trees of uneven height!"
They were all three pleased, delighted at this.

"And the ring!" exclaimed Gallus. "My father wears just such a ring, a silver serpent, entwined! And what now, if he can see so far away, can he unroll the book and read the future?"

"I see," said the old man, "three great, white pyramids of stone!" He murmured, his brows frowning. "Much of greatness here, many men, peacock fans, trumpets and hosts of warriors. . . ."

He opened his eyes and turned to Gallus, contemplating him with interest.

"You will be great indeed!" he said. "And I saw a stone beast, a carved god, the shape of a lion with the head of a man, a truly wonderous thing! You ruled in that land, you will indeed be very great, a King or a Governor of vast and rich dominions!"

Gallus turned away, but Valens gave a cry of excitement.

"You will govern Egypt!" he cried. "The three pyramids, the man-headed lion——"

"That is as the fates may decide," said Gallus, sharply, "and it is not yet."

He had always hoped to receive the Governorship of Egypt from Augustus. Would he receive that glittering prize, if he failed to take Arabia, and lost a Legion? Then he laughed. He had not meant to cast a gloom over them. He was to be Governor of Egypt? Good! Let them all become Governors of somewhere! Let the old man look at Valens and tell them when he would be a King too!

The old man's three companions were now in earnest conversation with him. They looked towards Gallus while they spoke.

"Who are these?" asked Gallus. "Are they also tellers of good fortune?"

They saw that he spoke of them and one came forward, a tall man of some forty years of age, hook-nosed, large and luminous of eye, his beard black and pointed. He addressed himself to Valens and Lilleth drew in towards him, puzzled, helping with a word here and there.

"What does he say?" asked Gallus.

"It is some riddle," answered Valens, "if indeed he does not make sport of us. He and his two companions await the rising of a star, a new star, brighter than any in the heavens, far away there to the north. They are astrologers. But, when that star rises, it shall not set, so he says, for it is no part of the moving vault of heaven. It will lead them to the north by night and day, until they stand at last beneath it. For there, beneath the star, will be born a Babe who will be King of the world."

"It is a riddle, then," said Gallus, thinking deeply, his heel grinding a small hollow in the sand. "A riddle— once I had much skill in their unravelling, as a boy. Ask him, who is to be the father of the child?"

"The very spirit of heaven and earth!" replied the astrologer. "And his mother the most blessed among women. See," he continued, unwrapping a linen bundle "see, here are gifts which we have prepared, gifts in token of our homage to the infant King."

And he spread out before them a small incense burner of gold and two sandalwood boxes, containing frankincense and myrrh. They would have laughed, had it not been for his humility, and his dignity.

"Why so small a gift for the King of the world?" asked Lilleth.

"Small, indeed, my lady; but we are poor as we are wise." He smiled, then, his eyes on her face. "Have you children? Often they like small things. See the gold of the incense burner is egg-shell thin, and a babe can hold it in his hands! And He will not know riches, for He will be found swaddled in linen and He will be born where the humble asses are stabled and laid in a manger for His cradle."

But Gallus had had enough of riddles. They had come here to divert themselves and first he was to be Governor of Egypt and then the King of the world was to be born in a manger—that could be diverting had a clown said it, but this astrologer had an uncomfortable presence. One could smile, but one could not laugh at what he said. And Gallus wanted to laugh.

"Come," he said, impatiently, "let the old fellow tell your future, Valens."

The old seer looked at Valens. He took a pace away from him, regarding him, frowning in perplexity. He studied his hand and then dropped it, turning away and looking across the desert to the south.

"My fortune?" asked Valens in a low voice.

"There is no fortune in your hand," he replied and Lilleth paled.

"What does he say?" asked Gallus. Here was more gloom, when they had come for merriment. But Valens did not reply. He had asked for his fortune to be told. He would not accept the answer that fortune was not his.

"Why have I no fortune in my palm?" he demanded, sharply.

The old man turned to him, his hands outspread, a gesture of incomprehension.

"There is an end," he said, "and that is all I see. Yet I will look into the ink, if you will?"

He filled an earthenware bowl with dark fluid and sat down upon the ground, the bowl between his hands, gazing absorbed into its black, shining surface. Gradually a frown gathered on his brow. His eyes widened, so that they wondered what things he saw moving beneath the dark mirror of the ink. He looked away suddenly, a swift movement of his head, shutting his eyes, and Lilleth cried out, dropping on her knees beside him, imploring him to look again, to look again——

246

"But, lady, I have seen all, all," said the old man gently, and, looking at her, he suddenly started back, his eyes narrowing, amazed recognition in his face.

"Look again!" pleaded Lilleth. "It is for him and so for me, as I believe. I would not have it end there, in the dark pool of the ink!"

He lowered his eyes and looked down into the bowl. And, when he had looked for a long time, his face expressionless, he poured out the ink on to the sand and rose, turning from them, walking away, his shoulders stooped, a tired old man, who had seen too much and who would look no more.

They stood unmoving and Gallus asked no questions, for, while he had not understood their words, he knew that he had seen a tragedy. And Lilleth still knelt, her eyes wide with fear, her hands to her breasts.

The three astrologers had watched them in silence. Now one came to Lilleth and took her hand, inclining his head towards Valens. "This," he asked, "is your man?"

She looked into his deep, compassionate eyes.

"Yes," she whispered.

"Roads meet," he said, "and they part, only to meet again. Behold, we wait for a sign, a star, and seek a Babe, who brings such love as the world has never known. Then, when we have worshipped Him, we shall return to our land, to Azzan. The Babe, in this life, we shall not see again. Yet we shall see Him otherwhere, when He comes into His Kingdom. Fear not, lady, if parting comes; you shall not lose your love."

CHAPTER 17

Mariba of the Springs

He besieged and assaulted the city . . . it was not by war,
but by disease, toil, hunger and the hardness of the road.

THEY looked from their ragged war-camp by the water pools on the strong, high walls of Mariba, glowing a rich red in the early sunlight. Between them and the city stood a small group of men, bright light shining and glittering on helmets and brazen medallions, as they moved here and there on the slope of rock, examining the city before them. Distantly, from the walls, came the occasional whip-lash crack of a sling. On battlements, bastions and frowning curtain wall, weapons glinted, where the warriors of Ma'in watched their deliberations.

Gallus looked up at the high red wall before him. Valens had said that the wall was a strong obstacle and he had been right. With only the four heavy engines remaining to them, the wall was unbreachable. For four days now they had skirmished and tested the defences of the city, while a ram and scaling ladders had been built. They had scoured the bare country for timber. Now but two days' water remained in the pools. To-day and to-morrow the city must be assaulted and, if they failed, there was no other course open to them but to retrace their steps to Athrula and Nejran.

248

Four heavy engines, twenty-six dart throwers and each of his ten Cohorts well under half their strength: that was the force he could dispose to attack this city with its un-breachable wall and with but one entrance, a double iron postern, counterpoised. It was a formidable problem. Lacking weapons and men, he must throw against the city all his ingenuity in the art of assault.

They had built a swinging ram, a stout trunk of wild fig tree, slung in a high frame of lashed timbers, its steeply-sloping walls covered with a shield of ox and camel hides. The frame had been constructed to fit exactly between the bastions, so that the iron-bound ram head could be adjusted by ropes and pulleys to strike at any part of the postern gate. They could not judge the strength of the postern, nor of the stone grooves in which it moved, but they would give it a testing tap or two. At Athrula, they had gathered a store of country bows, sufficient to arm two Cohorts, the Ninth and Tenth. Every man carried, rolled on his belt, a long sling, a deadly weapon against unarmoured men in skilled hands. They had prepared scaling ladders of rope and timber, and quantities of heavy cloth, to be soaked in oil, and bundles of faggots, prepared for burning. Now the men, watching from the camp, looked down on Gallus and his Centurions, seeing him turn and gather them round him with a gesture, to hear his final orders for the morrow's attack.

"We cannot lay siege to this city," he said, "since time presses. It must be taken by assault. The gateway is held by a double postern, working on a counterpoise, so that when the outer plate is lowered, the inner rises. Between the two is a passage. You see that smoke rising between the bastions? That is hot oil prepared, in balanced tanks. If you force the outer postern, those whose task it is will spill the tanks and the passageway will be a cascade and a river of hot oil. But if we break the tanks, that part of their defence is gone. That is your task to-day, Repetinus. A Cohort will accompany you. You will break the roof over the oil tanks with the heavy engines. There is a risk in this, can you tell it to me?"

"Yes, Praefectus," replied Repetinus, with a grin, "the counterpoise chamber may catch fire."

"It is a risk we must take. But, if you see fire from the oil tanks, suspend throwing. I have little doubt that the barbarians trust in the strength of the outer postern and that they will do all they can to preserve the counterpoise and its mechanism. So it is a slow business, this, and after it you have another task. To-morrow we will fire the city, burn it down. The wind by day is northerly, a strong steady wind for our purpose. By evening, you should move your engines to the north wall and commence the destruction of the upper parts of the houses near the wall. Break the walls down and expose the roof timbers. All these houses have floors and ceilings of plaster, resting on slats and laths. Break down the upper storeys. The ram will reach the postern at the rising of the morning star. When the star rises, and you hear the first blow of the ram, throw in balls wrapped in burning cloth, and brands, bound and aflame.

"And now, Priscus: the First, Second and Third Cohorts are yours for the assault on the north wall. The Ninth will support you with arrows and you will pick and use slingers as you will. When the fires gain strength in the city, that is your time. Up on to the wall with you and clear a strong lodgement on it. Do not leave the wall;

hold it and we will join you there and take the city by sections from within.

"You, Pudens, command the ram. The Tenth will support you with their arrows. We will block the lower loopholes of the bastions for you with flaming brands. I and the remaining Cohorts will wait until there is a breach. Take your time and strike at the centre first, to bend the plate and jam the postern in its grooves. Then break a narrow opening in its side, but do not free it, or the inner postern will drop down. I want it opened and jammed tight. Is that clear? To your work, then, all of you."

The four heavy engines rolled up the rocky hill, their throwing arms jolting and swaying, a watchful Cohort spread to either flank. From the tower of the bastion, Farid looked down on them, his eyes alight with interest. He had heard of these strange machines and he was now to see their work. They came to rest about two hundred paces from the gate and the valley rang with hammer blows, as wedges were driven between the frames and the rock. Naked men, their bodies white and shining against the dark ground, heaved at ropes and winch levers. First one throwing arm and then another moved back, until they lay horizontal and the trigger pins held down the power of thick, twisted sinew ropes. Other men ran forward, placing roughly-shaped granite balls in the throwing-cups, while engine commanders measured distance and height with their eyes and ordered the positioning of the heavy check-balks, forward in the frames.

"Let fly!"

The throwing arms sprang up and forward. Four thirty-pound blocks of stone shot into the sky, with a rushing sound, curved in high trajectory and fell beyond the wall. At the strike of throwing arm on check-balk, the men seized ropes and winches, heaving back the throwing-arm once more, while engine commanders snapped out their swift orders for the repositioning of the balks. Farid and his men crouched behind the battlements. A stone struck the wall below him, chips and splinters flying from it, leaving the granite hardly marked. Others fell in the city behind the wall, breaking ornamental stone work on the house fronts but causing no damage to the strong lower courses of the houses. Then he noticed that the stones began to fall closer together and three, one after another, suddenly struck and crashed through the timber roof above the oil tanks, unbalancing a tank, so that it spilled its hot oil into the passage below. At once he understood the object of the bombardment. Two more stone balls crashed through the timber roof and, as he rose to give orders from his crouched position, a flood of oil gushed over the fires and flame rose in the air hissing, followed by rolling black smoke. He ran down the steps to the bastion. At all costs the counterpoise chamber must be preserved.

"Spill the tanks!" he shouted. "Spill the tanks! Bring water, let men stand by the counterpoise with water!"

Repetinus, too, had seen the smoke. He raised his hand in a signal to stop throwing. He watched men running from the battlements. That would be fire in the counter-poise chamber, he knew. Let them put it out, the fools. He turned, shading his eyes against the sun, towards a man he had posted on a high crag, who could look down upon the bastions. His hand, also, was raised. He waited till the man turned sideways to him, making a throwing motion with his arm. He turned to the catapult teams.

"Let fly!" he ordered.

Once more the air was full of rushing sound. All four engines were striking accurately now, their crews taking their time, adjusting check-balks, tapping the wedges below the frames to keep them in position. The timber roof above the oil tanks and the balance mechanism must be destroyed beyond repair. Repetinus was a thorough man, and Farid crouched under the battlements, watching this accurate, steady pounding of the timber roof, until it and the mechanism below it were a splintered, tangled mass, the tanks smashed and useless. His Ma'ini warriors watched, grim and impotent in silence. But they were not alarmed. This was without doubt a clever thing, done with strong weapons. But these balls of stone could never breach their granite wall or avail against the iron posterns and, in the passage between the posterns, loophole after loophole still held its steady arrow, its dark watchful eyes.

By midday Repetinus was satisfied with his work. Gallus rubbed his hands together in pleasure.

"Well done," he said; "let the men rest now and shade themselves. Let food be brought. There is yet the preparation of the city for fire, but you have ample time."

In the late afternoon, they once more set the machines in motion, trundling them over the rock to their new position, facing the north wall. This time they hung hide screens to the frames, cunningly placed to protect the crews, for their work must now be done close in to the wall, within range of sling stones. As the sun inclined to the right, they battered at the closely-spaced house-tops. The Arabs on the wall looked back at their city, murmuring, bewildered by this peculiar form of war. Why break the house-tops and belvederes thus, one by one?

"What think you, Farid," asked one, Ahmed, a grizzled warrior who commanded the north wall. "What purpose have they? The oil, yes, one can see that. But first the postern faces them and that they cannot break. And now this stoning of the house-tops. It is a truly wonderful thing!"

Farid frowned and shook his head.

"They are warriors," he said, "such as before this land has not seen. Look how they move in blocks of men, each in his own place! See their weapons and their armour! And this—I do not know, but there is some devilry in it. Tell your tribesmen to use the sling no more; they cannot hurt men hidden behind hides."

Round stones, jagged stones, rocks from the hillsides, they crashed and thudded into the city. One by one they broke open roofs and upper storeys, exposing beams, opening plaster ceilings and floors, where slats and light timbers lay hidden. The sun sank below the mountains. They rested until moonrise. Then once more they moved up and down the wall. From the camp above, the resting Cohorts could hear the steady smack and whirr of the catapults, the strike of their missiles and the rattle of falling masonry. Until past midnight the work went on. Then the crews rested, sleeping exhausted on the hard rock of the hill, while round their engines others stacked high the oil-soaked cloths and bundles of dry timber, for the morning's work.

Slowly, on its heavy wheels and rollers, showing against the last stars like the vast bulk of some prehistoric animal, the hide-covered battering-ram moved towards the gate. Within the frame, torches flared, casting weird shadows of men and timbers on the raw-hide walls and roof. In the torchlight they watched the swinging tree-trunk, steadying it with ropes, while others heaved and pushed the heavy frame up the steep slope of rock.

From the city wall they had seen this strange, shadowy thing looming out of the night, red light glowing and flashing from its sides. High-pitched, trilling war-cries alarmed the garrison. A crackle of slings greeted the ram, stones striking the hide screen with dull smacks, or spinning off the rocks, humming away into the darkness. From below the wall, slings answered and arrows hissed upwards at the embrasures as the Ninth Cohort came into action.

Stones from the wall now struck the hides with force and here and there, within the ram's torchlit interior, arrow-heads appeared, flashing suddenly and hanging, held from penetration of the hide by their rough feathering.

The frame of the ram jarred between the bastions. Men sprang from the frame, burning branches and brands in their hands, thrusting and forcing them into the loop-holes within reach. Heavy blocks of stone crashed down on the hide shield from the wall above. Within the shield, they heaved on pulley ropes positioning the swinging tree-trunk, until it almost rested on the postern face. The Centurion Pudens stood under the forward edge of the hide shield, within a few paces of the ram head. Men on the positioning ropes, the ropes which swung the ram, and high in the roof of the frame by the fulcrum points, watched him intently for signals, for speech here, once the ram began to swing, would be impossible. He lifted his hand palm outward now, a sign that angle and proximity had been obtained. Then, with both hands, he waved them back and the ram moved backwards to its full extent. His hand cut downwards. Released, the iron-bound butt of the tree-trunk swung forward into the postern, a ringing blow of iron on iron. It moved back and swung again and again, striking, striking, striking with a deep booming sound, which rang and echoed in the hills.

Since midnight fires had burned by the catapults, under the north wall, small at first, but blazing up now as heavy bundles of dry timber were set to them. Ahmed and his warriors on the north wall watched these rising flames, wondering what new devilry they portended, distracted by the tumult of fighting on their left. As the ram struck its first blow, Repetinus gave the order. The catapults let fly. Stones wrapped in blazing cloth, bundles of flaming timber rushed into the air over the walls, crashing down upon the exposed timbers of broken roof-tops, scattering their sparks far and wide. A faint breath from the north heralded the coming wind. In shadow, behind the fires, Priscus and his three Cohorts crouched close together, long lines of ladder teams before them, waiting for their chance.

In a moment six or seven house-tops burst into flame. The Arabs turned from the wall in panic, running down into the city. But Ahmed was before them, opposing them, striking them with his spear butt, driving them back.

"Back! Back!" he cried. "Leave not the wall, fools! Back to the wall!"

They stopped, distracted between the wall and the burning houses. But he forced them back to their duty and as they turned to the wall again they saw it against the spreading light—two curved claws of iron, scraping, gripping and sinking down within an embrasure, the

256

grapnel-head of a scaling ladder, and another, like the claws of a blind monster, swaying over the wall, feeling for a grip.

A helmeted head rose above the first grapnel. Ahmed drove his heavy spear at it. Beside him another warrior lifted a great rock in the air and hurled it down upon the ascending men. Eight ladders gripped the wall. Once their claws were fast in an embrasure they could not be released. They struck down at the climbing men. Arrows hissed upwards at them, but they were careless of their lives, exposing their blue-stained breasts to the storm of death, spurning their wounded from beneath their feet, slipping in the blood which spread on the battlement floor, striking the Romans down. And from below the wall came the blare of horns and the hunting call of the *tubas*.

From the war-camp they looked down upon the city as dawn broke. Wind whipped the flaming house-tops, spreading fire through the north quarter, as burning logs flew high over the wall, leaving ragged trails of smoke behind them. Tumult from the gate and the wall filled the air, the cries of men, the hoarse blaring of war horns, the falling of broken masonry and the boom . . . boom . . . boom of the ram, a deep ringing sound like a gong, under-lying in its long echoes, overriding in its ringing stroke, all the other tumult of the battle.

Pudens, under the forward-hanging hide shield, watched the hammering of the postern. After forty counted strokes it held. He gave the signal to cease striking. Once more within the shield they heaved and tugged at the positioning ropes, moving the ram head to face one side of the iron plate opposing it. Then again it swung and struck, swung and struck, shaking him, deafening him in this clanging place. A heavy silver-bound spear, hurled from above, cut through the hides and glanced off his armoured shoulder. He hardly felt the blow, for the postern moved—he was sure of it—very little, but it moved. He signalled to cease once more, while positioning ropes took the weight of the tree-trunk and men moved the fulcrum points a handsbreadth forward. Once again he ordered them to strike, blow after ringing blow.

In the city fire leapt and spread towards the street of tombs. Farid looked down into it, his heart sinking. The two granaries, squat, pillared buildings, stood on the north of the street, in the path of the spreading fire. The tall houses, close packed, burned downwards with tremendous speed, as ceilings and floors gave way and flaring beams crashed down through them. Unsupported, their stone walls bulged outwards and split, plunging in ruin, casting hot stones and flaming timbers far and wide. Already flames spread south of the tombs and one tall tower there had fallen. The fire roared and a house by the granaries crumpled down, spilling a mass of burning debris among the sacks. What could he do? For there lay all the grain and oil they had. They had lost it and however the fight went to-day, to-night they must find food otherwhere, they must leave the city in the dark before moonrise; and this was the central keep of Ma'in.

Priscus, his shield held high above his head, leapt upwards on the ladder. A spear thrust down on him, between his shield and the wall, glancing from his armour. His right hand gripped the iron of a grapnel claw and he heaved himself through an embrasure. His sword flashed out and he sprang at the defenders, stabbing and thrusting, a raging, black-bearded Hercules. Behind him, four of his men sprang from the ladder-head to the wall, as a rock hurled downwards, struck the lashed joints of the ladder and split it in two, the lower part falling, scraping and slipping against the wall, spilling the men who held it down upon the rock. High above them on the wall, abandoned to their fate, Priscus and his four men raged against the warriors of Ma'in. They sprang at the defenders of the next ladder-head, slaughtering them, turning outwards, their backs to the ladder. Ahmed saw the danger and its dire remedy. As Priscus cleared his sword point from a falling man, he leapt at him, weaponless, gripping with his hands and knees, hurling him back through the embrasure and down, down, crashing together on the hard rock beneath, in an embrace of death. After them, locked together Ma'inis and Romans swayed grappling and fell out from the walls, their knives stabbing as they fell. With redoubled fury they swarmed up the ladders, arrows flashing over them, but where one Ma'ini fell, two stepped to take his place, and others ran up to the wall from the city with flaming beams from their fallen houses and cast them down upon the frail ladders and the climbing men.

And they drew back from the high wall of Mariba, snarling, their strength spent, their ladders smashed and broken.

Pudens watched the iron plate before him, as the ram struck low and to the left. He took a pace nearer and signalled cease. Yes, it was ready to move. He studied it carefully. He must not altogether burst it from its grooves. It must be struck to wedge sideways, so that it jammed the counterpoise and held the inner postern open. He signalled to his men. Once again they moved the fulcrum points, a little backwards this time. Word passed from the ram back to Gallus and the waiting Cohorts, a horn blew and they moved forward, closing in on the gateway, their shields held high. Once more the ram swung and struck, this time with no ringing stroke, but a dead, crushing blow and Gallus, Clemens and their men, ran for the postern, a storm of arrows flashing over them at the battlements above.

The iron plate was wedged and twisted. Picked men thrust their shields against breast-high loopholes, as Gallus and his men raced down the passage for the inner postern. But the city beyond was not to be theirs. The last blow of the ram had broken a main cable of the counter-poise, the other had been charred by fire. Gallus had a brief view, as he ran, of the street of tombs, smoke billowing across it, when he heard a rumble of wheels above his head and the inner postern fell, crashing down into its groove in the living rock, forbidding entry to Mariba of the springs. And as they retreated out of the passage and back from the now useless ram, Gallus spoke to a trumpeter and a call echoed over the flaming city and the jagged mountains, an unfamiliar tune to the Legion's ears, calling them away from the city they had failed to take.

The archers spread out from each other, crouched, nimble, pressing in under the battlements. They withheld their arrows, their bows full-drawn, until a spear or a head showed in an embrasure. Then they loosed them in a volley, a hissing tongue of bright iron, while behind them the Cohorts reformed their triple lines.

Beak open, head lowered for the strike, golden pinions widespread, the Eagle faced the city of the moon. Pace by backward pace its fierce guards bore it from its prey, their pride untamed, menace in their slow, deliberate movements and in their baleful, narrowed eyes.

The assaulting Cohorts, reformed, stood ready just beyond arrow-shot of the bastions and of the wall. The archers, obedient to a short trumpet call, ran back from the wall, gathering together in a loose formation, moving back towards the camp. One by one the Cohorts retreated down the slope of rock.

Once more the embrasures of the city wall sparkled with the light of many spears—not now aimed downwards in defence, but thrown high in the air, brandished in exultation, spinning and twirling as the warriors of Ma'in leaped and stamped in a wild dance of victory! While behind them other spears, of fire, orange and scarlet, leaped upward from the dying city of Mariba of the springs. And on the mountain above the water pools, the warriors of Rome filed through the gates of their war-camp and went each one to his own place.

*   *   *

As the sun sank and mountain shadow spread out over the land, they looked down on Mariba, no longer afire but misted in smoke. And they looked away, their faces grim, as they splashed the last water from the rock pools into their water skins. That night they could rest a little. At the rising of the morning star they must march away, back over the desolate land to the Well of Thirst.

Gallus sat alone, absorbed in his thoughts. He had eaten, heartily, a meal of millet cakes cooked in oil and he had drunk a bowl of foaming camel's milk. Now, as he sat, his mind roved over the two years and more of this expedition. The inimical country! Perhaps he had erred in his choice of alternatives. Syllaeus, the crafty fellow—

they would lay him by the heels yet, he was sure of it.   The poor old nomad King!   And Aretas, whom they might well have defended better, he slept soundly by the war-camp in Nejran, his death avenged in full.   The moon-priest was dead too, so they had told him.   And now they left Mariba, where they had failed.   Yes, and it was he who had failed and he who must return and explain that failure and these enormous losses for no gain.   He shook his head.   How could one explain that Arabia the Happy was a desert, a long desolate road, until you came to Mariba, in the mountain of springs?   It was time for sleep, before to-morrow's marching.   He rose and stretched his arms wide, a smile on his lips.   He had no bitter thoughts.   If he had failed, at least he had endured.   He lay down on a couch of spread sacks and, in an instant, he was asleep.

Valens could not sleep.   He had laid off his heavy armour and drawn a woollen cloak over his shoulders. Nightfall found him beyond the camp, sitting on a boulder overlooking the city.   In the stillness, he could hear a mur-mur of many voices from the ruined streets; here and there torches flared redly.

He had not climbed those long steps in the street of tombs, to the temple of the moon.   It drew him still, the small white temple, even now, before the moon-rise, when it was hidden from his eyes.   All his life he would remember that strange excitement which had shaken him, when first he gazed down on Mariba and its temple. Now its secret would never be his, he never would stand there by the pool, looking up at the pillars and the low temple court and know the reason for its strong, insistent call.   And what remained now but return from disaster, with a tired remnant of a Legion, failure for its prize?

His thoughts grew sombre, a darkening of the spirit. The long road, the hard road they had traversed, must be retraced. As once again they set forth in the dawning, marching back on the narrow path away from this land of mirage, would the ghosts of their dead companions rise from the sand and march with them, a shadow Legion, to stand grey and empty-handed before Caesar? Or were they here, with him, looking down on the ruined, impregnable city? For they had left, on the long Arabian road, a ghost Legion, who would walk beside the tired traveller touching his sleeve and whispering, "Wander no more!" or who might flit before him, beckoning, crying, "Hurry! Hurry! For the horns are calling and we must scale the walls of Mariba, at the rising of the morning star!"

He lifted his head from his hands and looked down again on the city. The quarter moon was rising, red as blood, above sharp mountain peaks. He watched it as it paled, flooding the rocks with a mist of light. The city was dark, silent.

Silent! He held his breath, straining to catch the faintest sound. But there was no sound, only the breathing of the night wind in his ears. He rose, his heart beating swiftly, lightly with excitement. He went down towards the city, his dark red cloak black in the moonlight, on soundless feet, pausing now and again, listening, keeping to the shadows.

He stood beneath the wall. He looked up at it, so tall and lowering, a mighty obstacle. No silver-bound spear-point shone above the battlements. No swift arrow sped at him, flashing in the moonlight. He walked towards the gateway bastions. He gazed between them at the twisted postern and the dark passage beyond. Above him, the strong curtain wall was unguarded, no tower warden cried his high challenge in the night. He hesitated here, between the bastions, torn by he knew not what forces of duty and desire. He should go back now, at once to alarm the camp. Mariba was theirs! No need, now, to sound the trumpets and to swing the ram. They could enter the city which they had burned and broken to their will.

It called to him, pleading with him to come, to enter the city, to climb the long steps to the temple. He passed the bastion. Before him, like a black knife-cut in the wall, was the narrow aqueduct which led from the city to the field cistern below the camp. He entered it, edging his way through the darkness. He turned from it and stood in a broad street, white tombs flanking its long black steps, which led upwards to the temple on the mountain peak. He turned, startled at a sound, and Lilleth stood beside him.

They did not speak. They gazed at each other in silence, and the magic of the city held them, the stillness, the white tombs, the fallen houses and, above them, the stars and the rising crescent moon.

They climbed the long steps side by side. They stood on a marble pavement, high on the mountain above the city, a pool of water at their feet and, beyond, the four delicate pillars of the temple, flanked by marble statues of kneeling ibex; the low, dark temple court before them. There were two temples, as they looked down, one built on rock, the other unreal, floating in the still water at their feet.

"If you move a little to the left," said Lilleth, "you can see the ibex statue in the water. Do you see? It is as if it knelt there, in worship to the moon!"

264

He moved as she told him. It was as she had said and the moon glowed in the water as no moon ever glowed in the heavens.

"My pool, Antonius," she whispered.

"It is my pool," he said, "but I will share it with you."

She knelt down beside the water.

"If I put in my hands," she said unsteadily, "I will shatter everything—kneel by me, Antonius; I am afraid!"

He knelt by her.

"Of what are you afraid? Put in your hands. If you shatter the images in the pool, in a little time stillness will rebuild them."

"Yes," she whispered, "yes; we can change nothing, you and I. We can break nothing that stillness will not mend."

She bent over the edge of the pool. She looked at the images in its depths. Her breath fluttered in a sigh of fear. She put her hands into the water.

A sharp, unbearable pain pierced her heart and the stars in the water reeled and the pillars bent and staggered, the marble ibex split into a thousand gleaming fragments and the pool had gone!

He heard the hiss and the strike of the arrow. He saw her body suddenly rigid and erect. Then her eyes closed and she fell sideways into his arms, the arrow deep in her heart. And a second shaft from the dark court of the temple struck into his side.

Life was ebbing from him. He did not hear the sound of swift, bare feet, running from the temple down the long, dark steps. He lay beside her, pillowing her head on his arm, covering her from the wind with the wide folds of his cloak. His tired mind looked no more for meanings, for interpretations. He turned her face to his, loving its marble beauty, content that, when she died, his strength should fail him.

He lay back his eyes closed.

A trumpet called, loudly, stridently commanding: "Awake!" it called. "Awake, soldiers! Awake in the dawning . . .!"

It called to the camp above the water-holes; its fierce voice echoed over the pointed mountains; its last note, high and clear, saluted the rising of the morning star! And it called to Valens, Centurion, rousing him from fading dreams, halting the feet of his spirit for a moment on the doorstep of death, with a harsh voice of bitter accusation.

He struggled up, leaning on an elbow, and the arrow shaft which pierced him was heavy, dragging him downward with a deathly weight. Born of past experience and present urgency, scenes shone and faded in his mind. Under closed eyelids, he imagined the waking camp. He saw the horsemen, leading their horses among boulders in the darkness. He saw the Eagle rising, above glinting armour, bright gold in the light of the flaming palisade! And for a moment he saw Gallus, his handsome face calm, as he looked down for the last time on Mariba, the city which had been denied to him.

Yet the city was empty, defenceless and, if the Arabs had blocked the springs, at once they could be made to flow again! Nothing now barred the Romans from Mariba and, with the springs of Mariba to sustain them, with Athrula and Nejran behind them, all the golden road was theirs, from Yenbo' to the southern sea!

Who could tell Gallus of his fortune? Who should stand now before Gallus and show him, with a strong, outstretched arm, his captive city, which held in its burnt and tumbled ruin the key to all the treasures of the sun? Who but Antonius Valens, the Centurion—none but he. Gallus had said that the great Augustus could safely lean on Valens' wisdom—he must rise up, he must go now, he must cry out to Gallus, "Mariba is yours, yours is Arabia the Happy, the southern sea awaits the commands of Rome!"

With terrible effort he rose from his elbow to his spread hand. Slowly he turned his head from the temple pool towards the camp above. For a moment he opened his eyes, seeing only swaying mountain peaks below a bright and rising star of morning. But there was no way for his feet from the dead city to the living camp. Roads parted here. For Gallus, brightly sunlit, there lay the long, hard road to high command. And for Valens? Already his spirit drifted to the land of shades. There was no fortune in his hand.

And, as he died, from afar a horn sounded, echoing in the mountains, where a Legion turned from Mariba and marched away, on the road to Rome, over the hills into the far lands of history and legend.

POSTSCRIPT

Postscript

THE first Augustan Governor of Egypt was Cornelius Gallus. His short term of office was distinguished by tumult and riots and, in 26 B.C. Augustus recalled him to Rome and appointed Publius Petronius in his place. Cornelius Gallus was charged with tyranny before the Senate and, faced with banishment, killed himself by falling on his sword.

In 25 B.C. Augustus Caesar determined upon his enterprise of conquering Arabia. He appointed Aelius Gallus General of this expedition. While Aelius Gallus set off on his ill-fated march, Candace, Queen of Ethiopia, invaded the southern borders of Egypt and Publius Petronius, the Governor, led a punitive expedition eight hundred miles to the south and, after a series of victories, a lasting peace was concluded between the Queen and Augustus. Aelius Gallus had meanwhile returned with the remnant of his army and, in 18 B.C. Augustus appointed him to relieve Petronius as Governor of Egypt. His career as Governor was a most distinguished one.

Aelius Gallus was the friend and patron of the famous geographer Strabo, who accompanied him on his inspection of the southern frontier of Egypt and together they travelled up the Nile as far as the borders of Ethiopia. We may imagine that it was on this march, by the great river, that Gallus told Strabo the story of his Arabian adventures.

In Strabo's bare description, four places are all-important. The first two are the cities of Yathrib, now Al Medina, and Nejran. These two cities are identifiable without question, since both are well known to-day. Then there is the river where "the barbarians were assembled for battle", six days' march south from Nejran. This is the perennial stream which flows from the mountains of Jauf al Yemen, then the country of Sheba. It was an uneven battle, since we are told that "ten thousand of them fell, but only three of the Romans". The fourth place is the city of Mariba, where Gallus turned back. Strabo writes, "he besieged and assaulted the city for six days, but gave up for lack of

270

water." Some have supposed that Mariba is the city of Marib, the capital of the Kingdom of Sheba, but there is no lack of water near Marib and we must look elsewhere.

I have therefore opened my ears to a legend current among the tribes of Ma'in, in the Qor Range of mountains, at present within the British Aden Protectorate, that in ancient times an army of the Frankish people destroyed the city of Mariba, near the modern settlement of 'ain ar Rasas and then retreated to the west, "no man knows whither". The Arab legend accuses this army of blocking the sources of the springs at Mariba. The Romans say that they were defeated by lack of water. In all that is important to the identification of this Mariba as the city where Gallus turned back, both accounts agree—that an army came to the city of Mariba and went no farther, leaving the city waterless and desolate.

Where are the cities of Arata, Aska and Athrula? Some day the archaeologists may find the answer. That they are close to the positions I have assigned to them on the map there can be no doubt, and by the known cities of Yathrib and Nejran, Gallus' achievement is made plain, startling in its magnitude.

In reconstructing the story, I was struck by the division of the desert march into two distinct parts—from Arata to the "land of the nomads" and thence to Nejran. Something sinister happened at Arata and the treachery of Syllaeus is mentioned. This treachery cast Gallus out into trackless desert, to wander for thirty days. Only one thing could have saved him, to meet with nomads. This he must have done and he names their Sheikh as "Sabus". His wandering is now over. There is a sense of direction and of confidence in the words, "on for fifty days through trackless wastes as far as the city of Negrana." And he arrived before Nejran ready for war, for Strabo writes, "the city fell at the first assault."

No less remarkable than his invasion of Arabia is Gallus' retreat. From Mariba, returning in his tracks to collect his garrisons from Athrula and Nejran, he struck west across the northern Yemen, fighting a battle at "Seven Wells", and encamped on the Red Sea coast. There he built ships and in them returned to the known world.

Nothing is duller than a bibliography. Among several sources, I am most indebted to Forestier and Parker for my description of the Roman soldier. Forestier[1] in his beautiful illustrations shows the

[1] *The Roman Soldier*, Amadee Forestier, A. and C. Black, Ltd. 1928.

progress of Roman arms and equipment through the centuries. Parker[1] goes deeper into many controversies, discussing their organization, their conditions of service and promotion, their march and battle formations and their light and heavy weapons. For the construction and the powers of their engines of war, I have turned to Payne-Gallwey,[2] who spent many years building these machines and experimenting on them, on his estate.

Gallus and his men are the heroes of this story. Syllaeus is the villain. We read of him in *Josephus' Antiquities*, that he "was a shrewd man, although he was but young, and handsome withal". The notorious Salome, who danced before Herod for the prize of the Baptist's head, "looked upon Syllaeus with some passion" and desired to marry him. Syllaeus proposed to King Herod that if he consented to the match, there might be a union between Judah and Arabia, "the government of which country was already in effect under his power and more evidently would be his hereafter." For he was then the first Minister to the King Abodas of Nabataea. Herod agreed, on the condition that Syllaeus embraced the Jewish faith, but this Syllaeus refused to do, saying that if he did so the Arabs would stone him. There is little doubt that, later, he was the instigator of a plot to murder Herod. Later still, he was accused before the ageing Augustus of manifold crimes and was beheaded.

Three ancient Kingdoms divided South Arabia at the time of this story, Sheba, Qataban and Himyar. All three were destined to endure for many years but, in the end, the Kings of Himyar were to style themselves, "Tobba of Himyar, Axum and Sheba and Masters of Reidan."

According to tradition, the Three Wise Kings came from South Arabia and were astrologers. Three centuries after Christ, the Empress Helena sent emissaries into Arabia to discover "Sessania Adrumatorum"—'Azzan of the Hadhramis—and to search for the bones of the Magi. These they found and brought back to Constantinople and these sacred relics are now supposed to lie in Cologne Cathedral.

My story is told, through the kindness of John Murray. Fifteen years have passed since a night in the desert when I hoped that I might, in some way, be Gallus' chronicler. If there should be in the tale some colour too crude or some error in the telling, I ask for pardon. My theme needs an artistry far beyond my powers.

[1] *The Roman Legions*, H. M. D. Parker, Oxford, at the Clarendon Press, 1928.
[2] *The Crossbow, with a Treatise on the Ballista and Catapult*, Payne-Gallwey.